PREDATOR PRIEST

■ ■ ■

Robert J. McAllister, M.D., Ph.D.

DORRANCE
PUBLISHING CO
EST. 1920
PITTSBURGH, PENNSYLVANIA 15238

Dorrance Publishing Co
585 Alpha Drive
Pittsburgh, PA 15238
Visit our website at *www.dorrancebookstore.com*

ISBN: 978-1-4809-4425-1
eISBN: 978-1-4809-4448-0

To
My Constant Companions

Peace & Blessings
Bob McAllister

CHAPTER ONE

He was standing alone the first day I met him. I watched him for several minutes before we went over to say hello. He stood erect and studiously scanned the parishioners coming out the church door. I watched and wondered. What's he thinking? And more importantly: what's he feeling? You see, my life work has been in that rather intricate and often mysterious field of human emotions. For those few minutes he was my *subject*. Normally I don't scour my brain in such casual encounters, but this was different.

This is the new pastor recently assigned to our small but loyal and active Catholic parish. He has been transferred from one of the larger towns in Montana and our understanding is this is a temporary assignment. He is filling the gap left when Father Joe retired five years ago and returned to Ireland. Joseph Donovan came from Ireland, and the parish has been staffed by priests from Ireland as far back as records show, probably since the parish was established in the 1880s.

After Joe left we had a visiting priest, Father Kevin Brunner, from Highland. He came and said evening Mass the second and fourth Saturdays of the month. On Sundays, other than the second and fourth, one of the laymen (heaven forbid laywomen be allowed) held a communion service with prayers, scripture reading, and distribution of Communion. We are all wondering: when this man goes, then who? Without a replacement the closest parish to our town is in Highland, seventy miles away. Will we have our own pastor, or will the diocese continue to cover the need unsatisfactorily with another visiting priest? Our frequently discussed concern is the lack of vocations to fill growing vacancies in the priesthood.

Thoughts like these flitted through my head as I "took the new pastor's measure." To be a bit more honest, the subject has been a distraction to me for the past hour during the celebration of Mass. It is still on my mind. It often is.

The new man looks to be in his early fifties, full head of brown hair, about 5'10", a little paunchy, erect. Perhaps "stiff" would better describe his stance. Doesn't look like an outdoorsman. Most of the parishioners are lining up to welcome him and shake hands. It's a bit more formal than I expected. For the most part we're a rather casual bunch, mostly ranchers and farmers plus the merchants of the town. He seems gracious enough, but a lack of warmth in his responsiveness to those he greets is quite apparent.

I took my wife's hand and we joined the line. Before we got within earshot Jane leaned over and quietly said, "A bit wooden, don't you agree." It was a private label we use. The two of us have assigned "stick of wood" to people who exhibit a very limited emotional response or none at all. So early on, we judged Father Fred to be not necessarily unfriendly, but distant, perhaps a loner. Of course he came to the parish *as a loaner*.

When we finally came face to face, I smiled, extended my hand, and said, "It's good to meet you, Father Fred. Welcome to St. Cyril's. I'm Bob Lee, and this is my wife Jane." His reply, "It's Father Brown, and I am glad to be here." "Well, thank you very much, you stuffed shirt" was my unspoken thought. I was tempted to tell him we don't stand on a lot of formality here and we don't stand in awe of parish priests. We called the previous pastor "Father Joe" or just "Joe" ever since we'd been coming to the parish. Before we moved to Montana we always came to Mass here when we visited the ranch. We saw Joe as one of us. Most pastors these days are comfortable with that familiarity. If they're not they should be.

I commented on the lovely day, and we walked away as the line of greeters moved up. He didn't even look at Jane and had no exchange with her, which struck me as extremely rude. She obviously had no desire to extend herself to "Father Brown" after his opening comment. Generally people find Jane to be a friendly person. He acted like she wasn't there.

Jane and I chatted for a time with various friends about the beautiful day, the lack of rain, the generous yield of hay this year, the price of cattle, our gardens, how the locusts seemed to be increasing—the usual country talk. Some of us also engage in typical after-church talk evaluating the service, the music, and the homilies; all areas where we normally accept what we get without serious complaint. There is really no one to complain to, particularly in the area of bad homilies. Someone usually brings up which parishioners were not in attendance, often adding whether or not they've been absent before and, if so, how many times.

In the past five years our congregation has decreased by almost fifteen percent while the population of the town has increased by nearly twenty-five percent. The majority of those who no longer attend Mass still live in town but, according to general understanding, have conflicts with the rigidity of certain dogmatic attitudes and practices no longer acceptable to them. Instead of being "cafeteria Catholics" as most of us have become, their consciences apparently cannot skim the surface quite so easily. The visiting priest, Brunner, who filled-in the last five years, brought up the subject of birth control, abortion, and homosexuality in nearly every homily he gave. It was enough to drive almost anyone away.

After half an hour of chatting we said our goodbyes and headed home. During our short drive to the ranch we exchanged thoughts about the morning. We commonly exchange our thoughts about everything. While I tend to be on the quiet side, Jane is a "talker," and I must admit I enjoy all the talking we do especially since she does most of it.

Meeting Fred was number one on the agenda, of course. Jane has an uncanny ability not just to see people but to intuit them. I rarely find her first impressions off the mark. She opened the conversation. "Father Brown seems rather sensitive about familiarity and wants to be sure we keep our place. I thought he was rather rude. If this is the kind of attitude he's going to continue around here, I doubt he'll be very popular. Maybe he needs to be in a parish with sophisticated people, people who will kowtow to him and give him 'yes, Reverend Brown, and no, Reverend Brown and whatever you say, Reverend Brown.' He should come out here and help me in the garden, get some dirt in his hands."

"You said it right on, Janey. You spotted his 'woodenness' before we even met him. I totally agree. If this is the best he's got he's not going to fit in well at all. I thought it was extremely rude he didn't even acknowledge your presence. Right then he lost about nine and a half points with me on a scale of ten.

"He's here on a temporary assignment. No one ever told us where he came from or where he served before. We don't know the name of every priest in the diocese, but we sure know most of them or at least have heard their names." I continued to mull it over and then added, "I was in the seminary with Jack Tracey who is now the chancellor. You met Jack a year or two ago when we attended Sunday Mass in Back Eagle. I'll give him a call someday next week and see what he's willing to tell us about this guy."

"That's a good idea," Jane replied. "I don't think priests get moved around as often as they used to in the diocese. Remember when Kennedy was bishop, he said he planned to move all parish priests every three years. He didn't want them 'to get too familiar with the parishioners.' I don't think he had in mind the old saying 'familiarity breeds contempt.' I think he was afraid familiarity might breed hanky-panky. I don't think there's much chance of that with Reverend Brown."

We were driving into our yard. "You're right about that, Love. Not to change the subject, but it looks like that weaned calf got out of the corral and is back with its mother. They'll be okay together now because her milk has dried up. Besides, it's lunch time and I'm hungry."

Jane and I have been managing the ranch the last three years. It feels much longer for both of us. Ever since we married forty-two years ago, we visited here two or three times a year and kept up with all the relatives and friends in the town of Springer. I always loved the ranch, the foothills, the Little Belt Mountain Range three miles to the south, the Highwoods thirty miles to the north. Our frequent visits made it feel like a second home.

The "Big Sky Country" was always welcoming and took me back to wonderful memories of my childhood and teenage years. Back then ranch life was primitive and poor; it was hard work and long hours; challenging and wonderful. By age eight I was riding my little mare, Red, and when I was ten I was driving a team of horses in the hay fields.

Shortly after we married I brought Jane on her first visit to the ranch. It was quite an experience for a Philadelphia girl to be in "the Wild West." During the visit Jane rode a horse for the first time. We saddled up two horses (an especially gentle one for Jane) and off we went down the county road. Once she got the rhythm of it she loved it. These days she rides with me quite often and proves herself a capable "cowpoke" when we move cattle from one pasture to another.

My next older brother, Don, took over the ranch/wheat farm after Dad died in 1950. Actually Don had managed the ranch about ten years before Dad's death. Helen, Don's wife, and Jane were always close, more like sisters. Jane was an only child, and Helen had one sister who was a Benedictine nun.

When I was a boy Dad had ten or more men on the haying crew and the same for the threshing crew. The crew included Dad, my five older brothers and me, and a couple of cousins from Springer. Hired men worked for a dollar a day with room and board. It was a six-day week of ten-hour days.

Over the years the ranch had become a one-man operation. A self-propelled combine cut the wheat, separated it from the straw, and emptied it into a truck from which the grain was mechanically elevated into a granary for storage. Cutting hay required one machine to cut it and leave it in windrows and another to bind it in covered bales. Currently many of these machines are run by remote control as the owner rests leisurely nearby. Don never changed to the use of such expensive, and perhaps not as efficient, equipment.

Helen died five years ago. It was just before Father Joe left for Ireland. Of course, we flew out for the funeral and arrived in time to help Don with the preparations. I still remember Jane and I were with him when he picked out the coffin.

We flew out again when Don died a little over three years ago. On the plane from Baltimore, I said to Jane, "Babe, the thought of retiring has recently been on my mind. I've been treating patients, teaching, and lecturing all over the country for the last thirty years. I'm beginning to wonder about getting out of the mental health field. How would you feel about making the change, maybe moving on to something else or maybe just hanging up the shingle for good? I really don't know what else I would want to do. Think about it and we'll talk about it when we have more time. Your thoughts and especially that eerie instinct of yours have always been important in decisions we've made and as I recall quite accurate."

Jane looked at me as if she were reading the mind behind my thoughts. Sometimes I think she reads my mind even when I'm only daydreaming. She gave me that look, somewhere between quizzical and all-knowing. "Are you thinking you'd like to go back to the ranch? I know you've always loved it there."

Her comment startled me. Actually the thought never occurred to me except for the fantasy I've always had about returning to my boyhood there. That's more likely just a daydream of being young again (some sort of rebirth illusion) rather than being a rancher again. During this trip I anticipated we would go out from Springer and visit the land and the ranch-house this one last time; but Jane's comment certainly added a totally new feature to the trip.

It felt like she was reading thoughts that hadn't quite surfaced in my mind. I considered her words for several minutes. I *knew* what she meant without further explanation. Our communication channels were so deep and so clear this sort of thing happened all the time.

The question of "What will happen to the ranch?" never even crossed my mind. Don's step-nephew Ted lives about five hundred yards from Don and Helen's house. Ted lives with his wife and two kids in a mobile home. He rents some land in the area and does his own farming with his own equipment. Occasionally Ted helped Don herding cattle or trucking them to cattle sales. Ted and his wife have always been available and were helpful during Don's and Helen's illnesses. They are just automatically "filling in" since Don's death. Their two boys are teenagers and at times helped Don. Ted negotiated his move to the ranch about nine years ago, and their presence has truly been a Godsend.

Don and Helen have two children and five grandchildren, none of whom we have seen for several years. Their son, John, is a dentist in Seattle, and their daughter, Loretta, is teaching in Carson City, Nevada. They will inherit the ranch, but it isn't likely either of them will want to live there. Selling it will be the most probable alternative. Getting someone to manage it for them "on shares" is a possibility, but it would have to be someone dependable, because grain and hay need to be sowed and harvested at the right time and livestock need to be cared for all the time.

Jane clearly had no intention of delaying this discussion. She didn't need "to think it over" because we could think it through now as we talked it out. Not an unusual approach for my enthusiastic and practical wife.

Obvious questions bounced back and forth between us. Can we manage it for them? Do we want to manage it for them? Would they want us to do it? Is this a realistic thing to even consider? I always worked with Don during our visits to the ranch and often ran the combine, the hay baler and the other farm implements while Don was busy doing something else. I always felt comfortable and capable with the livestock. But to take on the responsibility for it all—that would be a major undertaking.

And was Jane really as interested as she appeared to be when I mentioned making some kind of change? Or was this idea something she thought would please me? That would be so like her. What Robbie wanted would be what she wanted. The first time we met Jane called me "Robbie." No one, not even our three children, ever use that name. It's her coinage and believe me it is valued and brings her good returns.

Don's funeral must have been one of the most attended, I should really say celebrated, in many years. The church was totally filled, and about two hundred people stood outside during the funeral Mass. Burial was in the town cemetery where my grandparents, parents, three of my siblings, aunts, uncles, cousins, and many Montana pioneers are buried. There must have been two thousand or more who came to pay their respects.

Only one dark cloud shadowed the whole event. The visiting priest, Father Kevin Bruner from Highland, was unavailable to say the funeral Mass. We had to get another priest from Culver City ninety miles away. I mentioned earlier how after-church talk sometimes covered the homily. There wasn't time for after-church talk this day because everyone immediately followed the hearse to the cemetery. If time had permitted immediate conversation about the homily, the vitriol would have darkened the day and been too malicious to pass any examination of conscience in regard to charity. This day, of all days, the priest exceeded even the worst of expectations.

He could give good sermons. We heard him preach a couple years ago when we were visiting in Culver City. He had the knowledge, the voice, the passion, and seemingly the compassion. In spite of all that, his sermon this day wandered all over his own life, not the Lord's and not Don's nor the life of anyone familiar to any of us. He told stories about his childhood, where his parents took him to buy ice cream, what his father said to his mother about the butcher shop owner, a story from seminary days, a comment he heard about a current movie starlet. He referred once to Don; holding up the memorial card with Don's picture, he said, "Don't you think Don looked like Robert Redford?" And he went on in that endless way he had; just when you

7

think he's wound down he comes up with another meaningless, unattached, out-of-nowhere comment. It was agony. It was embarrassing. I was ashamed. For the first time I wished I was a Protestant. I guess I was that day, at least in regard to the homily.

After the burial we ate lunch with Don's children, John and Loretta, and the three grandchildren. We spent almost three hours telling stories about Don and Helen and the visits we all made to the ranch. Once they were aware Don had cancer of the spleen, John and Loretta obviously had been talking about what they would do with the ranch after Don's death. *They* brought the subject up and asked us what our thoughts were. They knew we were their parents' confidantes. They were clearly undecided, but it seemed obvious they desired to keep it within the family. I told them I really believed Don would want the ranch to remain the Lee Ranch. In addition, I said one of their children or even a grandchild might someday wish to return and be a rancher. Providence smiled on us again. They asked us to manage the ranch.

We contacted each of our three children and all heartily approved. Each of them spent time there with us when they still lived at home. They have their own fond memories of the ranch and Don and Helen. Laura, our oldest, is married, has two children, and is teaching at St. Agnes College in Minneapolis. Joe is unmarried, an electrical engineer employed at NASA, and lives in Columbia, Maryland. Edward, our youngest, owns an IT company in Boise, Idaho. He and his wife have one child.

Over the next several months Ted took care of the ranch while Jane and I managed our personal affairs and negotiated terms with John and Loretta. The ranch remained in their names. Jane and I would manage it on a suitable share basis, getting a portion of the profit from the sale of cattle and wheat.

One of my brothers, Larry, was in the Bataan Death March of World War II. His granddaughter is an attorney in Highland, so we asked her to handle the legal documents. She was well acquainted with all parties involved.

I closed my practice, canceled any future engagements, and resigned from my teaching position effective the end of the semester. We moved to the ranch and took up residence in Don and Helen's house. The Philadelphia girl and the wandering Montanan were home.

Jane and I made a number of major decisions in our life; this was one of them. Our first major decision was to get married. Our love grew rapidly once we met. We quickly found we had an unusual compatibility with common interests, common needs and common values. Each of us had been through some patches of life that had potential for permanent damage. We shared the history of those years and found healing factors in our togetherness. We attributed our union to divine providence. It became a fixed pattern for us to maintain openness and fully share our daily lives. As our bonding deepened we adopted affectionate terms in our conversations and no hesitation about displaying our love openly.

CHAPTER TWO

For years my brother Don taught Sunday school in the parish during the school year. After Father Joe retired to Ireland, life in the parish faded or at least greatly diminished. Sunday school was gradually discontinued for lack of interest and attendance. Kevin, the visiting priest, showed no interest in its continuance and never mentioned it to Don. Coming to say Mass twice a month seemed to be a burden for him. He wasn't very pastoral in his attitude or his homilies.

Now that the parish has a full time pastor, it occurred to me there might be enough interest to start Sunday school again, especially if the pastor would support the idea. I had some teaching experience at the college level, and I thought I could tailor it sufficiently to be acceptable to the youth of the parish.

One day when I was in Springer to buy a new scoop shovel, I stopped by the rectory (the pastor's home). He responded immediately to the bell, almost as if he were expecting me. I wondered if he was sitting in the arm chair near the window, a spot where he could see anyone approaching the house.

"Hello, Father Brown. I was in town and decided to come by and ask you about something that's been on my mind the last couple of months. My brother, who managed the ranch until his death three years ago, used to teach Sunday school twice a month during the school year. Attendance dropped after Father Joe went back to Ireland and ended completely before my brother died. I'm wondering if you would be interested in starting it up again. If you are, I'd be willing to take it on starting in September."

11

"Please, come in and let's sit down and talk about it," he replied without hesitation, "Yes, I would be interested. Let's sit over here," pointing toward his desk. The room was rather stark and uninviting. There were two arm chairs with a lamp table (but no lamp) between them, a medium size table (his desk) with three chairs around it, a couple of file cabinets nearby, and a four-shelf bookcase with half a dozen books. There was a television on a small table across from the windows. A wall-to-wall dark gray carpet covered the floor. Besides the overhead ceiling light, there was a lamp on his desk and a small floor lamp near one of the arm chairs. There were a couple of nondescript pictures on two of the walls. It looked more monastic than home-like.

As we sat down Fred said, "I'm surprised Sunday school has been discontinued so long. How many children do you think would attend? Or better to ask, how many should attend?"

I answered, "Off hand, I'd say ten or twelve. Of course, it all depends on what age group we're considering. If we have the class for kids ages nine to fifteen, we should have about twelve attending. You probably don't yet know all the families, so let me mention those who would be likely to attend. Let me sort of search through the congregation as I see it in my head and try to come up with the names. The Brills have two, the Klines have two, Mansfields have three, Kemps have one, the Kirbys have three, and Mrs. Quirk has one. That gives us twelve. You'll get to know them all after you've been here a few weeks."

Father Brown responded, "I know them all now. I've been studying family names and members over the three weeks since I got here. I know where each of them lives and what they do for a living."

Springer is a town of about fifteen thousand people, and the businesses depend primarily on the farmers and ranchers living within a thirty- to forty-mile radius. There are eight or ten small towns within that radius. Those are typical western small towns with a grocery store, a couple of gas stations, two or three bars with or without a small restaurant, and sometimes a rundown motel.

Springer's population has grown considerably in the last ten years. When Dad arrived in the late 1800s on a stagecoach, the town was big enough not only to be a stage coach stop, but it was a station where there was a change of horses, but not of drivers. At that time there were probably more horses in the town than people. Almost everyone had either a saddle horse or a team of horses. And they kept from sixteen to twenty horses in the corral for the stage coach. There was an old expression people used when there was a person they didn't like: "He's one of the reasons there are more horses' asses in town than horses." In Springer today there are some who would say if you counted all the horses and all the horses' asses, you might come up a few short on horses.

Springer became something of a small boom town about ten years ago when a divided four-lane federal highway came through. Black Eagle was eighty miles to the west and Culver City was ninety miles to the east, both with populations of seventy to eighty thousand. During a period of ten years or more, Montana had no speed limit; which made Black Eagle a little over an hour away. As a result Springer became a bedroom community for people wanting to escape the "big city life." Eventually the federal government insisted there be a speed limit on all federally constructed and maintained highways. Montana posted seventy-five as a speed limit at night only. It satisfies the feds, at least for now.

Enough history, let's get back to Fred's comment about knowing families and where they lived. I said, "I'm surprised you've had time to visit them all. I thought you would spend at least several weeks just settling in and becoming familiar with the layout of the town."

He replied without hesitation, "Oh, I know the town. I drove through it several times once I knew of my assignment a month or more ago. I stopped in several of the stores and talked a bit with the clerks and sometimes the owners. In a town this size you don't have to talk long before you start hearing some of the town gossip. I have the town pretty well mapped out in my mind so I could get to any address where I might be called in an emergency. And I've been by the farms and ranches in the area so I know who lives where."

I expressed my surprise. "It's strange none of the people mentioned meeting you before or recognizing you when you said your first Mass a few weeks ago."

He replied, "When a priest doesn't wear a Roman collar, he's just another guy." His reply often came to mind a few weeks later when events occurred which brought mental, emotional and spiritual burdens not just to the parish but to the people of the town.

As we continued talking about the Sunday school class he showed growing enthusiasm. Sunday Mass is at 9 A.M. We agreed class should begin right after Mass, approximately 10 A.M., and would have a little flexibility about ending. I would plan to end at 10:30 but could extend the time a bit if necessary.

Father Brown added, "Especially if someone has a question and should not go home without an answer." His phrase, "should not go home without an answer," caught my attention. I thought it sounded defensive and superfluous. Obviously parents from the country wait for their children and lateness is not a big problem.

Father's next question, "How many of the children are boys and how many are girls?"

I sorted them out on my fingers and arrived at, "Five girls and seven boys." I continued, "Since you raised that question, let me ask you something else. The Bishop recently gave notice that parishes may have girls serving at the altar as well as boys. We didn't do anything about that, waiting for you to arrive. What's your pleasure?" As I think back on this day, the question stands out like a sore thumb but I didn't know it was pointing somewhere.

Brown replied, "Let's just keep it with boys for now. The parish just had a change of priests, better not to make too many changes too quickly. Who is in charge of the altar boys and how many are there?"

"I guess you're in charge, and there are five of them." I continued, "The boys more or less pass the job down to younger brothers or to cousins or some friend whose family attends Sunday Mass regularly. It seems to me the boys almost routinely limit the age from nine to fourteen. Kids under nine don't seem quite ready for it. They tend to become inattentive or distracted, sort of itchy. And around age fourteen the boys generally want to discontinue serving.

"The five of them arrange among themselves who will be serving each Sunday. The boys always plan to have two available to serve Mass. Four of them are from ranch-farm families, and occasionally field work prevents someone's attendance. Jim Mansfield, Pat and Joe Kirby, and Tom Brill are from ranches. Tim Quirk lives in Springer with his mother who works at the Double Bar Saloon. Tim is always available to fill in if any of the others are missing. Tim comes to Mass whether or not his mother is sleeping in that morning." Fred gave a knowing nod to my last comment, which I thought we could have done without.

We moved on to small talk for a while before I said I should really be on my way and added, "Are you getting settled in okay? Is there anything I can do to help? Anything you need and can't find? We're all happy you are here and want to accommodate your needs as well as we can."

14

He seemed to relax a little with me, and his voice held a new ease. "No, I'm doing fine and so far I have everything in hand. I appreciate your offer. I don't see many parishioners during the week unless I go downtown for something. I spend most of my time in the rectory. By nature I'm not much of a socializer. I read a lot and watch television in the evening. I subscribe to the *Culver City Gazette* for the general news and, of course, I get the weekly *Catholic Register*.

"By the way, I was a bit curt the first day we met. It was not an easy day for me being in a new parish and having the usual concerns about being accepted. I do prefer to be called Father Brown when there are others around. I think it maintains a certain respect and I'm uncomfortable with familiarity. But when you and I are talking or doing something together, 'Fred' would be fine."

I was on my way out the door. "Thanks for mentioning our meeting that day. It is difficult to be confronted by so many strangers all at once." I had forgotten the town's people weren't all *strangers* to him due to his earlier *clandestine* visits.

On the way back to the ranch I sorted through the conversation, the sort of thing I typically do in an attempt to clarify any additional meaning in the exchange of words. This "examination of conversation" became a habit during my years as a psychiatrist. It enabled me to compile accurate notes after a session with a patient. Currently it just seems natural to keep all the events fresh in my mind so I can review them with Jane as I typically do.

We were in a busy time of year on the ranch. I had 160 acres of hay laying in windrows in the field. Rain was predicted later in the week, and I wanted to get it baled before it got wet again. Once that field was finished the haying would be completed for the present. I can stack the bales later in the places where I'll need them most, come winter.

It was a busy time when Father Fred called me one morning a week or so later and asked if I could come into town to meet with him. I suggested he drive out to the ranch and maybe have lunch with us.

He responded, "I would really rather talk to you privately and confidentially if I could. I may want to take a note or two while we talk."

I tried again, saying, "Jane can find something to do outside, and we can sit in our living room. Or we can go out to my tool-shop or down to the barn to talk. There are plenty of places for privacy here."

Even over the phone his voice carried a persuasive, tense quality as he ignored my offer. "Maybe we can make it another time. It doesn't have to be today. I just wanted to get some things settled in my mind so I can go ahead with better understanding for necessary planning."

He *is* our pastor, and I had offered to do whatever I could, so I agreed to the town meeting. "What time do you want me to come in? It's nine o'clock. If I come in now, will we be finished in time for me to get home by noon?"

He assured me we would finish in an hour or two. I told Jane about the call and asked if she'd like to ride in with me. "I can drop you at Penney's or Sears; and you haven't had much time in the new H&M store. You can shop while I talk with Fred." We both wondered what was so pressing for him. Jane decided not to go. She had a small load of wash to do and some gardening and she'd prepare lunch.

When I got to Springer, I went directly to the rectory. This time Fred must have been watching for me because he opened the door as I walked up the sidewalk. I wondered what was so important and why so secretive.

He extended his hand. "This is very kind of you to come on such short notice. Perhaps I'm over-reacting to the multitude of situations confronting me as I become more involved in parish life. I believe you are someone I can confide in and someone whose judgment I can trust. Please, come in and let's sit at my desk again so I can make a note or two if necessary."

His living room was as sparse as it had been on my first visit. As he became more settled I expected some pictures, knickknacks, mementos, or at least some personal items would be unpacked and placed somewhere to alleviate the painful starkness of the room. I'm not a decorator, but I know the soothing presence of such things.

After we sat down, Fred began in a prepared sort of manner, like he'd been rehearsing what he was going to say. "First, I'd like to talk about the altar boys and second, I'd like to talk about your Sunday school class. I've had each of the five altar boys as servers at Mass. They are respectful and behave in an appropriate way during the service and they seem to relate to me well. Before too long I would like to do something special for them or perhaps with them, an outing of some kind, maybe a picnic together. Do you have any suggestions about what we might do?"

It took me some time to think about his request and to come up with some appropriate suggestions. It's been a long time since I had to find entertainment for young boys. Fred made a few notes as I spoke. "Whatever you plan, it should probably be on a Sunday because, except for Tim Quirk, they are all farm boys and usually not available during the week. You could take them swimming at the Nelson reservoir three miles north of town. There are bathrooms available and a couple of changing huts. You might take them fishing on Otter Creek where it runs within a mile of the road to Black Eagle. You turn off the highway at Spinekop to get to the area. There's a well-equipped town picnic ground off Hamilton Street. They might enjoy an evening cookout or a picnic there. You could arrange an evening cookout on a Saturday or Sunday. Some of the locals like to climb Wolf Butte. It's about twelve miles south of Springer. You can see it from town. The mountain is shaped like the tip of an arrow. The climb would be a bit of a challenge for you unless you're in pretty good physical condition. I may come up with some additional ideas, but that's the best I can do on the spur of the moment."

Fred's enthusiasm surprised me. "Those are great suggestions and all sound like good possibilities. I'll scout out each spot you've mentioned. Let me bring up an associated question. I'm sure you know the Church has become a sort of watch dog over their clergy and not without good cause. Basically the hierarchy is placing so many restrictions regarding contact with persons under age eighteen, it sometimes interferes directly with good ministry. Their code of conduct does not allow me to walk along the street with a young person who is alone. I could not take a youngster in my car even if he or she were ill or in need of transportation in a storm or late at night. If I met Tim Quirk or one of the other altar boys on the street, I could speak but I could not stop and talk. Since regulations state I should not be with one child alone, if I followed the letter of the law I would not be able to begin preparation for Mass until two altar boys are present in the sacristy (the room where the priest puts on vestments). And what if only one altar boy shows up? Can I still vest and say Mass? I'm sure you see how the restrictions become rather ridiculous.

"The Catholic hierarchy is almost ludicrous in the limitations they place on priests; it becomes difficult to move about in the parish and even in the town. I feel like I should wear a sign saying: 'All people under the age of eighteen must avoid this man. He is considered dangerous.' Do you understand my position, my dilemma? How can I be of value in the parish with these impossible boundaries?"

Fred was looking intently at me obviously expecting a supportive response to his remarks. I felt I needed to be careful about what I said. I certainly didn't want to expand his rebellious irritation nor did I want to readily expose my own criticism of the hierarchy and their inadequacy in dealing with the worldwide child abuse scandals.

After some thought I replied, "Your point about these regulations limiting effective ministry is certainly well taken. These guidelines take some of the humanity out of the clergy, and a number of them don't appear to have a surplus of humanity to begin with. In order to function in a meaningful manner I assume you almost need to cross the boundaries on occasion. But to do so presents a hazard you've probably considered. If you haven't, you should. Cases of child abuse by priests have become so notorious, the general public is quite conscious of the possibility and suspicions are easily aroused. If someone sees a priest alone with an eight-year-old boy, a thirteen-year-old girl, a seventeen-year-old adolescent or a two-year-old child, they could conclude the situation is almost parallel to that of terrorism— *'If you see something, say something.'* Alarms go off in their heads. A call is made to the police or a call to Bishop Butler, and you could be contacted for questioning possibly by the police and certainly by the diocese. If your history in the church is unsullied, your explanation will probably suffice with a stern warning about 'the next time.' Over time as you become better known in the parish there will certainly be parishioners ready to vouch for you. At the moment you would have to rely on a clean slate in the past."

I thought I saw a shadow of anxiety on Fred's face as he sat deep in thought for several minutes. He dropped his head and for a moment I wondered if he might be praying. Then he raised his head and said calmly and sincerely, "Thank you, Bob. You are an understanding man and I appreciate your frankness. You obviously have a remarkable sensitivity for the complexities of our lives as priests and now with the added burden of public suspicion."

I was about to ask if we were finished, but then I remembered he had two concerns. He addressed the second one. "I would like to hear your plans for Sunday school. When do you expect to begin and how will you deal with the Sunday school guide sent out by the diocese for all Sunday school teachers?"

I replied, "If you're agreeable, I'd suggest we begin Sunday school class the second Sunday in September and then continue on the second and fourth Sundays of each month through the school year. We'll skip the fourth Sunday in December."

Fred said, "That sounds fine to me. What's your attitude about the Sunday school guide, Bob?"

"I plan to follow the general guidelines about what to take up in class. But I have some difficulty with the harsh and highly critical stance the guide takes in relation to contraception, abortion, and sexual identity. This parish, including the children of course, went through three years of Father Kevin Bruner's harangues about those three subjects.

"You can be sure I will approach them much differently, and I believe far more charitably. I will ask the children to pray for women who are carrying unwanted fetuses. I will try to help the students appreciate the anguish a woman may go through knowing she is too poor to feed another child or too ill or too overworked to care for another child. If the pregnancy is the result of rape, then we should at least understand the woman's desire to, in a sense, regain her feeling of integrity. She has been violated. Although one may not agree with her decision to have an abortion, one can still have compassion for her situation and treat her with respect and not condemnation. As far as I'm concerned her decision is between her and her God. I will not discuss Thomas Aquinas's argument that the beginning of life in the fetus may be quite sometime after conception. That position which is reasonable to me would only muddy the water for them. You may be aware some current well-known theologians argue that abortion before viability is acceptable. In all of this there is a principle of 'the lesser of two evils.' But that too is not appropriate to bring into a discussion with children in this age group or at this time.

"In regard to contraception, again I will try to help students know that people sometimes need or want to limit the number of children they have. Poverty, physical or emotional limitations, a conflicted marital situation, and general fear of the future may be major factors for couples deciding not to have a child or additional children. But their love goes on and may well need the nourishment and bond of sexual intimacy which is also one of the purposes of marriage. I believe the use of contraceptives is an appropriate measure for a married couple in their desire to maintain the love and intimacy of their bond.

19

"If a class discussion leads into the subject of premarital sex, I would certainly bring up the appropriateness of contraception. I think the 'lesser of two evils' might then be a suitable principle to discuss.

"With regard to sexual diversities, I will provide information and scientific opinions regarding inborn diversities including those related to sexuality. In the Letter to the Galatians, St. Paul says: 'There does not exist among you Jew or Greek, slave or freeman, male or female. All are one in Christ Jesus.' That's solid ground for me. And yes, I would argue in favor of same sex marriages.

"So if you want a teacher who follows the orthodoxy of the church as outlined in the Guide, you will need to look for someone else. It ain't ME."

Fred went into a thoughtful phase again before he spoke. "I'd like you to stay in the job. I'm a bit shaken by your description of these three areas that seemed so settled for me in my understanding of doctrine. But I truly admire the manner in which you address them, and in so doing you seem to make the sinfulness less damning.

"It occurs to me one of your students might carry some of your comments home to parents who may be staunch, traditional Catholics. Your comments may go up the chain to Bishop Butler and then return to my lap. How do you think we should proceed then?"

I had a quick answer for that one. "Don't worry about the Bishop. I spent two years with Charles in the seminary. He's a pussycat."

After a lengthy pause, he responded, "Interesting comments. You've thought a lot about all these areas we've talked about. And I thought you were just a rancher."

I gave him a bit of my past. "For a number of years I was involved, in one way or another, with all the topics we've discussed today. Normally I keep my opinions to myself other than to discuss them with my wife. Jane and I see eye to eye on all matters related to the church and our faith. In fact, it is rare for us to disagree on anything. I hope you don't feel I was trying to convince you to see things differently than you do."

Fred replied, "No indeed. I'm grateful you shared so freely with me and it has expanded my thinking. I believe you are someone I can rely on and I value your opinion. I trust our conversations will remain private. I appreciate your coming into town, and now I'm afraid I've kept you much longer than the hour I promised."

I responded to his words about privacy. "Fred, I discuss everything in my life with my wife. Essentially we share all that happens."

He replied, "That's a reasonable exception to my request."

We said goodbye and I left for the ranch. When I entered the house, Jane had lunch waiting on the table. As I expected she was full of questions and I was full of information. And as usual lunch time became conversation time. It always is unless we've spent the entire morning in one another's company. Even then there are always things to talk about.

CHAPTER THREE

During lunch I went over my conversation with Fred and except for a few questions Jane asked along the way, I think it was a fairly complete and sequential report of our meeting. When I finished, Jane asked the question I knew she would ask. "What do you think of him?"

It made me smile. "I knew you would ask that. I don't know. I'm not sure. He's looking for information, and he probably sees me both as a source and as a potentially supportive figure in the parish. I suspect he has singled me out as his confidante.

"The altar boys and diocesan regulations regarding contact with youngsters seem to be a priority for him. He presents an interesting regulation conflict when he suggests he shouldn't be in the sacristy unless two altar boys are there. But I can understand his concern when we see the continuing headline news about clergy abuse of children. There was an article in Sunday's paper about another case of abuse by some monks back in Pennsylvania somewhere. It continues to be front page stuff, so no wonder it's front and center in his mind.

"He apparently was comfortable with my plan to deal with the Sunday school guide as I said I'll do in class. I thought he might give me a bad time about that. When I told him I'd been in the seminary with Butler, that eased his mind."

I looked at Jane and knew she was framing a thought for words. "He really had two subjects to talk about. One was young boys, the other was sex.

23

Note the combination. Granted he may have many other questions and topics and interests, but he picks these two and insists on a private, confidential if not secretive, meeting in the rectory. I know you will be teaching Sunday school and we're nearing September, so it is obvious that particular item does need to be settled now.

"There is something about it all and maybe about him that leaves me uneasy. I know you've had a lot of contact and interaction with religious men and women, and you have a keen awareness of the conflicts which may occur in their state of life. And I'm also well aware of your natural compassion for them. But remember Father Peter in Minneapolis and the sleepless nights that caused us both."

Indeed I did remember even though it was several years ago. Peter was referred to me by the Jesuit Superior of their local community. During the first two or three visits I learned Peter was smuggled out of the Oklahoma City Diocese in the past year. Back in the sixties there was a scandal related to numerous cases of sexual abuse by several priests in Oklahoma. I believe those cases helped bring to light the scandal of clerical abuse of children in the United States. Undoubtedly the behavior was known to exist in several dioceses here and in Europe but had not yet *come to light,* i.e. was not yet known to the legal authorities. The *light of the church* is not always the *light of the law* nor is it always the *light of God.*

Peter had previously studied for a graduate degree in theology at the Jesuit University in Minneapolis. During that time he made many friends among the Jesuits and they had encouraged him to return anytime for a visit or to take some courses at the University if there was a later opportunity.

When Peter was accused of child abuse in Oklahoma, the case was argued for years and revolved primarily around the statute of limitations. The state legislature had just extended the statute of limitations regarding sexual abuse of minors. Realizing that Peter was now within the grasp of the law, his bishop appealed to the Jesuits to shelter Peter until the decision regarding limitations could be appealed. The Jesuits accepted the secret request. The diocese fabricated the story that Peter unexpectedly disappeared from the diocese and his whereabouts were unknown.

His bishop recommended he seek psychiatric care once he was settled in Minneapolis. I taught at one of the Jesuit colleges in the area. I knew the Superior, hence the referral.

I have always refrained from considering any one patient as typical of any psychiatric illness or even of any particular behavioral proclivities. I believe people are too complex to attempt to group them in narrow categories. But Peter does come to mind when child abusers are mentioned. He was congenial, mild mannered, and appeared cooperative with any suggestions I made. He never displayed anxiety or irritability or depression. He *said* he was depressed but showed no symptoms of the illness. (I wondered if he thought it was appropriate for him to *be* depressed.) He stated definitively he would not, could not discuss the accusations made against him. He said there was always the possibility I and my records could be subpoenaed and he did not want to put me in "that uncomfortable position." More importantly his bishop instructed him under the vow of obedience to hold to "no comment" regarding the allegations. So let's play "checkers or cards," what else can we do with the time in my office?

A psychiatrist must assume the patient is telling the truth. If the patient lies, the patient is wasting money. If the patient tells the truth, the patient may benefit from treatment if they are willing to talk about important and pertinent matters as determined by the psychiatrist. That's how the process works. A psychiatrist is not a detective, not an investigator. He is a listener, a questioner, and an honest and determined helper.

I assumed Peter was telling the truth, but his stated limitations closed the door on anything meaningful. I continued to see him at two week intervals thinking he might become more open with me. He talked readily about his current situation, saying he read a lot, took long walks, and had lengthy visits with his Jesuit friends.

One day he mentioned meeting a Boy Scout leader and he expressed an interest in working with the man. I picked up on it immediately and advised him to think carefully about any such decision and to talk to me again before he signed on for anything of that kind. He made another appointment with me but didn't keep it. Before Peter left that day I asked if he would want a referral to see another psychiatrist after my departure. His declining did not surprise me.

Jane and I had decided three months earlier to move back to Maryland with Joe, the one child still living with us. My patients, including Peter, had received a letter with a thirty-day notice of my office closing.

About eighteen months after our move, someone rang the doorbell at our home in Olney, Maryland. Jane was home alone. When she opened the door, the man standing there asked if she was Jane Lee. When she replied in the affirmative, he handed her a subpoena and walked away. Sixteen youths in Minneapolis were suing the Jesuits, the Bishop in Minneapolis, the Bishop in Oklahoma, and my wife and me. They were accusing me of complicity, neglect, or some kind of involvement (I forget the particulars) in Peter's alleged sexual abuse of each plaintiff. They included Jane in the suit in case I put all our assets in her name.

The dates of abuse specified by the boys occurred several weeks after I left Minneapolis. They accused me of neglect in not arranging continued counseling for Peter when I left the area. A group of attorneys representing the plaintiffs and all the defendants flew back to Maryland and took my deposition. I was eventually dismissed from the case because of the timeframe and my notes which detailed my recommendations and Peter's response to them. Until our dismissal Jane and I underwent weeks of worry.

My attorney later informed me Peter was found guilty of the charges and each plaintiff was awarded $250,000 by court decree to be paid by the aggregate of defendants. The incident remains fresh in our minds.

I was later informed by one of my Jesuit friends that Peter was taken back to Oklahoma by the police and was being held in jail to stand trial for several charges of sexual abuse of minors in Oklahoma, now covered by the statutes of limitations. I had no desire to follow the case either through the media or friends.

During my years of practice I saw several priests in regard to alleged incidents of child abuse. Proper treatment was thwarted by limitations similar to those exhibited by Peter. They were silenced by the religious superior and/or showed personal unwillingness to discuss their behavior. The alleged perpetrators were much like Peter in affect and demeanor—friendly and almost eagerly cooperative but only to a point. Regardless of the charges they rarely showed signs of anxiety or discomfort in the office. General questions were answered easily and without hesitation. When asked about family history and childhood experiences they reported general details of everyday living but glossed over intimate details of family interaction. They withheld, concealed, or perhaps had no appreciation of the emotionally significant exchanges that regularly and naturally occur in family life. *The important information was always missing.*

Jane's mention of Peter brought the whole episode back. It was a timely comment. She wasn't disagreeing with me. She was stretching my thinking as she has always done.

I said to her, "You're right, my love. But we do need more time and more interaction with Fred before we draw any conclusions. During the time I've spent with him, he seemed quite open, direct and thoughtful. But all of that doesn't tell me much about *him*. And that reminds me, I intended to call Jack Tracey in the Chancery office and get whatever information he might be willing to give me. Jack must at least know where Fred previously served in this diocese and whether or not he's a Montana native. I seriously doubt he is. He's a big city guy."

As we got up from the table, Jane's final comment, "Watch yourself, Robbie, and watch Reverend Brown."

The warm days of August continue to ripen our five hundred and sixty acres of wheat. I need to do what I remember so well watching my father do. He'd walk a few yards into the wheat field, take a head of wheat and shell it in his hand. Readiness for harvesting depends on how easily and completely the kernels come out of the shells. I think of this every time I hear the Gospel reading in which the Pharisees question Jesus because he and his disciples, walking in a wheat field and hungry, shell the wheat on the Sabbath. Dad had a strict rule never to work on Sunday. But Sunday was an acceptable day to check the readiness of wheat for harvest.

Early this morning Jane and I drove to Springer. I needed a couple of parts for the baler, and Jane came along to pick up some spices to replace the empties. I went to Spencer's Machine Shop to pick up the parts and get bolts to go with them. As I came out, Father Brown was waiting for me.

His opening comment: "I'm glad I saw you. Do you have a few minutes? I've thought of something related to our recent conversation and I'm interested in your opinion. I guarantee not more than fifteen minutes."

"Jane's in the grocery store around the corner. Let me go and tell her where I'll be." I walked around and found Jane. "Sweetheart, could you get a cup of coffee and sit and wait for me while I go over to the rectory and talk to Father Brown? I just ran into him when I came out of Spencer's. I'll be back in fifteen minutes or so." She gave me "that look" and took off toward the coffee counter.

I drove to the rectory. Fred was welcoming and apologetic for his request, so he quickly moved to his question. "Let me ask your opinion about another subject: general sex education for the young. I have a friend who is a member of a religious community that specializes in retreats. He gives parish retreats specifically for young people. What would you think of my asking him to give a retreat here at St. Cyril's for our youth?"

I was quick to reply. "I realize we didn't get into that area very deeply a week or two ago when we talked about some of my opinions and the Sunday school guide. Sex information is an important topic for the kids in the class. It is a subheading for teenagers and at the same time a more critical issue than it is for adults and should, in my judgment, be handled in a careful but thorough manner.

"When I was in Catholic grade school, we had a couple of retreats by members of the community you mentioned. They made you feel sinful if you even thought about a girl or looked at her twice. They were 'hell fire and damnation' all the way. And I doubt their approach has changed. I say this in spite of the fact that their founder reportedly stressed the value of human liberty, the importance of informed consent, and the significance of concrete circumstances in evaluating moral behavior. I think those principles fell by the wayside somewhere through the years.

"These kids are mostly farm kids, and if they don't live on a farm they've certainly visited one. They are well aware of the fundamentals of sex in their observation of cattle and chickens and other animals. They are far ahead of the 'birds and bees' stuff nor do they need the frightening sex information provided by any group of preachers. In fact, I'm uncomfortable with priests or nuns discussing a topic about which they presumably have no personal knowledge. I have a scholarly work filled with valuable information about love, sexual behaviors, and justice. I will loan it to you sometime if you're interested. *Just Love* was written a few years ago by a nun-theologian named Farley. Of course, the Catholic Bishops have been highly critical of it, which makes it more likely to be read by less conservative Catholics and not by the doctrinaires.

"Fundamentally, what you're probably interested in is the morality of sexuality. In our fast moving society, kids are going to have to sort out much of that for themselves. They have guidelines coming from their parents, their reading, their teachers, and from talking with one another. And don't forget the social media available to all of them and carrying information on any topic they want to pursue. Sexual behavior has become a bit like the question of drug use. Parents, teachers, coaches, et cetera can talk and talk, but today's kids at some point are going to have to say 'yes' or 'no' on their own. These days they are less likely to make that decision on religious grounds or faith-based models. Peer pressure too often dominates their decisions. They need a broad knowledge base to deal with the complexities of sex as presented in our present society. I don't think a spiritual retreat would be acceptable or of any value to them."

I think Fred felt overwhelmed with this onslaught of words in reply to his simple question. I admit I get worked up about some issues. Although he did not differ openly with me, I had the impression Fred was not in total agreement with my comments. We engaged in a few general remarks about the weather and then said our goodbyes.

I called Jane on my cell as I drove away and she was waiting for me on the corner of Central and Yates just outside Safeway. On the way home I filled her in on my conversation with Fred. Her comment, "Sounds like you were pretty direct and laid it out clearly. Do you realize how much we think the same way but you are so adept at finding words for it while I just stumble around?"

I thought it was a good time for some levity. (Jane always regretted never learning to ride a bike.) I said, "You know I truly believe that's because you never learned to ride a bike. Bike riding enables a person to develop all kinds of skills that make the rest of life simple." I got a punch on the shoulder but not hard enough to interfere with my driving.

Jane and I did a sort of "pick-up" lunch, which is always fine with me. She's a great cook so I have to restrain my eating when she fixes one of her usual meals. As we ate we continued to talk about my meeting with Fred. She smiled as she asked, "Do you think Fred's looking for sex information for the teenagers or for himself?" I didn't reply and I'm quite sure she wasn't expecting one.

As I left the table and started for the door I said, "I'm going to ride up and check our cattle grazing on the state land near Wolf Butte. I'll be leaving in about half an hour. How about riding up with me and enjoy this nice day?" We have a four-month lease on one hundred and twenty acres of grazing land from the Montana Department of Natural Resources and Conservation.

Jane replied, "I'd love to come along. Let me tidy up first. If you'll bring Kate in and saddle her, I'll be down at the barn before two o'clock." Jane's horse (Kate) had a gentle disposition and was well trained with cattle. I rode a gelding named Ben. Don left four horses on the ranch. The other two were draft horses (work horses to us).

The saddle horses were in a five-acre pasture by the barn. I went out with a gallon can holding a few cups of oats. I called the horses and shook the can. They respond to their names, but the sound of oats gets their attention and brings them more quickly. I let each of them dip into the oat can for a few nibbles as they passed me and went into the barn. I bridled and saddled them with a saddle bag on each. I was just finishing when Jane walked in, ready to go, boots and all.

We rode four miles up the county road toward Wolf Butte. Then we crossed a cattle pass and headed directly toward the butte. A cattle pass is made of strips of wood or metal separated from each other by a space so large a cow's hoof will go between the strips. As a result cows are afraid to cross them; but one can cross in any kind of vehicle or on horseback. I always thought it was strange to call them "cattle passes" when they were just the opposite.

We had sixty-six heifers grazing on the rented land since July after they had pastured a couple of months in the company of our two bulls. Each tested positive for pregnancy before the move. I planned to move them in late October to winter pasture at the ranch where there were sheds to shelter them in storms and for calving in January and February. The baled hay would be nearby.

We crossed a second cattle pass into the leased pasture. I wanted to get a count today to be sure they were all there. Theft remains a possibility. Brand inspectors pay close attention when a person is transporting a horse out of the county. If the horse doesn't have your brand, you need papers showing you bought it. Someone who steals a cow is more likely to butcher it than to sell it. Pretty hard to find or reclaim a butchered cow.

The cattle were scattered in the field. We rode by all the treed areas and counted cattle as we went along. I also wanted to check the mountain creek to be certain it was not dry. The snow pack in the mountains had been light the previous winter and the water table might be low.

Black Angus cattle are difficult to see especially in patches of trees or lying down in areas of heavy buckbrush. Their natural pattern is to graze in the morning and lie down in the afternoon. Like people, it's their lazy time of day. I chose this time because it's easier to get an accurate count. We counted separately and checked with each other as we left each area. It took over an hour to ride through and we both ended up with sixty-six.

It was such a beautiful day with the gentle westerly breeze and the big sky of Montana deeply blue. I said, "Janey, let's ride up to that area at the base of the butte, the spot we used to go to with Don and Helen during summer visits. Remember, Helen would fix us a picnic lunch to take along. There's that old log cabin there."

Jane didn't hesitate. "Fine with me. It would be a shame not to take advantage of such a divine day. And I love it up there. It's a great place to look for forest loot. I found a few arrow heads when we were there with Don and Helen."

We left the State land and headed toward the base of the mountain about a mile off to the south and with a sharp rise in the terrain. When we arrived we dismounted, dropped the reins, and walked toward the cabin, ten yards away.

No one in the county knew when the cabin was built, but it must have been back in the early or mid-eighteen hundreds. Dad came from Canada in the 1880s, and the first job he had was cutting timber in this area for the Great Northern Railroad. The cabin was there at the time. It's made of roughly hewn logs, with no windows and an old weathered door with a rusted latch. Hunters still use it as a haven in an early winter blizzard during the deer and elk hunting season.

As we approached the cabin, Jane wandered to the right toward the surrounding woods as I expected she would do. I loved the way nature seemed to call her and then bless her with an unusual find to take home or to enrich her with a memorable view. She often found a stone or a small branch or a mountain flower or a special piece of bark to bring home, already knowing which shelf or table it would go on. The small metal box in her saddle bag rarely went home empty.

She was walking toward rough terrain with dead fallen trees, exposed tree roots and large rocks in the timbered areas. I said, "I'm going to have a look inside the cabin. Be careful in that area." I opened the cabin door and went in. It didn't smell musty because the rough logs allowed constant ventilation. With the light from the open door behind me my eyes accommodated quickly. Where the floor dust was thick there were shoe prints, none of them distinct.

I saw a few candy wrappers and an empty cookie box. Someone had been there since early August when I came by. Nothing remarkable about that. But it did seem unusual. I've rarely found evidence of visitors and I always come by when I'm in the area. I feel like I'm the caretaker because I know the cabin was meaningful to my father.

I turned and Jane was standing in the doorway. "Look what I found," she said, holding up a Sprite can and a Coke can. "They were over in those trees," and she pointed to the trees south of the cabin.

I replied, "Someone has been here since I came by in August. There are candy wrappers and a cookie box from Albertson's. I'd guess it was someone from Springer. Strangers aren't likely to come up across the fields to this out-of-the-way place. Whoever was here must know the area pretty well. Most likely it was more than one person coming to walk around a little, do some mountain climbing, get some clean fresh air, and have some lunch. They tidied up but didn't quite get it all."

I showed Jane the shoe marks in the dust. She looked closely and commented, "I think there are prints of at least two or three different shoes." She showed me where she was looking, and I agreed there were different markings. She found one print that looked smaller than the others. It was hard to be sure because they were all somewhat blurred, one on top of the other.

It was time to start back home. Our horses were standing where we dropped the reins. We put the empty cans, candy wrappers and cookie box in my saddle bag. I don't like to leave trash anywhere but especially in the mountains. Trash is an insult to mountain majesty.

During the ride home we talked about work we need to do. The wheat looks ready to harvest, but I'll check some heads in another day or two. Jane said the corn in her garden would soon be ready to eat. Fresh corn on the table is one of the joys of raising one's own garden. When I was a boy our garden must have covered two acres. Mom canned at least thirty quarts of various vegetables for the winter months, including corn off the cob. We said nothing further about the log cabin scene, but it continued to linger in my mind. When we rode into the yard Jane said, "If you take care of Kate, I'll start fixing dinner. We'll have the other half of the prairie chicken you shot yesterday and I dug up some new potatoes early this morning."

I replied, "That sounds good to me. I'll put Kate in the pasture and then I'll ride Ben to get the cows." I milk two cows twice a day. They're in a small pasture just across the county road. They provide plenty of milk and cream for Jane's cooking.

While we were eating supper (called dinner when we are in town), Jane reminded me I was going to call Jack Tracey in the chancery office. I asked, "Any particular reason you mentioned that now?"

"No, Robbie. I just got thinking about it on the ride home. Now that you ask, for some reason that smaller shoe mark in the cabin sticks in my mind."

I said, "I'll try to reach Jack after dinner. I have his home phone number and I don't think he'll mind. He called me at ten o'clock one night about two months ago when he had a parishioner in his office threatening to commit suicide unless he baptized her baby there and then. I'm curious as to what he did. I encouraged him to baptize the child or encourage her to do it herself. But if she wouldn't then he ought to. I said it wouldn't do the child any harm and it would send the mom home satisfied and presumably safe. Suicide is prevented, and God would bless the three of them. Jack owes me."

I made the call about eight o'clock. He answered, "Hey, Bob, how are you? It's good to hear from you. Is there something special on your mind?"

I replied, "First of all, how did you resolve the situation with the suicidal woman and her unbaptized child?"

Jack answered, "I took your advice and stretched my conscience a little and baptized the child as requested. I wasn't sure she was calm enough to accept the idea of baptizing the child herself. The mother continues to show up at my Sunday Mass, all smiles and a crying Christian baby. The husband never comes to Mass, and it was my concern they might not raise the child in the Catholic Church."

I said, "Does it really matter that much? Must they guarantee the child will be raised as a Catholic in order to baptize the baby? How many baptized raised-in- the-Church Catholics were once in your parish and no longer show up because they are going to some other church or none at all?" He admitted my comment was accurate.

I brought up the reason for my call. "Can you give me any information about Fred Brown, our new temporary pastor? What parish was he in before he came to St. Cyril's? Is he from this diocese? I never heard of him before. What's the story? Or better, what *can* you tell me?"

He responded, "There isn't much I know, and there's probably less I can tell you. Fred has been in the diocese about six years. He served as assistant pastor in a group of small churches in the Cut Bank area. The pastor there raised a question a couple of times with Bishop Butler regarding Fred's aloofness toward the general public. Some of the townspeople made complaints but always with the subheading that he was overly friendly with the boys of the town. He apparently was joining them in their pick-up touch football. The Bishop didn't like the sound of it. You needed a parish priest at St. Cyril's so Bishop Butler decided to give Fred a try on his own. That's the story."

I wasn't satisfied. "There must be more information about his background. Where did he originally come from? What seminary did he go to? Where was he ordained and when? He had a life prior to these past six years."

There was a long pause before Jack responded. I knew he was wondering how far he could go. "He came from somewhere in the southcentral U.S. I don't know why he left his original diocese, but I think he may have spent several years in another diocese or maybe two others before he came here. Information regarding his past service is either not available to Bishop Butler or else he keeps it to himself. And that's about all I can tell you. I have no idea where he went to the seminary, but somehow I heard it was a Sulpician seminary in St. Louis. I believe he came here from a Missouri Diocese." I thanked Jack for the information although I didn't see much real value in it. It was all very vague. We said the usual cordial goodbye.

Jane and I talked for an hour or more about the little I had just learned and about our own experience of Fred. Then I suggested we go to bed. I had to work on the combine in the morning to make some minor repairs and have it ready for the wheat harvest, next on the ranch agenda.

CHAPTER FOUR

The next Sunday was the first Sunday of September. Fred and I agreed I would say a few words after Mass to announce the opening of Sunday school classes. Jane and I left the ranch a little earlier than usual because I wanted to remind Fred about the arrangement. When we arrived at St. Cyril's, Jane went into the church and I went around the left to the sacristy, a small room located on that side toward the farther end of the church. The sacristy was entered by a separate outside door. The rectory was on that side of the church with the pastor's garage between the rectory and the sacristy. I was surprised to see a new black Toyota Tundra pickup parked in front of the garage.

Fred was in the sacristy vesting for Mass. After we greeted each other I said, "Is that beautiful truck yours, or do you have a visitor?"

Fred said with a smile, "No, it's mine. Do you like it? I bought it in Highland two weeks ago. I thought it would be more useful in a rural parish. I traded my three-year-old Lexus in on it. I really like to drive the pickup. It's higher; it has more power; it feels bigger and is bigger. "

My fleeting thought, "*Is that what this man needs: To be higher, bigger, more powerful?*" I was in a cheerful mood and decided I'd tease him a little. "Does that meet Bishop Butler's rules about 'no expensive cars for members of the diocesan clergy?' And have you given it a name?"

He was apparently in a good mood too. He countered with a smile and the comment, "This isn't a car. It's a truck, and the Bishop said nothing about

35

trucks. And I rarely see the Bishop anyway." After a moment he added, "It does need a name. I'll call it *The Bear*."

I responded, "Good name for a Montana truck." In a sense of levity I continued, "Yeah, how about the Freddy Bear, as in Teddy Bear?"

His face froze and seemed to darken. My attempted humor obviously hit a tender spot. He tried unsuccessfully to conceal his deep hurt and moved on quickly saying, "About this morning, at the end of Mass I will ask the congregation to remain to hear a few words about the start of Sunday school." He was actually turning away as he said those words and began picking up his vestments. It seemed like a very strange response. Months later I came to know the painful meaning it held for him. I left and went in to kneel beside Jane in the church.

After the last blessing Father Brown did the brief introduction. I know some of our parishioners are anxious to get out and get home; others will stand around and visit for thirty or forty minutes if it's a nice day and this one was nice. I wanted to make the message brief: "I recently talked with our new pastor, Father Brown, and suggested he might want to consider starting regular Sunday school again. As you all know it continued for a time after Father Joe left and then it just fell apart during the visits of Father Bruner. My brother was the teacher for many years prior to the demise of Sunday school during the Bruner period. I volunteered to start the program again, and Father Brown accepted my offer.

"I assume you who are parents will appreciate having Sunday school again during the school year. I suggested we have classes right after Mass on the second and fourth Sundays of the month from September through May. We will of course skip the fourth Sunday of December. Class will normally be over promptly at 10:30 unless there is a particular discussion that should be completed before the children leave. I promise that will not occur often.

"I don't believe there are any clear guidelines about who should attend. We think the classes will be appropriate for children between the ages of nine and fourteen. If older children want to attend they would be welcome, but we think younger children should learn about their faith from their parents and their attendance at Mass. Preparation for First Communion in this parish has traditionally been done by the parents. Father Brown and I will help you with that if you so desire. We anticipate there will be approximately twelve youngsters attending. Does anyone have a question or wish to comment?"

John Mansfield raised his hand and asked about preparation for the Sacrament of Confirmation. Fred and I previously talked about that so I responded, "I'll ask Father Brown to answer your question, John."

Father Brown said, "We never know when Bishop Butler will come to the parish to confirm those teenagers who are the proper age. We cannot expect him every year. He will notify us well in advance of the time he has chosen, and Mr. Lee and I will arrange the preparation for those due to be confirmed."

There were no more questions. I thanked them for their time and they filed out of the church. Father Brown usually stands at the door and speaks with people as they leave. He's not much of a hand-shaker. This morning he went directly to the sacristy. I didn't see him again. I wondered if it was because of my earlier comment about the bear. We visited for a half hour with the Kirbys and the Brills; both families were grateful for the restart of Sunday school. Together they have five who will be attending.

On our way home Jane said she thought it was a good idea to restart Sunday school and she was glad I not only volunteered but brought the whole idea back into circulation. I asked if she noticed Fred's new Tundra. She had not. I told her of my exchange with Fred about a name for the truck and how angry he appeared when I made my comment "Freddy Bear as in Teddy Bear." Jane agreed it was a strange reaction to an attempt at humor.

After lunch I decided it was a good day for the harvest ritual of shelling a few kernels of wheat. While I helped Jane with the dishes I told her what I planned to do and asked her to join me. We went from the ranch house to the 160 acre wheat field we called the "east field" because it was east of the county road. We walked about five yards into the wheat. I pulled off a head, gave it to Jane and then took one in my hand and showed her how to shell it. I shelled a couple and all three shelled out quite easily. It's time to begin the harvest.

Before we went home, I drove two miles to the one hundred and forty-acre "north field" as in north of the ranch house. The wheat shelled nicely but not quite as completely as in the first field. I'll begin the harvest in the other field.

Monday I finished milking by the time Jane had breakfast ready. After we ate, Jane began doing the dishes. I said, "I'll take the combine up to the east field and begin cutting. If you bring the grain truck by 8:30, I'll probably have a tank full and will need to empty."

Jane came over, gave me a kiss and said with a smile, "Happy harvest. I'll be there in plenty of time." Good start to my day.

The day passed quickly. Jane and I work well as a team. I run the combine, and she has the truck ready for me to unload the grain. She drives the truck to the granary and unloads using the electric auger.

By Thursday we moved to the north field and anticipated we might finish it early next week. Then we'll have another two hundred acres left to do on the O'Hara field (named after its prior owner). A self-propelled combine is a miracle compared to harvesting when I was a boy. Then there was a horse-pulled binder which cut and bound the grain in bundles to be picked up by hand and stacked in a group, later loaded on wagons and hauled to a machine that separated the wheat kernels from the straw and chaff. There was a crew of about twelve. Jane and I do it all now in two or three weeks depending on the weather. Can't cut grain when it's wet or too damp; won't shell.

We finished the second field late Tuesday of the following week. At the end of the day I still had time to move the combine to the last field for an early start on Wednesday morning. That final field was almost finished by Saturday evening. The rest remained to do next week.

Sunday was the second Sunday of the month, a Sunday school day. I went over the topic the night before. It related mostly to the founding of the Catholic Church, the missionary work of St. Paul, and the leadership of St. Peter.

As we drove to Mass I commented, "I hope Fred has gotten over his irritation of last Sunday. If I was sure I offended him and knew what the offense was, I would certainly apologize and try to soothe his feelings. But I'd feel foolish even bringing up the subject of Freddy Bears and Teddy Bears."

Jane took a few minutes before she spoke. "My guess is it will be over and he'll be his usual self. It must have something to do with another time, perhaps his childhood; but a time he has tried to forget and for the most part has forgotten. You just woke the sleeping tiger, or more likely a sleeping teddy bear, from his childhood or even his infancy. He'll get over it, and I doubt he'll ever mention it again. And I agree, I don't think you should bring it up."

The subject still bothered me. "I wonder whether or not he'll remind people of Sunday school class today. Maybe I'll walk around to the sacristy and remind him. Then I'll get a feel for what his attitude is."

We parked at the church, and as Jane went in, I walked around to the sacristy. The Tundra was parked as it was last week. I walked over to get a better look at the dashboard. I had considered buying one but thought they were too expensive for us. As I looked in the front seat, I saw a couple of candy wrappers on the floor. My thought was, "I guess Fred likes a candy bar sometimes when he's driving." I was moving away from the car when I noticed an empty cookie box on the back seat with *Albertson* marked on the top. I immediately thought of the log cabin in the woods. I decided it was not a good idea to speak to Fred right then. I joined Jane inside the church.

I was distracted from time to time during Mass, and it sort of annoyed me. I try to be prayerful and absorb the spirituality of the service. But there was a recurring question in my mind. Is there any connection between these two findings of candy bars and a cookie box? I tried to pray, but it kept popping back into my head. At the end of Mass Fred reminded the congregation I would conduct Sunday school in the basement. The basement room is a large pleasant room used for activities, lectures (which rarely happen), social gatherings, occasionally wedding receptions, and Sunday school.

All the expected kids were there except one of the Kline girls, but her sister, Helen, said Barbara was ill. I began the class. "I know all of you, and of course I know your parents. I would remind you my brother Don taught this class in past years and maybe some of you who are older were in his class." Three or four acknowledged that by raising hands.

"I'm going to read a scripture passage in which Jesus tells Peter he is the rock on which the Lord will build his church. Then I'll read a passage telling of the conversion of St. Paul, an early missionary.

"But before I do that let me give you some idea of how I want to conduct these classes throughout the year. I'll begin by telling you the keynote or focus of the morning and read some related scriptural passages. I may make a comment or two related to the topic of the day. Then I will ask you to share your thoughts with the class. Now *this is very important.* There are no right answers. I'm not looking for answers, just your thoughts, or maybe your feelings about the topic, questions you may have in your mind, something you want explained, something you don't agree with, whatever may come into your mind as I bring up a topic. This is a class where there are only two important rules:

first, we listen to and respect each other; second, we are free to say or ask whatever is on our minds."

As I'm saying the last few words, I notice Fred come in the door at the back of the room. I continued, "I see Father Brown coming in and perhaps he would like to say a few words to you. Come on up front, Father Brown. I'll have each member of the class introduce themselves."

Fred continued to come toward me, smiling and looking relaxed. He seemed comfortable with the youngsters and as he walked, he said, "I think I've probably met all of you or at least I've seen you at Mass with your parents. I want to welcome all of you to Mr. Lee's class and hope it will be a valuable experience for you. I know Mr. Lee had experience teaching in three or four different colleges so teaching at this level may be somewhat of a new experience for him. But I know I can rely on his personal credentials so I feel confident leaving you in his Sunday classroom.

"There is one area that concerns me so I thought I would address it even though this is the first class or perhaps *because* this is the first class. I have been considering the possibility of having someone from outside the parish come and provide a couple of talks in a special program for all of you."

Inside my head I dreaded hearing what he was going to say. I knew he was going to bring up the topic of sex and inside I'm screaming at him, "Brown, don't do it! Leave it alone! This you cannot handle! Walk away, man!" But I didn't dare open my mouth for his sake *and* for the kids' sake. I knew interfering would destroy Sunday school on the spot. I have seen Fred's anger, how he shuts down and walks away.

Off he went on Gullible's Travels. "I'm going to say a little about sexual sins today, at least a few fundamental things I think you should be aware of. Most sexual sins are mortally sinful. And you know you must tell mortal sins to a priest for them to be forgiven. So you cannot go to Communion unless you have been to confession."

I'm thinking, "Where have you been these last thirty or forty years? What a harsh, poorly informed confessor you would be?"

He continued, "I think young people these days, young people your age need to have some basic knowledge about matters related to sex. To get some idea of where you are on the subject, let me, for a few minutes, open it up to any questions you might have regarding the subject of sex."

I'm thinking, "You're a fool to encourage this group, mixed by age and gender, to ask questions freely and especially in this first class. They use expressions they don't even understand and you haven't even heard, and you're going to come out looking like a fool."

Since the kids were more aware of and sensitive to the age and gender issues than Fred was, there were no responders. Fred waded knee-deep into the marsh and seemed determined to wait in the murky water until he got an answer. A long period of uneasy silence, especially with teenagers, can quickly become emotionally charged. I believe everyone in the class (myself included) was embarrassed by Fred's confrontational attitude and blunt introduction of the subject. Continuing silence only enhanced the growing anxiety in each of us.

I saw Tim Quirk beginning to fidget in his seat, and suddenly he sort of blurted out, "What's a hard-on? I heard my mother ask her boyfriend if he had one." You can imagine the snickers and the "looking somewhere else" reaction. I think some of the boys especially felt Tim's discomfort over the response to Fred's question. Their supportive reaction was to ask additional questions so Tim would not stand alone. Tom Brill asked, "Is it a sin to look up a girl's dress?" Helen Kline asked, "What does 'prick' mean? I hear my father use it all the time." Jim Mansfield asked, "Is it a sin to touch a girl's boobs? That's what my sister calls them." To which his sister Mary replied, "I DO NOT!"

I couldn't let Fred do *this* to *these* kids in *my class*. I was going to intrude whether he liked it or not. We had to move away from the sex subject. I spoke, "I don't want you to think I'm disagreeing with Father Brown about anything he said, but we'll be taking up the subject of sin in a later class. Let me just say, and I know Father Brown will agree, the church teaches a mortal sin must include three things. These are: first, a serious matter, second, sufficient reflection, and third, full consent of the will. Most sins you might commit are probably not serious matters. But let's assume the act is indeed a serious one. Sufficient reflection means you've thought about the act with a clear mind; so it's not something you do on impulse. Like my impulse when I hit my thumb with a hammer and let out a couple of bad words. There must also be full consent of the will. This part is a little tricky because here is where emotions come into play. If you do something because you're very angry or very sad or very lonely or very frightened, those feelings easily interfere and can have a major part in whether or not the behavior is sinful and also how sinful.

"Suppose you're walking on a dark street and someone starts chasing you. You just left a pick-up ball game with friends and you happen to be carrying a baseball and you have a pretty good throw. The pursuer is catching up and begins threatening to kill you when he catches you. Do you think it's a sin if you turn and take him down with your throw?" I realized my examples weren't too good, but this was total "spur of the moment" stuff.

"I'm sure Father Brown didn't want to go into all these details today. He's undoubtedly busy and he knows we will cover the matter of sin a few lessons from now. And as far as the questions you started asking about sexual matters, we can consider them at a more appropriate time."

The floor belonged to Fred. He seemed to have found his reasoning ability again and responded gracefully, "Mr. Lee is quite right, and I did speak rather freely but poorly because of the press of time. Some people are waiting to see me in my office so I'll be on my way and let your capable teacher take you down the road of religion." I was probably the only one who caught the note of sarcasm in his comment. He walked out *as if* in a hurry.

After he left the room, I added another clarification or really a correction. "Let me make one more thing clear: sins are forgiven when we ask God to forgive them either by saying the Act of Contrition you all know or simply by asking God in our own words to forgive us. It is God who forgives our sins, not the priest. If we have done something really serious, we should go to confession if possible before receiving Communion. We'll talk more about this in later classes."

There wasn't much time left so I made a few comments about the topic with which we began and then dismissed the class saying, "Have a good two weeks. Most of you will be busy helping your parents after you get home from school. Good luck in your class work. I should change that to 'good studying,' luck is not what you need. See you in two weeks."

When I left the church, Jane was visiting with the Mansfields and the Brills. The Mansfield kids were the two who brought up the "boobs instead of breasts" comments. I joined the conversation until Jim and Mary came up. Then Jane and I said goodbye and walked toward the car.

Before we got to the car, I heard Fred call my name. He was approaching as I turned around and took a few steps toward him. As he got close and out of the hearing of others, he quietly said, "Just wanted to thank you for bailing me out during your class. You probably knew I was in over my head. I think it's probably wiser for me not to address that certain subject unless it comes up in someone's confession. I appreciate your help. Have a good week." He didn't wait for a response but turned around and walked toward the rectory. I hated to think about these youngsters going to confession to this narrow-minded and poorly informed man, at least in the area of sexuality.

As we drove away, I expected Jane would be full of questions. The question she asked was certainly not the one I expected. "Do you realize Father Brown has been here almost three months and he has never once looked me in the eye?"

I could hardly believe what she said. Yet I know how observant she is and how carefully she zeros in on the behaviors of people about whom she has any question, doubt or discomfort. I replied, "If anyone else told me that, I don't think I'd believe them but I certainly have no reason to doubt you. Now that you mention it, I can't remember any situation in which I saw any exchange between the two of you. He ignored you the first day we met. I remember that well. We talked about it. Do you have any idea why this would be happening?"

Jane was quick to answer. "He doesn't trust me is my feeling. I have no idea why, other than the fact I don't trust him. Perhaps he senses my lack of trust."

I commented, "Maybe he is in some way aware of it, although I don't think you have overtly done anything that would give him cause to feel that way. I suspect he's always studying people and probably comes up with uncertainty about you. Deep down I believe he doesn't have a great deal of confidence in his own abilities and is fearful others will see behind the façade. The first day even before we met him you said he was kind of '*wooden.*' Do you remember that?

"But we're home now so let's continue this during lunch. I have some interesting things to tell you about this morning. If you'll ready the lunch, I'll go have a quick look at a sprocket on the combine. I may need to replace it before we start up again tomorrow. The weather report says we are going to have rain tonight so combining tomorrow morning is unlikely.

"After lunch, what would you think about our driving to Black Eagle? We could visit the Russel Art Gallery, check out a couple of antique stores, wander through the enlarged mall, maybe see a movie, have an early dinner at the Lewis and Clark Hotel and get back in time for me to do the milking. Or better, I'll ask Ted if he or one of the boys can do the milking and we'll come home whenever we please. We may even have time for a Southern Comfort Manhattan. Oh, by the way I believe there is a new Nordstrom store in Black Eagle. If you watch our time carefully, we could squeeze in a quick go-through."

Jane responded, "It sounds inviting. Of course I'd love to go, Robbie. We always enjoy our time together whatever we do. I have one added suggestion. Let's leave Fred Brown out of the rest of our day. Somehow he begins to feel like an intruder." The last part of her response surprised me, but I was grateful for the suggestion.

As I walked out the door I said, "It's a deal, Babe, and I'll be back before you have lunch ready."

CHAPTER FIVE

As predicted, it rained late Sunday night after we got home from Black Eagle. It measured about a quarter of an inch on the rain gauge but it was enough to keep me from cutting wheat Monday morning. I decided to buy another sprocket to replace the one on the combine so delay of a day would not be a major problem as long as the rain doesn't continue and we have sunny skies.

I told Jane I'd be going into Springer about ten o'clock and she decided to go in with me. She wanted to pick up some paint supplies at The Gallery store. She hasn't had time for painting this summer, but with leisurely days in the fall and winter months she'll undoubtedly be finding scenes in the foothills and the mountain ranges to put on canvas.

On the way to town I reminded Jane she suggested we should leave Fred Brown out of our Sunday afternoon trip. I commented it was a wise recommendation. The day and evening were free of any mention or any thought of him. But now it was time to share my Sunday morning experience. I summarized what occurred yesterday morning prior to Mass and then the Sunday school fiasco after Mass.

I gave a pretty accurate and sequential summary of events: seeing the candy wrappers and cookie box in Fred's truck and then a fairly detailed report of the Sunday school class. Jane digests information quickly and sometimes comes out with an immediate reaction often tinged if not tainted by emotion.

Then she mollifies her spontaneous reaction with a more thoughtful and more considered response. "That guy's an ass! He needs to be locked up somewhere. You should call Bishop Butler and let him know we have a lemon out here. Brown didn't show much sense bringing up sexuality in such a ridiculous manner. You certainly gave him a break intervening the way you did. Your comments must have cleared the air and brought some reassurance to the kids that at least you knew how to talk to them."

I pulled up at The Gallery and parked so we could finish the discussion. Jane went on, "Maybe you're beginning to wonder about Brown as I have from the beginning. You ought to pay close attention to things the kids might say about him when they come to your class. I'm sure you will. I'll get out and you go ahead to find the sprocket you need. Take your time because I could look around in here for an hour or two although I know we don't have that kind of time."

I responded, "It's nine-twenty. Suppose I pick you up about eleven o'-clock. I'll park and find you in the store. I'll look around Stenzel's for a while and see what new machinery is on the market." Jane kissed me and hopped out.

I parked outside Stenzel's and in no time found the sprocket I was looking for. I paid for it up front and took it to the car, planning to come back in and look around at the merchandize. As I turned to go back in the store, I saw Tim Quirk walking leisurely down the street.

Let me tell you a little about Tim and his mother, Lucy. They moved into Springer about four years ago. I remember my brother telling me about their arrival. Tim must have been five years old at the time. He's nine now. There was gossip about Lucy from the beginning. She used a lot of make-up and dressed with a maximum of legal exposure. She was also quite pretty and had a ready smile. She was a "friendly" woman. There was talk that different men used to visit her in the evening and stay late.

Tim was small for his age. He had difficulty fitting in with his peers and was somewhat shy around adults. He had an engaging smile, some clumsy mannerisms, and his verbal responses were slow and on occasion off target. Some of his difficulty must have been due to his home life, and there was also the fact that his peers often teased him because of his name, calling him "quirky kid" and "quirky queer."

In spite of his response patterns and name, or maybe because of them and because of his mother's behavior, Tim had more or less become the town waif. Everyone knew him and each in his or her own way sort of "looked after him." Even his peers had relented on their teasing and had become more supportive of him, as I noted before in the Sunday school class. I waited by the store as Tim approached. He smiled and cheerfully said, "Hello, Mister Lee."

I held out my hand and we shook hands rather formally. "Good morning, Tim. It's nice to see you. What have you been up to lately? And aren't you supposed to be in school this morning?" He said his mother was not feeling well and he was going to the drug store to pick up some medicine for her. He would go to school after he took it home. He didn't seem to be in a hurry.

I decided to walk with him a short distance, and we began to talk. I asked if he had time to stop at McDonald's and get a milkshake. He readily agreed and assured me he had the time. We were soon sitting down with chocolate shakes. Tim seemed relaxed and comfortable.

In retrospect I admit wanting to obtain information from Tim regarding his reaction to the Sunday school class and more importantly to Father Brown. I didn't want to be too direct about it, so I started with a few general comments about the day, the beginning of another school year and the rain of yesterday. Tim responded with limited remarks but stayed focused on each subject, which he often doesn't do. Perhaps the one to one of the situation made it easier for him and the milkshake helped keep his focus within the parameter of our table.

I got around to asking more about him, "Now that school has started, do you have any happy times, fun things to do, or chances to play with some of the other kids?"

He abandoned his straw momentarily and with a big smile replied. "We had a great time last night with Father Brown. He took Pat and Joe and Tom and Jim and me to Nelson Reservoir yesterday about five o'clock to swim, and afterwards we had a cookout.

"We all played around in the water for about an hour. No one else was around so Father Brown suggested we could skinny-dip since the sun was going down and it would be getting dark. I didn't want to at first, but the other kids took their suits off so I did too. Father Brown kept his suit on and continued to swim around with us. We had a beach ball we were tossing to each other.

"After a while Father Brown got out and started a charcoal fire. He brought all the stuff for the fire and had small camp chairs and a cooler with hotdogs and sodas and blankets to put on the grass. He hauls it all in the back of his new truck.

"When the fire was going well, he came over and hollered, 'Come on, guys. Hotdog time and then s'mores.' When we came out of the water, he said 'if you want to stay bare while you sit by the fire, you will dry out well before you put your clothes on.' I put my clothes on and Tom and Jim put on theirs, but Pat and Joe stayed naked. I thought it looked sort of funny to see them eating that way."

I asked, "Do you think Father Brown thought it was funny?"

Tim grinned a little as he replied, "He smiled a lot and teased them saying their hotdogs might get a bit too warm. Then a little later he asked them if he could warm their hotdogs a little. I wasn't sure what he meant, but they all seemed to think it was funny. The whole thing seemed a little strange to me, but it was a fun day to swim in the reservoir and to sit by the fire and eat."

In my practice I'd heard various stories from adults and children about how they were sexually seduced by others. I don't think I ever heard a story from a child who was witness to sexually seductive behavior but seemed totally unaware of its significance. I often wondered how seduction of children *typically begins.* I also wondered about what "funny" sexual scenes Tim may have seen in his own home.

I watched this innocent little nine-year-old finish his milkshake, wipe his mouth on his sleeve, and make squirming movements that indicated he should be on his way. He was clearly unaware of the rather shocking things he just finished telling me. As I think of it now, I realize they weren't shocking for him. They were just playful behaviors of peers in which he innocently participated. Not surprising he had asked the question in Sunday school class about what a "hard-on" was.

I was already wondering: Has he told others? Would he tell others? It seemed to spill out so easily and so innocently. He had no idea how damning the story could be in the ear of others. For some people the next stop might be the police or the Bishop. And what should I do? How could I or should I intervene?

As I kept thinking about it my mind came up with an alternative view. Is it possible this was all a pretty innocent, early teenage playful evening? Was I coloring a picture black when it may have been quite innocent? Am I the one who's making a mountain out of a simple, playful, goofy evening spent by five kids and one adult who could possibly have absolutely no sexual interest in anything the kids were doing? Tell that story to the judge or to the Bishop and see if either one buys it! No, I was not exaggerating.

As we left the shop, I put my hand on Tim's shoulder and said, "Thanks for joining me. It was pleasant to talk with you. We must have a milkshake again sometime. By the way, perhaps the things you told me about your evening with Father Brown and the other boys should be kept as kind of 'club' information just for the altar boys. Other kids might be jealous if they knew the pastor had a sort of special relationship with you guys."

"That's the same thing Father Brown said when he took us up to Wolf Butte last Sunday." Tim was adding another chapter to the tale of Fred Brown. "Tom Brill said he knew the way because his parents' farm is south of town and Tom had been there a couple of times. Father Brown said he was anxious to give us a ride in his new truck so we asked him to take us. I was never up there before. That was as much fun as the reservoir was last night." And after that last piece of information, Tim mumbled a "goodbye" and went on to the drug store.

I always suspected the shadow of autism appeared in Tim's behavior. After he left, I began to wonder why he was so verbal and coherent in our conversation today. I came up with several reasons that seemed valid to me. There was just the two of us. I sat directly across from him. I looked at him consistently and with a show of interest. There were no distractions. He could fidget with the straw in his milkshake without losing his theme. He was reporting on something still visible in his mind, something that had been pleasant and satisfying for him. In short, we both had his complete attention.

As Tim walked away, I got in the car and was at The Gallery about two minutes to eleven. Jane was looking out the door as I parked in front of the shop. She came out with a few packages in her hands. When she opened the car door she said, "Robbie, would you go in and pick up the three frames I bought? I couldn't manage them and the packages too."

"Of course, Love." The frames must have been twenty-four by eighteen. Good landscape sizes and well-suited for landscape scenes.

When I returned to the car, I said, "Would you like to go to lunch at The Canteen or shall we go home? And how was the shopping? Did you find all the items you wanted?"

She thought it over for a few seconds and then replied, "Let's go home. I have some beef stew left over from the other day, and the key lime pie I made on Saturday is still waiting for you." Jane knew my love for key lime pie. She knew all the dishes I liked and catered to them extravagantly. She continued, "And yes, the shopping went well. They are almost as well stocked as The Artist Nest in Minneapolis was."

On the way to the ranch, I told Jane about meeting Tim and the conversation we had. She expressed no surprise, made no interruptions, and listened carefully as I went over Tim's story close to word for word. I was a careful listener with an ability to remember details almost verbatim. It was, after all, a valued asset in an active psychiatric practice.

When I finished my story, Jane remained silent for what seemed a long time. I'm familiar with her thoughtfully sorting through the things I say. Her response was a surprise, but I should have known her compassion would trump everything else. "That poor little boy! What a shame to catch this sad little boy in such an unholy scene! Isn't his life already difficult enough with the mom he has! This Brown guy is way out of line with these kids. He needs to be stopped and the sooner the better. What are you going to do about this?"

We drove into the yard as Jane finished her comment. But there was no stopping this conversation now. It continued as we walked into the house and during preparation for lunch and the eating of lunch and the cleaning up after lunch. And then we went out to the shady porch and sat on the swing until we finished.

I was already feeling uncomfortable with what I learned from Tim, but I wasn't feeling any great responsibility for interfering in the situation. The whole thing may have been quite innocent. A bunch of boys skinny dipping is not such an unusual event. Tim may have felt uncomfortable because he wasn't really a close friend to any of them and they probably hang out together. Does the priest bystander make a great difference in the scene? If he were not a priest, maybe a father or an uncle, would that make it less questionable? Or perhaps not questionable at all? And his inviting them to remain naked when they came to eat, what's the big deal about that? They're just kids. They're all male. Let them dry out. Why make an "illicit sex scene" out of what may only have been an innocent swimming party and cookout?

I summarized the above thoughts for Jane, knowing she would undoubtedly disagree with me. Which is precisely what she did. "Come on, Rob, we've had our doubts about Brown from the first day we saw him. We know he was in the Wolf Butte cabin with those kids. What do you think they were doing there? Playing hopscotch or some kind of 'you show me yours and I'll show you mine'?"

"Okay, Janey, you've made your point, and I will acknowledge what you say may well be true. But I don't want to act too quickly. Let me see if I can find out more about Fred Brown's background. I'll get on the computer and see what dirt I can dig up or what past sins I can uncover. Tracey didn't give me much to go on when I talked to him. But we know Fred's from a Southern state and possibly went to a Sulpician Seminary in St. Louis. So let's try to guess his likely age. I'd put him at forty-eight. What's your guess?"

Jane said, "I'd say forty-eight to fifty. He's probably showing more age than he'd like to. Maybe he bought the Tundra to make him feel younger."

I continued our guesswork. "Okay, let's do some figuring. We'll say he's forty-nine. Let's assume he took a normal path to the priesthood. He graduated high school at eighteen. I doubt he's one of those geniuses who graduate early. Four years of college, and he'd be twenty-two.

"The guys studying for the priesthood are lucky these days. They probably don't even take Latin. I had four years of it in high school and another four in college with a couple of years of Greek. Remember, we recently saw our granddaughter's Latin book with active stories written in what we called 'a dead language.'

"Sorry, I'm digressing. Fred finishes college at age twenty-two. Then four years in the seminary for theology, church history, scripture, et cetera. He would be ordained at age twenty-six. We'll subtract twenty-six from forty-nine and come up with twenty-three. I'll search for ordination records approximately twenty-three years ago. I'll try to find the St. Louis seminary online. They may have some class photos. If I come up with a blank, then I'll look at other seminaries in the South. I'll do a search of five or six dioceses in the Southern states and see what I can find. We should be able to learn at least more than we currently know. I almost forgot, Jack said he believed Fred spent a few years in two or three different central Southern states.

"This is all going to take some time. You know I'm not very sharp on the computer, but I can always get help from our son Edward in Boise. He owns an IT company. And, my darling, I'm sorry, but I'm not likely to even get started on the project this week. We have harvesting to continue, and the weather looks like we can get back on the O'Hara field at dawn tomorrow. Well, not really at dawn. We'll wait for the sun to burn off any dew that falls during the night."

The weather was good the next morning, and after breakfast I left for the wheat field. As usual I needed Jane to come with the grain truck in about thirty to forty minutes. The combine was running well with the new sprocket. The sieve that caused trouble was working fine. I chided myself for not replacing it earlier.

At lunch time we sit in the shade of the truck to eat. Jane brings a cooler in the cab with sandwiches, canned Pepsi, and her wonderful oatmeal raisin cookies. We typically don't get into heavy conversations during these "field lunches." We are both focused on the work and the need to finish the harvest while the good weather lasts.

The next few days went quickly and productively. By noon on Thursday the field was finished and so was the harvesting. The wheat was in the granary. It was time for a celebratory lunch. Jane served sweet corn on the cob freshly picked from her garden along with some shepherds' pie from the evening before. We complimented each other for a job completed and well done.

There is always a sense of freedom and rejoicing when the harvest is finished. It is a spiritual experience. We are keenly aware we have contributed to something sacred, participated in the work of creation, providing bread for the hunger of God's people. We often talk about how much ranch life awakens our faith or perhaps more accurately our spirituality.

My father's faith and my brother Don's were securely rooted in the land they lived and worked on. They were aware of their dependence on God's Providence. They behaved like God's fellow gardeners. Jane and I feel the same alliance in our daily chores but especially when new calves are born in winter and garden vegetables are gleaned in summer. These events seem more personal than the wheat fields and hay fields. Do we feel more invested in the vegetables and the calves because we touched them, held them in our hands? It doesn't surprise me when we ask God to hold us in His Hands. Touch can have a sacred quality.

It was time to move to other pursuits and at the top of my list was to find information about Fred Brown. I promised Jane this would be first on my agenda once the harvest was finished. The computer was now my harvester. I used an old desktop with a regular keyboard. It felt more like tools in my hands, a familiar feeling these last few years.

We agreed on forty-nine as Fred's current age, so I focused my search twenty-three years ago. Since Fred's age was a guess, I spread my search three years in each direction, a total of seven years. First I looked for seminaries in eight south-central states. I found four currently listed, and in Fred's time there were seven. None were staffed by Sulpician Fathers. I searched available records in each seminary and found nothing. In many cases records were poorly kept or unavailable.

Next I searched diocesan records in those states for the same seven years. This was "a needle in a haystack" search. Records were incomplete, unavailable, or in some cases, I suspect, expunged. I assumed records became far more significant and possibly perilous due to the abuse of minors by Catholic clergy. It was rare to find records clearly intact with name, date of birth, birthplace, parish of origin, assignments, and similar information one would expect.

Finally I checked major newspapers for articles published in the spring and early summer of the seven years. The ordination of a priest apparently made the news only when the man was from that city or its environs. The accessible Catholic press carried coverage of local ordinations only.

My search bore some fruition. I came up with names of fifty-four newly ordained priests for the eight states during that seven year period. Of the fifty-four, Brown was not an uncommon name. There was Clarence Brown, Patrick C. Brown, George H. Brown, Charles F. Brown, and Terrance Brown. No Fred Brown.

After three hours of computer frustration I decided to put it aside for now and spend some time with Jane. But the afternoon was gone. It was time to do the evening chores. After dinner I told Jane my frustrating computer experience had no significant results. She didn't pressure me to continue but said, "If it's too exasperating, you can always let it go."

Saturday morning after I finished morning chores and ate my breakfast I tackled the computer again. I had searched available information during the seven years I was considering. Then it occurred to me to go back about ten years from now and see if Fred Brown showed up. This brought a result. Eight years ago there was a Fred Brown in the Missouri Diocese of St. Louis. I remembered Jack Tracey told me he thought Fred came here from Missouri.

My finding the name didn't do me a lot of good. There were just the basics: Frederick Brown, assistant priest in St. Anthony's parish in St. Louis. I searched records of ordinands in Missouri going back a total of twenty years with the expectation his name would show up. I found nothing more.

As a side result of this research, I noted how severely the number of ordinands gradually declined after the late sixties. Many left the priesthood in the sixties and seventies after the Second Vatican Council of 1962-65. Why the flight? Perhaps it was partly due to disappointment caused by the reactionary backlash of the conservative hierarchy to some of the conciliar positions. During the Council the factor of *emotions* had quietly and almost imperceptibly (mistakenly in the view of some) crept into the Vatican. Among other changes the Council had relaxed some of the stringent paths to obtaining a dispensation from a priest's vows.

In support of clergy requests for dispensations, I had over the years written numerous letters stating essentially "after a thorough psychiatric evaluation, it is my opinion that at the time of ordination Father So-And-So did not have the emotional clarity and stability to make such a weighty lifetime decision." Having had a couple of years in seminary, I had firsthand knowledge of the cookie-cutter training provided on the road to ordination.

I knew how the doubts and misgivings of ordinands were typically confronted by seminary advisors. "My son, doubts like you are having occur to everyone as they approach the solemn day of ordination. The devil tempts us all, especially if we want to dedicate ourselves to the service of the Lord. Continue to pray and the Lord will keep you on your path and give you all the graces you need to serve Him well." The least they could have said was, "Let's talk about it."

When one is drowning in doubts, it is natural to grab hold of anything someone hands you, even if it is a straw. These poor guys found no matter how many straws they were handed by bishops, confessors, and fellow priests they were slowly sinking in the loneliness and tedium of their priestly life.

An escape route was now accessible, and many of the clergy, who needed emotional closeness and/or feminine companionship or who were just not sufficiently adept at living in a monarchical setting, were freed. The vow of celibacy had constantly, and mercilessly for some, confronted them without relief.

And the vow of obedience had its own painful dynamic. Imagine being forty or fifty years old and having someone you hardly know tell you to pack your bags and move to another town two hundred miles away. This abrupt order might come after you lived in your present parish only two or three years, and you couldn't be sure how long you would be in the new one. Especially for those with relationship needs, it must feel like a vagabond life without roots and with ties abruptly and arbitrarily terminated and without significant cause.

Bishops and Diocesan Chancellors (bishops' right-hand men) would defend themselves and say no one was ever transferred without being called into the Chancery to discuss the matter. No amount of discussion would have changed the decision. It was an empty formality. The vow of obedience supersedes any argument, no matter how valid.

I remember in the seminary when we raised any questions with the Superior regarding theology, scripture, or certain behaviors, no matter how the discussion went, his final answer as he sternly shook his head, *"It's the mind of the Church."* End of discussion. Present day dogmatic-like declarations don't seem to come so easily, so clearly, so neatly packaged, like frozen dinners. *The mind of the Church* doesn't cut it for a majority of Catholics these days.

The recent and ongoing exodus of priests generally does not include those who are homosexual. They are rarely motivated to change their life choice since the situation provides an emotional closeness for them as well as opportunities for clandestine relationships. Priests who are cissexual are expected to avoid personal and private relationships with women other than family members. If they have such relationships, there will be raised eyebrows in the parish to say the least. However, there are countries and areas where marital-type relationships by clergy are apparently not uncommon but overlooked. For want of clergy perhaps?

Another factor probably at play in this exodus was a kind of sexual revolution taking place in the last half of the 1900s. During World War II, Rosy the Riveter unwittingly began a feminists' movement and the *seeming intrusion* of women into what had largely been a man's world. Catholic nuns apparently caught the fever of freedom and became restless under the often intrusive control of the local ordinary (bishop). The required and cumbersome garb of convent life was influenced by this call to move more freely into the world at large. Nuns began modifying their habits (referring to both dress and behavior), and after a few years many of them were no longer recognizable because they dressed as other women, though perhaps with greater modesty, and reached out to new ministries.

The door to laicization had opened for priests and now the release from vows became easier and more acceptable for sisters. One of the interesting confluences resulting was the many marriages that occurred between former priests and former nuns. I was for a time teaching in a graduate program where nuns were among the students and many teachers were priests. On occasion, graduation resulted not only in a diploma but also a marriage license.

Even housewives left the semi-cloister of the home and put on pants or mini-skirts, and joined the quest for equality. Regretfully that quest must still go on. Women have still not reached equal status in our society, and the nuns would be back in a cloistered setting if the conservative members of the hierarchy had their way.

The result of all this is a shortage of priests in almost every state and every diocese. I recently received an email from a college classmate who is now a priest in the Baltimore diocese. He wrote that twelve priests are retiring this year and there is only one to be ordained. In many areas the shortage is filled with priests from Africa. I doubt there are any *extras* from Ireland any more.

I recently read a scripture passage from the prophet Amos, written seven hundred years before the birth of Jesus. "Yes, days are coming, says the Lord God, when I will send famine upon the land: Not a famine of bread, or thirst for water, but for hearing the word of the Lord. Then shall they wander from sea to sea and rove from the north to the east in search of the word of the Lord, but they shall not find it." Amos 8:11-12.

There are, of course, solutions to the shortage of priests and everyone is aware of them. These solutions are favored by liberal Catholics but opposed by conservative lay persons and most of the hierarchy. To say "the number of vocations is significantly decreasing" raises the question "why?" One might imagine a dialogue between a liberal lay person (LL) and a conservative member of the haughty hierarchy (HH).

(LL) "If one follows the position of most church leaders, men become priests because it is a spiritual calling from God. If there are fewer priests, then is God making fewer calls?"

(HH) "No, God is not making fewer calls; it is the men who are not listening to God's call."

(LL) "So it is the fault of those men who are called by God to the priesthood but fail to respond as they should. How does freedom of conscience and of decision-making fare in all of this?

(HH) "God leaves men free to make mistakes and not accept His call."

(LL) "And what if a woman believes she has a call to the priesthood? Is it a real call from God?"

(HH) "No, of course not; women can't be priests."

(LL) "So does that mean God didn't really call the woman and she is just confused and thought she heard God's call?"

(HH) "She must be confused or she is just pushing into a man's world."

(LL) "Why would she push to get into a man's world when so many men are leaving? And how do we know women can't be priests?"

(HH) "Because God said so."

(LL) "Everyone knows God didn't say that. So why can't women be priests?"

(HH) "Because that's the way it's always been! Case closed."

(LL) "One more question. What if God wants there to be women priests and so has stopped calling as many men in order to make room for the women?"

(HH) "Ridiculous. The discussion is closed."

(LL) "Well, if they can't be priests, why can't they at least be wives of priests?"

(HH) "They can't be wives because priests can't get married."

(LL) "And are you going to tell me that's because God says so?"

(HH) "No, God didn't say so. The church says so."

(LL) "Is that an infallible teaching of the church?"

(HH) "It's a belief of the faithful."

(LL) "I'm faithful but I don't believe it. Am I a heretic?"

(HH) "You should discuss it with your confessor."

(LL) "And if priests could marry, would more men want to be priests?"

(HH) "Well, they can't marry. And that's the way we want it."

End of a delightful and enlightening conversation.

CHAPTER SIX

Tomorrow is the fourth Sunday of the month and a class day. I need to look at the Sunday school guide for the recommended lesson. The guide's lesson relates to the Immaculate Conception of Mary and the birth of Jesus. The appropriate scripture readings are listed in addition to some suggestions for elaborating on the two subjects.

Both of the recommended subjects are usually enshrined with words and left sacrosanct in homilies and spiritual writings. It occurred to me a discussion with children in this age group could stir questions for them which should be addressed even though they may not be raised. The stories include a pregnancy and a birth, both under unusual and sacred circumstances. Nevertheless, the Virgin Mary was truly pregnant, and the Baby Jesus exited her womb at the appropriate time and in the usual manner. I see no reason or logic or scripture to say otherwise or to prevent current discussion of these topics.

On the way to Mass this morning, I was in a thoughtful mood. Jane reads these moods quickly and carefully chooses whether or not to enter my mental space. She chose not to this morning, which was just as well. I'm not sure I could have put my thoughts into meaningful words. When we arrived, we silently walked into church, holding hands as we always do.

Father Brown entered to say Mass, following the two altar boys dressed in white cassocks. It was a surprise. To my knowledge Fred never spoke to anyone about this change. The parish once had a parish council with a finance committee. I believe Father Joe started it but it ceased to exist when all the parish had was a visiting priest. Father Brown has not brought up the subject of a parish council or anything of the kind. It is to be a one-man show, I guess. I doubt these ranchers were delighted to see their boys dressed in white cassocks. And I doubt these two boys, Jim Mansfield and Tom Brill, were delighted to be wearing what the kids would be certain to call "dresses."

Father Brown gave a reasonably good homily, a bit long for my taste, but good. Myrtle Sweeny sang well, accompanied by her daughter Louise at the piano. When Mass ended, I kissed Jane and said, "I'll see you after my class, Love. Why don't you ask John Mansfield and Archie Brill what they think of the cassocks? You might ask Mable and Joyce too." Mable is John's wife, and Joyce is Archie's.

When I began class, I asked if there was anything from the past week they would like to talk about. There were no takers. So I did the scripture readings as recommended by the Guide. I asked if anyone had any questions about the readings. No takers. There was no one in my class younger than twelve other than Tim Quirk, and sexuality was familiar to him but not the proper words.

So I began, "What does the scripture mean when it says 'Mary was with child'?"

Finally Mary Mansfield answered, "It means she was pregnant."

"And what does fruit of the womb mean, Mary?" I asked.

"The fruit of her womb was the baby Jesus," she responded.

"And what word do we use for womb, Mary?"

"The uterus," she replied.

"And who can tell me how Mary got pregnant?"

Again Mary responded, "By the Holy Spirit."

I asked the class, "How does pregnancy usually occur?"

Each person in the class suddenly had an itch to scratch, a distant space to look at, or a need to examine a shoe. So with this for introduction, I proceeded to talk about sexual body parts and their function, including reproduction. It took some time and careful selection of words. Everyone was attentive and, for the most part, looked down or somewhere other than at one another.

But when I said the word "penis," Tim Quirk once more burst forth with an impulsive and shocking contribution. "I know that's a 'hard-on.' Father Brown showed me one."

I'm sure everyone's eyes turned to look at Tim. There were no giggles, no smiles, just stares. I didn't know what to say. I was as startled as the others. When I finally recovered some clear thinking, I said, "Tell me when this happened, Tim, and tell me what Father Brown did."

Tim looked embarrassed and with all eyes on him, he struggled to get words out. "I saw him…in that little park…down by…the Safeway Store. He was sitting…on a bench in…the park. He was reading and…had a tablet with…some …written words on it. I said 'hello' and…he invited…me to… sit down.

…When I sat down…he said, 'I think you…were…embarrassed when… I…talked to your class…a couple…of Sundays ago. You asked what…a … 'hard-on' was…and the others…laughed at you. He said…'Let me…show you'…and he took…the tablet and…sketched a man…with a…'hard on' or what…he said…was…a 'penis.' That was all. I just…thanked …him and went…on…to the store."

What a relief! But not entirely. I needed to make sure everyone understood what happened and that it was not to be seen as a big issue. It was 10:30, but we definitely needed "a little more time to make sure the kids knew what they needed to know" before I let them go. I said, "If any of you decides to mention this to your parents, be sure to explain **clearly** what Tim says happened. I don't think I need to comment on what Father Brown did other than to say he was trying to do something **he thought might be** helpful for Tim.

"Have a good two weeks. I understand you have no school on Tuesday because we're celebrating the day Montana became a state. Enjoy the day off." The kids left the room as I gathered my notes.

As I left the church, I saw Father Brown talking with John Mansfield and Archie Brill. Jane was standing a bit apart from them talking with their wives, Mable and Joyce. I joined John and Archie. They stood facing Fred and me.

Suddenly a possibility occurred to me, maybe something I should have figured out sooner. I decided to go with it. Fred was looking at the two of them as I stood beside him. I said, almost as if calling someone, "CHARLES," a very brief pause, and then, "Butler maybe won't come for confirmation this year." As I said "Charles," out of the corner of my eye I saw Fred anxiously turn his face toward me, then quickly recover as he heard the word Butler. He looked back at John and Archie. It worked or at least I thought it did. I think his face showed a tinge of red. I said to myself, "His real name is not Fred, it's Charles." I remembered the references to Charles F. Brown I'd seen in my computer search. Somewhere along the way (probably Missouri) he dropped the "Charles" and became "Fred Brown." He was getting away from "a past." I felt a bit stupid for not having picked up earlier on that possibility.

On the way home I gave Jane a review of the morning class. About the penis story, she commented, "I hope that's all he showed Tim. Even that is going too far, and I can't help but think he has picked Tim for his next victim."

I responded, "Don't you think you may be stretching things a bit? We don't know there have been any victims as you suggest. Fred may have been trying to help the kid out. You know Tim is not the brightest diamond and he has difficulty saying things accurately. At least Fred may have ended Tim's use of the word 'hard-on.' I hope the kids from class are clear about it with their parents."

"Robbie, is it possible you've lost your objectivity about this guy Fred, or should we call him 'Charles' now? You know when it comes to priests and nuns you're a pretty easy mark. You had nuns in grade and high school and apparently they were a good bunch. You had priests teaching in college and seminary. You've probably seen the cream of them all. And we've had priests and nuns for friends during our married life, and all were admirable people. You need to remember they're not all cream; a few may be sour milk. In fact, I remember a couple of those, at least from my perspective, but we don't need to get into that discussion again. Possibly you're starting off a little high on the scale when you consider Fred. I don't trust the man. As I said about Peter, be careful, Rob."

Since we were back at the house, we let the subject drop but certainly not out of sight or mind. I helped Jane get lunch ready and as we ate we talked about our plans for the rest of the day and the night. Willie Nelson is giving a performance in Culver City this evening, and we've had tickets for a couple of weeks. Willie has been our favorite entertainer for several years. We plan to stay the night at the Montana Lodge and then drive home leisurely tomorrow afternoon. We want to check out some of the antique shops as well as some of our favorite junk shops. Sometimes I think that's the part Jane enjoys the most.

We left the ranch about two o'clock for a leisurely trip to Culver City. When Jane and I travel, we always find a lot to talk about, things we never seem to get around to talking about when we're home. We reminisce about other trips we've made. It's remarkable how a trip like this seems to shut the door on concerns or problems that were front and center before we left the house. We have an unspoken understanding of the freedom attached to leisure time.

Willie Nelson was at his best with his country songs. He dedicated the performance to the State of Montana's birthday on Tuesday. It was a delightful evening and ended with a Southern Comfort Manhattan in the Lodge bar. Well, the evening *didn't really end there.*

Monday was a pleasant fall day. We spent time in the shops familiar to Jane. We ate lunch at the Wild Horse Grill, a popular place in Culver City. On the way home we began talking about our three children and before we finished we were home. The children and their families always fill a good bit of our leisure conversation and both our hearts.

Tuesday began as another beautiful Montana autumn day. It ended up a tragic day for the people of Springer. It continues to haunt us all. It became the focus of the town and extended its evil tentacles through the county and eventually throughout the state. For months the story would fill the minds and hearts of all who knew it. But for me the story would continue to unfold as I quickly became more than an observer.

It was about two in the afternoon when Jane called me. I was in the shop repairing a saddle. The county sheriff Matt Wilson was on the phone. His first words, "Father Brown asked me to call you. At the moment, he's here at the Columbus Hospital with me and Deputy Ken Carr. Brown brought Tim Quirk to the hospital, and Tim is dead. Brown says you are the parish leader and he needs you to come."

I couldn't believe what I was hearing. I could hardly respond. I told the sheriff I'd be there as quickly as I could. I told Jane what Wilson said and asked if she wanted to go to Springer with me. Jane was as shocked as I was and tears filled her eyes. "No, Rob, it's better if you go alone. There is nothing I can do but wait in the background to support you and you know I do that whether I'm there or here. This may involve more time than you realize. Take whatever time you need. I'll be here waiting."

I left for the Columbus Hospital. When I met Wilson he gave me the story he got from staff and others. Father Brown drove up to the emergency entrance of the hospital about 2 P.M. He sat in the Tundra honking the horn until an orderly came out. The orderly found Father Brown in the driver's seat and Tim Quirk lying on the front seat with his head in the priest's arms and blood all over the two of them.

They brought a gurney and took Tim into the emergency room. He was pronounced dead on arrival. Father Brown followed the gurney in. He was described as "bloody, sobbing, hardly articulate." The hospital record describes him saying, "He fell, he fell, he was running, he fell, his head hit a rock, he was bleeding. Did I hurt him? I picked him up and brought him here. Is he all right? Is he alive? Is he all right? Did I do something?"

The sheriff continued, "By the time I arrived, Brown was a little calmer and more coherent. He immediately asked me to call you, saying, 'Bob Lee is the leader of the parish. I need him. Please, call him now.'

"I asked him to tell me what happened. I'll piece it together for you from my notes. He and Tim were at Wolf Butte to celebrate Montana Day. Tom Brill and Jim Mansfield and the two Kirby boys were supposed to go, but they were unable to come because of work at home. He and Tim finished their lunch and were playing tag. He was 'it' and was chasing Tim. He told Tim not to go into the thick trees where Brown would be unable to see him. They began the chase. Tim ran, and as he ran he tripped over an exposed tree root and fell headlong to the ground. He hit his head on a big rock. Tim cried in pain for a few minutes with Brown holding him and trying to comfort him. When he stopped crying, Brown carried him to the Tundra and laid him on the front seat. Brown got in and drove to the hospital with Tim's head on his lap. That sums up what I have."

It was overwhelming to completely grasp what the sheriff was telling me. Tim was dead, and Fred Brown brought him to the E.R. I knew the tree roots. I knew the rocks. I knew Tim fell and hit his head. But was he truly dead? Is this a bad dream?

Sheriff Wilson's words finally got through to me. Tim Quirk is dead! And where is Fred Brown? I asked about him. The Sheriff said Fred was in an office nearby and Deputy Ken Carr was with him. I asked Wilson what he planned to do.

The sheriff responded, "We have to keep Father Brown in custody until we review the death scene and verify as best we can the information he has given us. The physician who examined the body was unable to determine the cause of death. He could not definitively attribute death to the head injury. Since Tim died a violent death under questionable circumstances, the Coroner will be called and we will need his assessment before we release the priest. Would you like to see him for a few minutes before we take him to headquarters? I'll ask Deputy Carr to step out of the room so you can speak privately."

Ken Carr left as I entered the room. Fred was sitting with his face in his hands, dried blood covering them, the front of his shirt and his trousers. I sat in a chair beside him. He never looked up until I spoke. I said very quietly, "You know Tim is dead. Tell me what happened, Fred."

He told me essentially what the sheriff told me, but with pauses and tears and looking at me with agony in his eyes. He interrupted his own jumble of words with phrases: "Tim was a sweet boy." "I loved little Tim." "We were so close." "He was such a dear child." "Did I do something wrong?"

I put my hand on Fred's shoulder and said, "Sheriff Wilson told me they are going to take you to the police station now and you will be held there until an investigation is made. Yes, Tim is dead, Father, and the police are involved. Do you understand that?" He nodded as he slowly stood. We moved toward the door.

The sheriff had to sign some papers at the hospital, one of which was the request for the medical examiner's evaluation. I was already at the jail as they came in. Ken Carr had Brown by the arm and went past me to wait for the sheriff to decide where to place Brown.

As they walked away, Sheriff Wilson said to me, "Bob, I've been sheriff in this county over ten years but I've never been in the Wolf Butte area where Brown says this happened. I know you live out that way and assume you're familiar with the spot. Would you consider leading us up to the place? And it might be helpful to have you there to clarify some of the directions Brown has given us. I'd appreciate your help. I plan on taking one of my deputies, probably Carr; and we have a detective on the force, Brian Jenkins. I'll bring him along."

I responded, "I'll be glad to go. I graze cattle on some State Land right near the area we're talking about. But let me speak to Brown for a moment and I'll try to get some specifics about where he and Tim were when this happened."

As I approached Brown, Ken Carr stepped a few feet away. I spoke to Fred, "I think it's important for you to cooperate with the sheriff and his officers. Maybe you can give me some helpful information. Can you tell me what area you and Tim were in when this happened?" We engaged in a brief exchange.

Brown: "It was close to that old log cabin."

Me: "Did you drive up as far as you could go in that opening that leads to the cabin?"

Brown: "Yes, up to the heavy brush and rocky area. I stopped there and I carried the cooler up to the cabin. We had our lunch there."

Me: "Let's try to locate the area where Tim fell. If I stand looking at the door of the cabin, what direction was Tim when he was running, to my right or to my left?"

Brown: "Tim would be to your right and where the area becomes steeper."

Me: "Okay, that's good. Now was he into the thick trees or just where there are a few scattered trees and buckbrush?"

Brown: "He was just into the area where there are a few trees."

Me: "As best you can remember, was he running straight south from there or was it a little to the east or to the west."

Brown: "I'd say it was about straight south."

Me: "Those directions will help us find the spot we are looking for. Thanks for helping, Father."

I told the sheriff that Brown described the general area my wife and I recently visited. The sheriff was satisfied I knew the area we would be looking for. I said, "We'll be going right by the ranch so you can just follow me home. I'll leave my pickup there and ride with the three of you the rest of the way if that's okay." He said that would work well.

I stepped back to where Brown was standing and said, "As soon as I get an opportunity, I'll call Bishop Butler. The Bishop will want to know the details as they become clear and he will want the diocesan attorney to be made aware of any legal issues resulting from Tim's death. I should also tell you at this point it would probably be better if you don't talk anymore to anyone about what happened. I'll be in touch with you later today or tomorrow."

He kept nodding his head as he walked away with the deputy; he was slumped over with head down. Even from the back his "beaten look" showed. He looked a much older, weary, defeated man.

The three officers followed me in the sheriff's car. As I drove home I thought how heartbreaking Tim's death would be for Jane. I knew she would be angry and critical of Fred for his role in the death, no matter how it occurred. He was there. He shirked his responsibility in some way. And of course, Jane will ask the question everyone will eventually ask: Why was Father Brown there alone with a nine-year-old boy?

Jane saw me driving toward the house and came out on the porch to meet me. Her worried look only increased when the sheriff's car pulled up behind me. As she approached I said, "I'm going with Sheriff Wilson and his two deputies to the Wolf Butte area where Tim's accident occurred. But first you and I will go in the house and I'll tell you about it all. But let me introduce you to the three policemen."

The three men got out of the car. I introduced them to Jane and suggested they come over in the shade of the porch and sit for a few minutes while I talked to my wife. Jane offered them iced tea, coffee, or soda. We brought out two iced teas and one diet Coke for them.

Jane and I went inside and sat in the kitchen with iced tea. As I gave her the whole story, I felt I was watching the reflection of my emotions on her face as she listened. When I finished, she was thoughtful and then spoke. "I'm glad you are the person you are. And I understand why Father Brown would ask to see you. It's not that you are 'the parish leader;' you are someone he knows he can trust. We'll keep Tim in our prayers and also his mother. You should do what you can to help Father Brown. We don't know if he has any family or friends. Perhaps he's all alone. He's going to need a friend." It was so like Jane. "When the rubber hits the road," as they say, she's full of heart.

I explained why I was going with the sheriff and deputies. "They'll drop me off here on their way back to town. I have no idea how long we might be." She kissed me, gave me a warm hug and "Love you, Rob. I'll be waiting for you."

The sheriff followed my directions, and we were close to Wolf Butte in about ten minutes. The last part of the drive gets rough, steep and full of underbrush and rocks. Slow going. We stopped about forty yards from the cabin. It would be close to where Brown probably stopped.

The officers looked closely at the area and found fresh tire tracks. The detective took close pictures of them and some measurements. They continued to look around carefully as we walked toward the cabin. I suggested we have a look in the cabin first and then come out and look for the area where Tim fell. The sheriff agreed since this was what Father Brown and Tim probably did.

The door of the cabin was halfway open. To my surprise the thick dust on the floor was swept into one corner and there was a new broom by the gathered dirt. A medium sized cooler was close to one wall with a couple of fold-up camp chairs beside it. There were four empty Coke cans, some Hershey candy wrappers, a couple of paper sandwich bags from the Cowboy Shop with crushed up papers and napkins inside. There was an empty chocolate cookie box from Albertson's.

I stood back as the officers examined the area. I saw the detective with gloves picking up various items and bagging them. They were being thorough. Apparently Father Brown did not return to the cabin to pick things up after Tim fell. He must have taken Tim directly to the truck.

I waited outside until they finished. I was trying to get an idea of where Tim may have fallen. When the officers came out I led them toward the area Father Brown described to me. As we came near, I cautioned, "I think we must be close to the spot. I'll let the three of you walk in front and I'll follow."

The three of them spread out a little and continued in the same direction. We had only gone a few yards more when the deputy pointed a few feet away and said, "Here's a rock with dried blood on it." We came closer. The detective moved in and took pictures of the rock and the area from several angles. Then with gloves he lifted the rock from the ground and put it in a large evidence bag held by the sheriff. The rock was about three or four inches thick and sort of oblong about six by ten inches. The three of them continued looking around the area near the rock. There were several partially exposed tree roots and one that lined up directly with the route Tim must have taken before the fall. The detective took more pictures.

We left the area and walked toward the car. I noted the cabin door was still open. I asked, "Do you mind if I shut the cabin door? I wouldn't want a stray bear or a small deer or coyotes wandering in there and messing the place up." The detective said they would leave things inside at they were. He went over to the cabin, latched the door shut, and put up a crime scene tape.

They dropped me at the ranch and went on their way. Before leaving the sheriff said, "For the present I will regard you as the person to contact concerning Father Brown. He has not given me the name of a relative or anyone else with whom to communicate. I assume you will notify whoever should be aware of his current situation. Under the circumstances we cannot release him on his own recognizance without a judge's order. An attorney could get him released with bail or perhaps without. I'll leave it up to you to proceed." I told the sheriff I would be in touch with the Bishop and undoubtedly the diocese would want an attorney involved. We agreed to keep in touch.

After they left, Jane and I talked about the events of the day as we began fixing dinner. I reported on the trip to Wolf Butte, looking in the cabin, what we found there and then finding the rock. I said, "I noted how carefully they handled everything at the crime scene." Then I added, "That's interesting. I automatically call it a 'crime scene' because of their routine. There is no good reason to consider a crime has been committed, but their behavior heightens the possibility in my mind. From what we know it should still be considered an accident."

Jane responded, "Whether or not Brown committed a crime, his behavior will certainly be questioned by the Bishop. For him to be in that setting alone with a nine year old boy will raise a strong reaction in our congregation and appropriately so. What do you think about your Father Brown now?"

"He's not *my* Father Brown, but it's a fair question. I've had some doubts from the beginning, not as strong as yours, but nevertheless doubts. Currently I see him as a priest who is already responsible for an enormous mistake, who is now sitting in jail, who has some accountability for the death of a nine-year-old boy, and who has no one immediately helpful in his life except me. I have no obligation to him other than Christian charity. The death of Tim, possibly occurring with his head in Fred's lap as Fred drove to Springer, is in itself enough to fill him with remorse and apprehension. It must have been difficult for him to tell the hospital staff what happened even in a garbled manner. Now he sits in jail frightened and uncertain not just about tomorrow but about his whole future. Imagine all that must be going through his head: his past must be involved, his present is total turmoil, and his future is completely uncertain."

Jane responded, "I get the picture and what you say makes sense. He is in a sad situation, and I can't imagine what it would be like to have even a slight responsibility for the death of a nine-year-old child. Don't you think you should call Jack Tracey or the Bishop and let them know?"

"I was just thinking of doing that. I sort of dread making the call, but I shouldn't put it off any longer. I'll use the phone in the living room, and if you eavesdrop that's fine with me. What I know you will know."

I called the bishop first. When the secretary answered my call, I asked to speak to Bishop Butler. She requested my name. "Bob Lee," I responded. She said, "Just a moment. I'll see if he's available."

I soon heard his voice. "Hello, Bob. It's good to hear from you. Jack and I were talking about you the other day. How are you and Jane and how is the ranching business? Perhaps I should first hear why you're calling me."

"I'm calling with bad news, Charles. I'm not sure how bad it is, but as things stand I'd say it is definitely not good. Fred Brown is at the moment in the Springer jail." I continued and used my sequential remembering to give him pretty much a blow-by-blow account of the last four or five hours. As I told the story, I could hardly believe all this occurred in one day, in fact in just a few hours. I ended saying, "I imagine Fred should have an attorney to represent him and find out what the immediate possibilities are as well as long range issues. Of course, much will depend on the investigation. At this point I have no idea whether Fred will have to remain in jail and if so, for how long. Considering the likely response of the townspeople over the death of this well-known and greatly loved boy, Fred may be better off in jail a few days. Whatever the outcome of the investigation, I respectfully suggest you begin considering removing Brown from Springer. I think his usefulness in this area is totally gone."

Bishop Butler was ahead of me in regard to Fred's removal from the parish. "Well, you've certainly dumped a lot in my lap, Bob. Yes, yes, no possibility of his serving in Springer any further. Let me see what I can do to find a replacement. I'll try to find a priest who can be there full time at least for a few months. The community has suffered enough from this tragedy, and I want to keep their bleeding to a minimum. At the moment I have no idea what we'll be able to provide for the future.

"And yes, I will call Tom O'Rourke, our diocesan attorney, and ask him to get out there today if possible. I know it's almost six o'clock, so it's not likely he'll make it today but first thing in the morning. May I have him call you so you can tell him what you've told me and also give him some information about the people he'll be dealing with when he gets there?"

70

I responded, "Tell him to call me anytime. I'll meet him in Springer when he comes. It's possible Fred will be more comfortable if I accompany Mr. O'Rourke on their first meeting. Fred has spoken rather freely to me at times. He might be more guarded with an attorney. I'll help in any way I can."

The bishop ended the conversation saying, "Thanks for getting in touch directly with me. You have done a great service to the diocese and to me personally. And thank you for being supportive of Father Brown. I had some reservations about sending him to Springer, but I felt I needed to give him another chance. Greetings to your lovely wife. We'll undoubtedly have cause to talk again about this. Have a blessed day."

Tom O'Rourke called me about seven that evening. I read about Tom from time to time when we visited Montana in the past and since we've lived here. He has been prominent throughout the state and active in the State Bar Association. I understand he was offered a federal judgeship but turned it down. The rumor was he turned it down because he wanted to continue the practice of law and primarily because he was attorney for the diocese. He has been a personal friend of the bishop's back to their high school days together. In fact, I met him when I was a seminarian and he came to visit Charles.

On the phone he introduced himself and asked if I could possibly meet with him at the Springer jail the following morning at nine. I said, "It might be better if you and I get together before we go to the jail. That won't be a good place for us to talk freely. I imagine Bishop Butler gave you the information I have, but there may be pieces I can fill in and also give you a general sense of the sheriff and his officers. We can also talk about the likely mood of the townspeople." O'Rourke was agreeable and asked where we should meet. I suggested Starbucks just across the street from the jail.

Jane and I talked for at least two hours about the events of the day. We wondered about Fred's career in the priesthood, and from a more professional point of view, I wondered what kind of childhood he must have had that brought him at this time of life apparently afoul of the law. Even if the law does not accuse him of any crime, his reputation as a priest is in serious jeopardy. He will certainly not escape the condemnation of the townspeople and of his church.

CHAPTER SEVEN

The following morning was cloud covered. During breakfast Jane and I spoke of it as a *mourning* world. I was not looking forward to my meeting with O'Rourke. At the moment I couldn't picture any bright spots in the coming day. Jane noted my dark mood. She brought more coffee and pulled her chair closer to mine, placing her hand on my shoulder.

"This must be hard for you, Rob. Everything seems tied together for us these days. In a way, all of life feels entwined around us since we moved to the ranch, and I think it leaves us feeling helpless. People refer to this region as the 'wide open spaces.' Visually our world is wide open but emotionally it has a feel of being closed in, almost tied down. The interconnectedness of life is what I'm trying to describe. We're personally connected to the members of our parish, to the clerks and managers of the stores we go to and the places where we eat, to the people we meet on the streets. What has happened to one of us has happened to all. Tim's death will be a relatively meaningless article in state and national newspapers. But to us it is part of our day and the day of everyone we know. Does this make sense to you?"

Jane's words touched something sharply familiar to me, and it brought some clarity to my thinking. I've lived with this feeling many times before. During my years as a psychiatrist this same emotional bond often entered my life. The patients I treated had life stories filled with abandonment, physical and/or emotional abuse, injustices never to be resolved. I was so absorbed in and committed to the treatment relationship, I frequently found myself tied into their dilemmas, engulfed in their turmoil. I could "feel" what they were feeling.

The burden of this countertransference needed relief and release. And, as I used to advise student counselors, I found a person with whom I could share the burden of these "take-home" feelings. That person was Jane. It was a relief just to express them verbally to a good listener. It objectified them. It freed me from the crippling ties encountered in the office. The conflicts and the seeming helplessness were no longer 'mine.' There was no violation of confidence. Jane, my 'sounding board,' had no need to hear the whole story or know the persons experiencing the wounds.

The reason for my mood and its want became clear. I needed to verbalize it openly and to Jane. "I'm sure you remember how I sometimes brought a patient's story home to you and talked about the struggle she or he was having." Jane nodded knowingly and reassuringly. So I continued, "That's what's happening now to me and perhaps to you as you listen and inwardly reflect my feelings. I feel like I'm in over my head. I'm trying to be supportive of Fred, I'm providing information to the Bishop, I'm helping the sheriff, and now I have an attorney to meet and try to help. And all the while Tim is dead. I haven't contacted his mother whom I intended to visit, and Fred, I know, is relying on me to connect with members of the parish. I'm feeling lost and as you say, 'entwined,' hemmed in by it all. The result is to feel pretty helpless."

Jane moved closer with her arm around my back. "I'm here, Robbie, and I'll be here through whatever happens. I do inwardly share many of the feelings you speak of. We are together and we will be together for any eventualities. So finish your coffee and go meet O'Rourke. By the way, you forgot to shave."

On my way to Springer, I thanked the Lord for the blessing of Jane in my life. I doubt I'd have been able to continue my previous psychiatric practice without her. My own emotions had always been deeply affected by some of the life stories I heard. Once more she was my sounding board, my escape port where I could unload my own feelings to find distance and objectivity. I must be careful not to overload her with what's happening inside me.

I got a cup of coffee and sat at a corner table in Starbucks a few minutes before nine. A man walked in a few minutes later, obviously looking for someone. I raised my cup toward him. He nodded, picked up some coffee and came to the table. I stood and extended my hand, "Bob Lee. It's good to meet you again. I believe I met you once when you came to visit Charles at the seminary."

We shook hands. He said, "Tom O'Rourke. Now that I see you, I do remember that meeting. Charles told me some good things about you. Said you are old friends. But let's get to the business at hand. Do you mind if I take a few notes?"

"Notes are fine," I replied. For the first time I told the story all in one piece: the sheriff's call, the scene at the hospital, the time at the jail, the trip to Wolf Butte and what was found there. Then I gave him some highlights of my contacts with Father Brown.

I concluded my remarks. "Father Brown is comfortable with me and seems to have chosen me to be his liaison with the parish. Apparently he has no relatives or longtime friends with whom he is connected. To this point at least, I believe I have his confidence. I'm thinking he may speak more freely and feel more at ease if I accompany you when you talk to him; that is totally your choice."

After he absorbed all I told him, as well as the remainder of his coffee, he responded, "I appreciate your summary. Yes, it may be a good idea for you to be with me during this first interview. I will need Father Brown's permission for that. I will assure him his words to us will be regarded as privileged communication, not to be revealed to any member of the courts or the law. If we include you, I will authorize you to be my assistant during the time of the interview. Let me give you my card which on the back has an authorization statement. I will write your name in the blank.

"Now if we're settled with this let's go to the jail and hear what Father Brown has to say. By the way, we'll probably have continuing contact so please call me Tom." In return I told him to call me Bob.

Sheriff Wilson saw us entering the jail and came out of his office to greet us. He had been talking to Detective Brian Jenkins who now accompanied him. I made the introductions. The sheriff invited us into his office. As we sat down the sheriff spoke, "Things may be getting a little more complicated than we expected. I'll let Brian fill you in on the latest."

Brian was the detective who was with us at Wolf Butte. He cleared his throat and looking at me began, "As you know the medical examiner was called to the Columbus Hospital because the doctor who declared Tim dead was unable to determine the 'cause of death,' regardless of the obvious head injury. The county coroner, Laura Krantz, noted some darkened areas around the mouth and chin and also ocular petechiae in addition to the laceration, swelling and previous bleeding in the right frontal area of the head. She noted the possibility of death by asphyxia as well as the possibility of death by blunt injury to the head with severe intracranial bleeding. As a result of the conflicted findings she requested the medical examiner perform an autopsy. At the moment Deputy Pete Chum is on his way to inform Ms. Quirk of the autopsy. Do either of you have any questions?"

"Has Father Brown been made aware of all this?" I asked.

The sheriff responded, "We have not yet told Father Brown these latest developments Detective Jenkins just mentioned. These are all events of this morning. We thought Mr. O'Rourke might prefer to tell his client."

O'Rourke asked, "Do you have any idea when we might expect the autopsy report?"

Sheriff Wilson responded, "Probably in the next five or six days we'll have a preliminary report. But they'll need to check finger prints, stomach contents, the extent of brain injury, and various blood and tissue reports. We'll need Brown's DNA. We're looking at two to three weeks maximum."

Tom looked at me and nodded. We were ready to move on. Tom thanked them both and asked if we could meet with Father Brown in a secure room, adding, "Bob Lee will be acting in the capacity of my assistant during the interview. By the way, has Father Brown asked you to contact anyone or has he made any phone calls? I assume he has had no visitors."

The sheriff said Brown had not requested any contact be made on his behalf nor had he made any calls or had any visitors. "I assume you know about his request of yesterday when he asked me to call Bob Lee." We both nodded. My mind objected to the word "yesterday." It couldn't have been yesterday. It felt like it was several days ago. So much has happened in less than twenty-four hours!

Detective Jenkins took us to an interview room and soon brought Fred in. As Jenkins left, he told us to just open the door when we were finished and someone would come for Father Brown. He left and closed the door behind him.

Fred was dressed in jail garb and was not cuffed or shackled. I wondered if that was special treatment for a cleric. He looked like he hadn't slept in days.

His face was grim and gaunt. He attempted a smile but his face did not respond to his feeble wish. I introduced O'Rourke making sure Fred understood this was an attorney sent by Bishop Butler. Fred didn't offer his hand to either of us. He slumped into a chair. The words from scripture came to me, "he has eyes but does not see, he has ears but does not hear." We both took chairs at the table.

O'Rourke began. "Bishop Butler sends his prayers. He is concerned about what has occurred and has asked me to gather all the information available. Before we begin I want you to know Mr. Lee is acting as my associate today and anything you tell us will be confidential. Only with your permission would we reveal to a court or officer of the law the content of your statements made during this interview. I am going to begin recording this interview now for my further review and study." Tom produced a recorder, turned it on, and placed in on the table.

I wondered if any of this registered with Fred. He was listless. His mind was somewhere else. He looked at me and said, "Where is Tim's body? I want to see him. I'm sorry he's dead. I don't know what happened. I loved little Tim. I didn't mean to hurt him. Did I hurt him? What happened?"

Appearing rather impatient, O'Rourke began what needed to be done. He spoke quietly but enunciated clearly. He touched Fred's arm to get his attention. "Father Brown, I want you to talk to *me* and tell me everything you remember about what happened at Wolf Butte when you and Tim were there yesterday. I will ask questions to help you remember the details and I want you to respond as accurately as you can. If you don't understand the question let me know. If you're not sure of the answer let me know of your uncertainty. Is what I'm saying clear to you?"

Several seconds went by before Fred acknowledged O'Rourke's question with a "Yes."

O'Rourke said, "We're ready to go then. Begin by telling me about yesterday and all that happened between you and Tim."

Fred began, "Tim came to the rectory at ten o'clock as we had agreed when I talked to him on Sunday and promised we would go to Wolf Butte. Tim was so happy. I had food and soda already in the back of my Tundra." It seemed like Fred's mind wandered as he began to describe the road and various things they passed on the way to the mountain. He didn't seem to be deliberately digressing. I wondered if he was recalling the trip in such detail because subconsciously he *did not want to get to Wolf Butte.*

O'Rourke decided to take more control of the interview as he realized Fred's verbal wanderings would extend the interview with meaningless material. With questioning based on what he already knew, O'Rourke took Fred through general details until he had Fred and Tim in the cabin eating lunch.

O'Rourke continued: "What did Tim eat?"

Brown: "A hot dog in a bun."

Tom: "What was with the hot dog?"

Brown: "Mustard and a dill pickle."

Tom: "Where did you buy the hot dogs?"

Brown: "At the Cowboy Shop on 2nd Avenue."

Tom continued and covered all the food and sodas. Then he moved on: "What did you do after you finished eating?"

Fred: "We sat and talked for half an hour."

Tom: "What did you talk about?"

Fred: "Tim talked about his mother and the men who come to the house."

Tom: "Any details about the men?"

Fred: "Tim said he walks into his mother's room sometimes and she and the man are naked on the bed and doing what they do."

Tom: "And what do they do?"

Fred: "Tim calls it fucking."

Tom: "What else did you talk about?"

Fred: "How other kids tease him, call him 'quirky,' and 'jerky quirky.'"

Tom: "What did you say?"

Fred: "I told him what 'jerk off' means."

Tom: "Did anything else happen in the cabin before you and Tim went outside?"

Fred: "As we stood up to leave I put my arm around Tim and hugged him and said I would pray for him."

Tom: "Where was your arm?"

Fred: "Around his shoulders."

Tom: "Did you pull his body around in front of you in a hug or were you just side by side?"

Fred: After an uneasy look and hesitation, "Side by side" and he lowered his gaze as he spoke. Perhaps a 'tell'?

Tom: "Tell me about the race you and Tim had. How did that come about?"

Fred sighed as if in pain and with clear reluctance answered, "It wasn't a race. As we left the cabin Tim said, 'Let's play hide and seek.' I didn't know the area well and I was afraid there might be bears or snakes or cliffs and Tim might go too far into the woods and get lost or hurt. So I said, 'Let's play tag.' Tim said, 'Okay, you're it' and he touched me and began to run toward the woods. I couldn't run as fast as he could, but I started after him. He was calling, 'Can't catch me. Can't catch me.' And he was into the woods. Then there was a shout or a cry. I didn't know if it was fear or pain or surprise or what. Then silence.

"I ran in the direction Tim had taken and almost stumbled on his body. His head was still on the rock and bleeding badly. His arms were spread wide as if he had been falling forward. I sat beside him and lifted his body close and held his head in my lap. He was breathing but his eyes were closed and he didn't respond when I called his name. I bent over and kissed the place on his left cheek where there was no blood. I began to cry and call his name. I lost it!

"When I came back to my senses and was conscious of what I was doing, I was in the Tundra with Tim's head still in my lap and bleeding. I was in front of the Columbus Hospital. At first I wondered what the sound was and then I realized it was the horn of my truck. I was doing it."

O'Rourke waited a minute or two and watched Fred slumped in his chair occasionally looking up at the attorney as if waiting for more questions. I'm guessing Tom is thinking of what the Bishop will need to know, another area to be covered with Fred. And there it was. "Father Brown, how did you happen to be alone on that mountain with a nine-year old-boy? Don't you think that's an obvious question Bishop Butler is going to need you to answer?"

Fred answered, "I expected the question, and I realize how foolish it was to be there with little Tim. It happened quite unexpectedly. I asked all the altar boys if they would like to have a picnic at Wolf Butte on Montana Day and they all said 'yes.' I was expecting all five of them to come to the rectory that morning by eleven o'clock. Tim came about ten to eleven and talked about the great day we all were going to have and how happy he was we were going. I remember him saying his mother never took him anywhere after they moved to Springer. His father used to play with him and take him to games and parks and movies, but his father disappeared just before his sixth birthday. He sounded so sad. I felt so sorry for him.

"We waited until 11:15, but none of the other boys showed up. I kept expecting them, but I finally decided they must have had to work or perhaps went somewhere else. I had their phone numbers but never thought to call them. I'm reluctant to call parishioners unless it's an emergency.

"As time passed, Tim became increasingly eager to go asking me repeatedly, 'Aren't we ready? Can we go now? Will we go if they don't come? Please, please, we have to go. I want to go. I need to go. It's Montana Day and I'm a Montanan.' He started to cry. I felt so bad for him it almost made me cry. I know now it was poor judgment to go just with Tim. I planned it for all the altar boys. It was a mistake. Tell the bishop how sorry I am."

O'Rourke responded unsympathetically, "This is not something that will be taken lightly by Bishop Butler nor can it be. I feel quite certain you will not continue as pastor in Springer. People in the town, not just your parishioners, are angry and will be highly judgmental about your behavior. Tim is dead, and no matter how this turns out legally, the people will hold you responsible for Tim's death. They are also well aware you have violated strict policies of the church, and the Catholic Church will expect the Bishop to act accordingly.

"Now, is there anything you want to add or change from the things you have told me today? I should let you know it is quite possible you may face legal charges, and if that occurs I will serve as your attorney. At this point I recommend you say nothing further about this entire episode to anyone except Bob Lee or me. Mr. Lee will act in my behalf when I am unavailable. I have an active practice in Black Eagle and will only be coming here as needed. At this time I could go before a judge and ask for your release on your own recognizance, but considering the current hostility of the villagers, the wide publicity of the story and the fact that you have no place to go, I believe it is for your best welfare to remain in jail. An autopsy has been requested, and you can expect to be here until the results are reported."

The mention of an autopsy came as a surprise to Tom and me when we were informed. When Tom mentioned it now Fred's eyes widened and a look of fear flashed over his face. He quickly asked, "Why did you say an autopsy?"

Tom said, "There was some discoloration around Tim's mouth and throat and the coroner thought there might be signs of asphyxiation. The cause of death remains undetermined at this time."

Fred wiggled around in his chair as if to defend himself or argue a point, but then he slumped even farther and put his head between his knees. The possibility of an autopsy clearly disturbed him. I think Fred was finally fully confronted with the seriousness of his situation.

Fred raised his head slowly and looked directly at O'Rourke. "I want Mr. Lee to have power of attorney to take charge of all my temporal possessions and to act as my surrogate in all matters I am hindered from managing at this time. I also request Mr. Lee be my alternate in all financial matters including my bank account in the Cascade Bank of Montana. My account is in the Black Eagle branch. Please, draw up the papers and send them to me as soon as possible. I have no acknowledged relatives and no friends who might act on my behalf. Therefore, if Mr. Lee is willing to take this responsibility, I would like to finalize these matters quickly. There are decisions I must make very soon and from this cell. I cannot rest until some of these matters are handled by the only person I know who is both competent and trustworthy."

Tom looked at me. I was hesitant. I had no idea what might be involved. On the face of it, acceptance of his request would be a big responsibility. Here was a man who some twenty years ago dedicated himself to serving the Lord in a celibate priesthood. He took the vows of chastity and obedience. Fred was stuck with his vowed life whether or not the vows were valid. Fred was not only limited by his vows. He was limited by his emotional isolation from others, his inability to form meaningful adult relationships, his narrow view of life preventing his moving on to another profession, his fear of the future. I had seen a lot of patients in my practice whose illness in final analysis was *aloneness*. The relationship between Fred and me is relatively barren but is apparently the only one he has. I couldn't walk away even from a stick of wood.

I spoke. "I'll do what you ask, Fred. Your situation is serious, and your own resourcefulness is completely limited. I will work with you as closely as I can but there may be areas where I feel unable to oblige your request or areas where I might question your decision and therefore be unwilling to accept responsibility for a requested action. In addition, I want you to know I usually discuss with my wife details of any serious decisions I make. Permission to do that must be part of my arrangement with you. Do you understand what I'm saying and will you accept the limitations I'm placing on what I'm agreeing to do?"

Fred watched me and kept shaking his head in the affirmative during my comments. I turned to O'Rourke. "Will you prepare the necessary papers to cover what Father Brown is asking me to do?"

Tom said, "I'll work on them as soon as I get back to the office. They should be ready tomorrow and I'll get them to Father Brown in overnight delivery. You will have to get a notary to accompany you to the jail and arrange a time with the sheriff when both of you can sign the papers and have them notarized.

"As far as I'm concerned there is nothing else I need from Father Brown at this time. I'll wait for further information from you, Bob. If you will fax me a copy of the autopsy report when it's available, I'd be grateful. I'll head back to Black Eagle and prepare my initial report for Bishop Butler. Father Brown, you can contact me through Mr. Lee or you can call me directly if there is an immediate need. Here's my card. Goodbye to you both."

As O'Rourke got up to leave, there was a pleading look on Fred's face wordlessly asking me to stay. I went to the door and shook hands with Tom as he left. When I sat down again, Fred had much to say.

"I've been thinking about a lot of things the last twenty-four hours. I slept poorly. I need to take care of some things that are terribly important. Since I have no idea how long I'll be in here, I am begging you to cover some loose ends for me very soon. There are a couple of items that must be handled in a completely confidential manner. I know I can trust you, and there is no one else I can trust.

"First, let me talk about the immediate and the obvious. I have very few personal articles in the rectory other than my clothes. I would appreciate it if you will just bag up all my clothes and keep them somewhere in your house or shop or the barn if you want. There are some rosary beads and some medals and prayer books and of course my breviary. Can you put all those in a box or a bag and keep them with the clothes? All the furniture can be left in the rectory or given to some charity. The file cabinets are practically empty except for the file of bank statements. All other items can be destroyed, burned preferably. The bank statements should be kept in a safe place. I'll explain why in a moment.

"There is one item hidden in a special place. First I will tell you what it is. It is a letter written to me about twelve years ago. It is connected to a sexual relationship that began in the seminary with a fellow seminarian. It was an affair which he initiated and which was far more satisfying to him than it was to me. *His* satisfaction was the primary focus, and oral sex was my primary task. I rarely had any satisfaction from his attempts to bring me to an orgasm. It really wasn't my thing. Masturbation was more satisfying than anything he could do for me. We slept together in his room almost once a week. As you might guess, we would both have been banished from the seminary if the professors ever became aware of our clandestine encounters.

"I believe I was probably Bill's (let's just call him Bill for now) only sexual partner at the time. He was from the Denver diocese, and I was from Tulsa, so we were separated when we came to ordination time. The separation seemed much more difficult for him. He was in tears when we said goodbye, and I was relieved the relationship was over. At least I thought it was over.

"Of course, it was simple for him to find me once I was assigned to my first parish in Oklahoma. He wrote to me, and we began to correspond. His responses were always prompt, but I deliberately delayed my replies. I wasn't eager to maintain contact. After about a year he wrote and asked me to meet him in Chicago. He was attending a three-day workshop on *Scripture Based Homilies* by a famous Dominican. I thought the workshop would be interesting so I agreed to go.

"Once there, Bill's focus was not on the workshop but on the renewal of our sexual relationship. He told me he had not been involved with anyone since we left the seminary. He behaved like he was sexually starved. We did some drinking, and Bill came up with some marijuana. I 'loosened up' and sort of got into the mood of it all. We both came away seemingly satiated but apparently for Bill his need was only increased.

"Within a few days of getting home I received a passionate letter from Bill telling me in detail how wonderful the experience was for him and how anxious he was to continue the sexual ecstasy we experienced in Chicago. I had no reciprocal feelings. During the intervening time the experience became increasingly distasteful and rather abhorrent to me. I felt I had been used, seduced into a sexual encounter which did not correspond with my sexual needs. His letter only irritated me. I felt betrayed.

"I became increasingly angry with the passage of time. Then I began to feel vindictive. I never answered his letter, but I saved it. I had the thought it might be useful someday. Bill wrote again a few times. I never answered.

"Bill was a talented person, extremely bright and very social. I was not surprised when I saw he was advancing in church circles. He designed and introduced some new programs in his diocese, programs that brought increased interaction and cooperation between clergy and laity. There were articles about his work in our diocesan newspaper. He was promoted to be a Monsignor, and within another two years he was promoted to be auxiliary bishop in a northwestern diocese.

"I wouldn't be surprised if he is a cardinal before too long. His appointment as an auxiliary bishop was a fortuitous event for me. About nine years ago I was having some personal financial difficulties which I would rather not discuss at this time. It occurred to me Bill's letter was waiting to be used. I probably kept it with the thought of someday taking revenge for the Chicago event. Here was an opportunity for retaliation and at the same time preserve my financial solvency. I required funds to keep a family from making a report to my bishop about my inappropriate behavior with their son.

"By his lavish lifestyle, Bill made me well aware he came from a wealthy family. I contacted him by phone and gave him a choice: money or a copy of the letter to his bishop.

"Bill deposits ten thousand dollars into my Cascade Bank account by the fifteenth of every month. The letter is my leverage. I want you to take the letter, get a safety deposit box in your name at the local branch of Cascade Bank, and place the letter and my financial files in that box. You will find the letter under the cushion in the confessional box. I had a lock put on the little stall where I sat hearing confessions. The key to the stall is under the ciborium in the tabernacle. You will need to do this before Bishop Butler sends another priest into the parish." (Note to reader: the ciborium is a large chalice that holds the hosts in the tabernacle.)

Wow! Fred's wheels have sure been turning. I was surprised he unloaded so easily. Obviously he's been appropriately worried about the letter being found. He's aware he's running out of time. "It must have been difficult for you to tell me all this, Fred. I appreciate your trust and confidence. We'll have to ask the officer at the desk to give me your keys. I'll take care of these things by tomorrow at the latest. Which reminds me, what should I do about the Tundra? You might be able to return it to the dealer with a small financial loss. It doesn't have many miles on it."

Fred answered, "Let's take that up when we get the papers transferring authority for you to act in my behalf. The important thing is to get that letter and those files as soon as you possibly can and stash them away in a safe deposit box. They're not only dangerous to Auxiliary Bishop Bill. They're dangerous to me. Discovery of the letter would certainly not contribute to my current situation."

As I left, Fred and I went to the desk officer and after Fred signed for his keys they were given to me. Fred asked me to get word out to the parishioners there would be no service the coming Sunday. I told him I had an email list and would notify them. I was sure by now they all knew Fred was in jail. When I left the jail, I called Jane and told her I was on my way home.

As we sat down to eat, I said, "My morning might ruin your appetite." I suggested we quietly have our lunch and then go on the porch to talk. So Jane told me what she had been doing and we talked about the weather and a few things we would need to focus on as we face the coming winter.

After we cleaned up the kitchen we took our tea to the porch and sat side by side on the swing. Jane and I always had the pattern of getting physically close to each other when we talked about difficult or disturbing events in our life. Our physical closeness was a natural haven.

I was well aware of my promise of confidentiality, spoken or implied, regarding all I heard and all I said during the morning at the jail. O'Rourke took me as his assistant that morning and exposed me to confidential material. Jane had been my confidante for years. It was not going to end over this or over anything else that could happen in our lives. I had informed Fred of my interaction with Jane when I'm in the process of a serious decision.

Jane sat quietly attending to every word as I related the morning events. I noticed an approving nod of her head when I responded to Fred about the limitations I would impose if I agreed to take the responsibility he was asking me to take for his affairs. She nodded as I told her about Fred's blackmail scheme which I know we both related to his purchase of the Tundra. When I finished talking Jane just sat in thought until I finally said, "What are you thinking, Love?"

She responded, "It all sounds quite complicated and also quite sad. I feel sorry for Father Brown. He must feel alone and very helpless. It must be humiliating for him to reveal his behavior to you and to ask you to become involved in minimizing its impact on his current situation. The future must look very bleak to him. Where is he going to go when he's released from jail? I suppose Bishop Butler has some responsibility for him and to him, but Butler must not have many choices about what to do with him. As you are well aware Fred was not a favorite of mine, but I hate to see him in such trouble now."

Before speaking I waited a bit for Jane to continue, but she was still reviewing what was said. I added, "His future is uncertain no matter what happens. We have to realize there may be a crime here. I was struck by the decision to request an autopsy. Cause of death seemed so obvious from the initial reports about Tim's head injury and how it happened. But after examination the coroner was not comfortable in making a decision.

"There is an interesting bit of information in Fred's report regarding his sexual reaction to his seminary partner. People often get confused about gays and child abusers and assume a relationship between the two. They are not connected. Fred had no desire for homosexual relationships. He entered into them passively. It is fairly clear his sexual interest is in children, and at this point presumably male children, making him a homosexual pedophile. Statistically most pedophiles are heterosexual. If priest pedophiles were studied separately, I would expect there would be more homosexual pedophiles among priests than in the general population of males.

"Before the advent of altar serving girls, there was the common picture of 'priest and altar boy.' A natural attraction for a homosexual pedophile! Priest pedophiles seem to follow the basic ecclesiastical attitude—keep women at a distance. If a person were a heterosexual pedophile, I presume he would be less attracted to the priesthood."

Jane and I talked for about two hours and even then we knew it would be a recurring subject of our conversations.

CHAPTER EIGHT

As Jane and I were talking, I said, "I better go back to Springer this afternoon, Love. I want to visit Lucy Quirk briefly and then I want to go to the rectory and church and take care of the essentials there. I'll probably be a couple of hours. Why don't you come along and have a look around again in the new H&M store? I don't think you had much time when you were there before."

"Yes, I'll join you today. I can look at some material for my sewing. Maybe getting in town for a while will help me get a better perspective on events of the last few days. Give me five minutes to fix my hair and change my dress."

I said, "While you do that, I'll call Ted and ask him if he'll get one of his boys to do the milking for me tonight. Then, if it's agreeable with you, we'll drive to that little Chinese restaurant in Spinekop and have a leisurely dinner."

We were relaxed on the drive into town. The lengthy conversation after lunch seemed to have eased some of the strong feelings we have struggled with for the last couple of days. As I dropped Jane at the Mall, I said, "I expect to be about two hours, maybe more. So take your time, wander around, and I'll find you when I get back here. You have your cell, so I'll call you if I have any problem finding you. I plan to see Mrs. Quirk and then go to the rectory. I don't plan to go by the jail again today."

Jane responded, "Take your time, and I'll be thinking about you. Is there anything you need or anything I can buy you while I'm here?" I answered in the negative and said I would see her in a couple of hours.

I decided Mrs. Quirk should be first on my list. I knew the way to her house, so I was standing at her door in no time. She answered the bell quickly, recognized me, and invited me in. I offered my condolences. She seemed pleased I came and was quick to mention how much Tim appreciated the Sunday school class. Tim told her about the day he and I met and had milkshakes together. She said he was quite proud of that and saw it as a special event in his day. She appeared comfortable and at ease when I first came in, but as we talked her voice took a more somber tone and sadness began to show on her face. "I know I wasn't a very good mother to Tim a lot of the time. I've had a hard enough time getting my own life together since his father disappeared just before I moved to Springer. He was a drunk and was mean to Tim, and he used to beat on me. I called the police a number of times. I really should've left him, but I hated to see Tim without a father even though his father wasn't much good.

"People in Springer have been very good to Tim although I haven't worked on any helpful relationships for myself. Maybe Tim will look down on me from heaven and help me live a better life. I hope they have chocolate cookies in heaven. They were his favorite."

My thought—they won't be from Albertson's. But I said, "I'm sure Tim's death has been a great loss for you, Lucy. If there is anything I can do or the parish can do for you, please let me know. I'm sure Tim's needs were sometimes a burden for you as a single mother. Let me know if Jane or I can be of help. I'm sure Tim will be helping now from his place in heaven."

Lucy stopped me as I was going toward the door. "There is one thing. If it is possible could a Catholic funeral be arranged for Tim? I'm Catholic, but I don't attend Mass much. But Tim was a church-goer, and I know he would want a Catholic burial."

I answered, "Of course he should have a Catholic funeral. He was our altar boy. I'm sure we can arrange a funeral, Lucy. I'll contact the bishop directly and see what can be done. Would one day next week be all right with you?" As I said that, I realized the time for a funeral would depend on when the autopsy is complete and the body is released. I quickly added, "Why don't you get in touch with me when the authorities notify you the body will be ready for burial?"

Lucy said, "I appreciate your coming by. I'll contact you regarding the funeral when it is time. Thank you. May the Lord bless you."

As I drove away, I thought how difficult it is going to be for Lucy Quirk to go on without Tim. Many people accused her of neglecting him, and undoubtedly she did to some extent. The sad part now is she may increasingly neglect herself. His death will probably have one of two results: it will create an emptiness that will overwhelm her and cause further deterioration, or it will light some new spark of life and stir her desire to become a person of whom Tim would be proud. I pray it will be the latter.

The possibility of a funeral in the next week or two was all the more reason I should clean things up at the rectory and church. I brought a couple of large Hefty Cinch Saks and three sturdy cardboard boxes. I put all Fred's shoes and boots in one of the bags. I packed all his clothes and shaving kit in two of the boxes, cleaning out all his closets and drawers in the bedroom and throughout the rest of the house. Besides the living room, kitchen, bath, and bedroom, there was one small "guest room" with no furniture and an empty closet. Most if not all the kitchenware belonged to the parish. I put his four or five books in a box along with the financial files from the file cabinet. I could look through them later for things to be saved. There was a small television with the remote laying on his table. I wondered if he ever watched TV. I put the TV and remote in with the books. The few pictures were too plain to bother with.

I kept thinking how depressing it must have been for Fred to live in such an isolated and barren world. I doubt he ever had any visitors other than me. There were recent newspapers on the floor by one of the arm chairs. The last few looked like they had not even been opened. These newspapers and the ones on the porch I put in the trash as I neatened the place.

My next task was to find and again hide *the letter*. I left the packed items in the rectory and found the key to enter the sacristy next door. I stopped by the garage but then remembered the Tundra was still impounded by the police.

As I entered the sacristy, I remembered the last time I was there. It was the day Fred got so angry when I suggested he call the Tundra "Freddy Bear as in Teddy Bear." I've never seen him that angry before or after. Now that I think about it, I'm quite sure I've never seen him angry or even irritated. He can be critical and a bit caustic, as he was in his comments about diocesan regulations. I wonder if his placidity is an inner peace or just a character flaw of excessive passivity.

I looked in the closet and drawers of the sacristy in case Fred left his breviary or a jacket or something that belonged to him. I found his breviary and rosary beads and decided to put them in the box of books. There was a scale in the corner of the sacristy. It seemed an unusual object to have in the sacristy. If Fred was watching his weight, he wouldn't come here to check it. I made a mental note to "find out about the scale." I left it.

I took the tabernacle key and entered the church. I stepped up to the altar and opened the tabernacle. I lifted the ciborium and picked up the key to the door of the priest's confessional box. I unlocked the door, lifted the cushion and picked up the fate-filled letter. It was in an open envelope addressed to Fred with a return address (no name). My behavior in all of this was so secretive and careful, I had a growing sense of being involved in something sinister. I almost felt afraid to touch it, afraid my fingerprints would be found.

Then I returned to the reality of why I was there and what I was doing. I picked up the letter, locked the doors I had unlocked, and left the sacristy to return to the rectory. I put the breviary and rosary in one of the boxes and put all I had collected in the back of the pickup. I kept the letter in my hand until I placed it in the glove compartment of the car and locked the compartment. As I left the area, I couldn't help wonder if someone saw me and would I someday have to testify as to why I was there and what I was doing there. I don't think I'd make a good criminal unless I toughened up for the work.

H&M is in the new mall and right next to the Gallery Store, so I knew I would find Jane in one or the other store. I looked first in H&M and found her in a few minutes. I was surprised when she looked at me with concern. "Are you all right, Robbie? You look stern. Is everything okay?"

"I'm fine, Love. Maybe I'm feeling a little anxious or intense since I just picked up Fred's belongings and I wasn't too keen about some items. I'll tell you about it later. This is not the best place to talk about it. Did you find anything you like? I don't see any packages in your hand but maybe you're just having it all delivered. Or do we have to go to the warehouse to pick it up?"

Jane smiled and said, "No, I didn't find anything I liked until you showed up. Then I decided I'll take one of those. Didn't you say something about having dinner at the New Moon Restaurant in Spinekop? When does that happen?"

We headed for Spinekop which was about ten minutes out of town. I told Jane about getting Fred's belongings. I treated the letter as a separate issue and told her the step by step details.

Jane was curious. "What's in the letter? You must have looked at it. What does it say? Who is it from? And it's addressed to Fred, I presume." She couldn't believe it when I said I hadn't read the letter. She was smiling as she said, "Well, Rob, I refuse to go into the restaurant until we've looked at the letter."

I calmly responded, "Okay, I'll bring something out for you after I've finished eating. What would go well for you in the car? Remember, no mess, no crumbs. We have car rules. Sweetheart, we can read the letter now if you insist, but I suspect it is going to be full of explicit sexual comments and suggestions. It's likely to lessen our appetite and require some discussion that would not be suitable in a restaurant where others might pick up on something we say."

"You're right as always, or at least sometimes, Rob. If you've resisted reading it up to this point, I guess I can stir up enough patience to wait until after dinner. Perhaps the best thing to do is to wait until we get home. Then we can sit and read it together."

I commented, "Very wise thought. I agree. Now let's get some food."

We had a pleasant hour with our Chinese dishes and talking about a variety of things that seem to show up when we have leisurely time together. The subject that has filled the last few days was put on hold during the meal and the drive home.

I left the bags and boxes in the pickup when we first got to the ranch. I unlocked the glove compartment and retrieved the special letter. We walked up on the porch and in the fading daylight sat together on the swing to read. It was two pages, each written on one side.

It began, "My dear sweet carnal Fred," and it ended, "Your constant lover and carnivore, James." With regard to the letter itself, I will censor it as words are censored on television or radio. By maintaining that standard it is not worth putting down the few words that would remain; there would be two pages essentially full of dashes. I've never had an interest in erotic material but this letter would hit the top of any charts I could even imagine. It was embarrassing to me that Jane was reading it with me. When we finished reading it, Jane simply said, "What a filthy man with a filthy mind!"

I replied, "You're right about that. And do you realize the man who wrote this may someday be a Cardinal in our church. There is no last name, but with his first name and the postmark it is easy to find him. Fred gave me 'Bill' as the name when he first spoke about him. He didn't use the correct name but when he decided to have me get the letter and safely hide it, he was aware I could easily discover who 'Bill' really is. Fred never asked me *not* to read the letter. This letter brings Fred a $10,000 deposit to his account at the Cascade Bank the fifteenth of each month.

"Fred insisted I get a safety deposit box at our bank to keep the letter. I wonder if attempts have been made to either steal it from him or try to buy it from him. Maybe that's why he always seemed to be looking out the window when I approached the rectory. The date on it is nine years ago. This man of the cloth has come up with approximately one million eighty thousand dollars over the past nine years. I wonder what *donations* contribute to these payments. Other than expensive cars, I wonder what else this money buys for Fred."

"Maybe young boys." Jane looked sad as she made the comment. She just sat quietly trying to sort through the debris of these past few days. It was a little easier for me to digest it all because my talk with Fred had prepared me for something sleazy, although not quite as sleazy as "Bill's" letter turned out to be.

Jane and I often take a walk in the evenings on the nearby county road. There is no traffic. Only two families live farther up the road past our ranch. The sun was just setting, and it wouldn't be dark for another forty-five minutes. I reached for her hand, and without a word we both stood up and took our sad troubled thoughts out into the cool, fresh, comforting evening air. The walk served as a vigil for Tim and his mother and for Fred and for an auxiliary bishop named "Bill." A boy had lost his life. A mother had lost her only son. A man was in jail with no one to mark his absence. A bishop was the one most in need and didn't know it. When we got home, we quietly went through the routines of bedtime. The vigil ended in our night prayers and a peaceful sleep.

After breakfast the following morning, I sent an email to the parishioners with a brief update regarding Father Brown and to let them know there will be no Sunday Mass until further notice. I wrote that Father Brown was currently in jail because of uncertainties regarding the death of Tim Quirk and the diocesan attorney had come and talked to Father Brown. I added Bishop Butler would try to send a priest to the parish at least for an extended period and a Catholic funeral for Tim Quirk is to be arranged. I'll provide further information as it becomes available.

The news of Tim's death and the circumstances of his death were repeated during every news program. The story was on the front page of Montana newspapers and a couple of national papers. The news also reported stories of people marching through the center of town with placards commemorating the death of Tim and signs condemning the Catholic Church. Some marchers went by the jail shouting threatening and vile slogans and calling for Father Brown to be released to *their* justice.

As I was finishing my email, Jane came in and sat in the chair near me. I said, "Babe, I'm wondering how long they might hold Father Brown in jail without formal charges. I assume no formal charges have been filed and unless the district attorney files charges I expect Fred could be released any day. If he is, it would probably be better for him not to remain in Springer. Some of the townspeople are becoming extremely hostile and some loose cannon might decide to harm him. Wrath has been rightfully raised. I'm going to call O'Rourke and ask if it's possible he could arrange Fred's release. If Fred can leave the jail I think the bishop might have O'Rourke bring him to Black Eagle and find one of the town's parishes to take him in temporarily. Rather than call O'Rourke, maybe it would be wiser for me to call Charles and talk to him about it. I also have to ask him about getting a priest for Tim's funeral Mass."

Jane responded, "You must feel you're in the center of this whole thing, Robbie. And that's okay with me. The more you can do to help work it out, the sooner it will be over for everyone and life will get back to normal. It's going to take a long time to be forgotten even when it's over."

I said, "I'll call Charles now and see what he wants to do. You're welcome to stay close. Then I won't need to repeat my part of the conversation and you'll probably pick up on the direction he decides to take."

I called the bishop and presented my two questions: "What's the possibility of getting Fred out of jail because he has not been formally charged; and what's the possibility of getting a priest for Tim's funeral when they release his remains for burial?" We discussed the two issues. He agreed the diocese should request Fred be released with the provision he basically be under house arrest in one of the four Black Eagle parishes. The bishop would determine which one later today if O'Rourke is successful in getting Fred released. Regarding the priest for Tim's funeral, Charles asked me to let him know as soon as I have a possible date from Mrs. Quirk. He would like to say the funeral Mass himself if he is available. Before we hung up I told Charles I'd call O'Rourke and ask him to check the possibility of getting Fred released.

My next call was to O'Rourke. When he came on the line, I said, "Hi, Tom, I just talked to Bishop Butler and he is agreeable to using whatever legal means are available to get Brown out of jail with the stipulation he will be under voluntary house arrest in a Black Eagle parish. If Brown can be released the Bishop will decide on the parish within the next few hours and let us know."

Tom responded, "That's a good idea. I'm sure we can get him released. There are no clear grounds for him even being there, so they can hardly insist on keeping him in jail until they get the results of the autopsy. As you know the autopsy may take another eight to twelve days depending on the availability of lab techs and the promptness of their reports. If Brown is released, the sheriff will want someone to sign responsibility for Father Brown, a responsibility basically saying the signatory will produce Father Brown when requested by the court to do so. I assume you will be willing to sign for his release and transport him to Black Eagle."

I thought about Father Peter and the story of his being smuggled out of his diocese with his bishop's approval when he was court ordered not to leave the state. But in for a penny, in for a dollar—or however the saying goes. "I'll sign for him if you get an okay from the sheriff for his release. I'll plan to pick him up this afternoon and bring him to the parish Butler chooses. By the way, I have the keys to the rectory and the church. I have removed his belongings and have them outside in my car. His car is still impounded by the police."

Tom replied, "I'll call the sheriff now, and if they are unable or unwilling to release Fred, I will call you back within the next half-hour. It would save me some trips to Springer to have Father Brown in Black Eagle. I'll expect to have some meetings with him over the next few weeks regarding autopsy findings, various legal issues and issues related to his future as a priest. If they okay his release, I'll let Charles know so he can decide which parish will take Fred. Good luck in your new role of guardian."

As we sat down for lunch, Jane and I talked about it all, mostly wondering how it will eventually turn out for Fred. The prospects don't appear to be good. I summarized the situation. "Bishop Butler is not likely to want him in this diocese anymore, and since he has apparently been in a couple of others, there is hardly a positive opportunity for his future. I suppose the diocese where he was ordained has the ultimate responsibility for him. He could probably obtain laicization if he requested it, but what would he do outside the priesthood? I can't see him in a regular job; there's none I can think of that would suit him. Perhaps his best bet would be to remain in the priesthood and let his bishop keep him on a short leash in some way. In the past I believe a priest in his situation might serve as chaplain in a convent somewhere. The problem is there aren't many convents anymore. Of course, much will depend on whether or not he's charged with a crime. 'House arrest' in a monastery or convent might be necessary until after the trial.

"If he had the rank of bishop, they might consider transferring him to the Vatican. That appears to be the solution when some of the 'higher-ups' of the church find themselves in trouble, especially when it has to do with sexual behaviors. It's an unusual way to escape the arm of the law, but it seems to work.

"I'll plan on going to Springer later this afternoon. In the meantime, I'm going to take the fork loader up to the east field. Can you take the time to drive the flatbed truck and meet me there? We'll do it just like we did last year. I pick up the bales and you drive the truck. In the next few days I want to get them stacked inside the corral because in October we'll bring the cows down from the Wolf Butte pasture. We'll only do a run-through today to see if everything is working."

Jane replied, "I'll clean up the dishes, Rob, and be right behind you with the truck."

We returned to the house a little before three. There were no calls from O'Rourke which meant Fred could be released. "Janey, I'll go to Springer now and get Fred out of the pokey and take him to Black Eagle. I'll check with

Charles on the way and find out which parish he'll be going to. I'll keep Fred's shoes, clothes, and books in the car, and he can pick out what he needs. Not sure when I'll be home, probably close to six. I'll call you when I'm on my way."

"I hope it all goes smoothly, Rob. I'm glad Fred is getting out of jail. I can't imagine how isolating and lonely a cell must be, no matter how 'wooden' a person is. You are truly going out of your way to help Fred, and I'm in full agreement with what you're doing. Whatever he is responsible for, he must be feeling very much alone. You know the experiences of my childhood. I can easily sympathize with him. Tell him I send my regards and he will be in my prayers."

"You're being gracious and generous, Babe. I know it will be meaningful to him even in his 'woodenness.'"

On the drive to Springer, I kept wondering what really happened at Wolf Butte. Fred showed some increased discomfort at times during O'Rourke's questioning. I felt there was more to it than he told us. No matter how much he might be placing his affairs in my hands, I doubted he would confide in me regarding Tim. It was too close to home, too recent, too risky. He knew I cared about Tim, not as he apparently did, but as most of the people in town did.

I parked in front of the jail and went in. Sheriff Wilson came out of his office to greet me. "Hi, Bob, I'm glad to see you and I can say I'm glad you're taking Father Brown off our hands. He certainly hasn't been a problem, but his presence makes things a little awkward for us. We're not used to having priests or ministers here. And I imagine you know we use a lot of unsavory language working around here.

"We've also been concerned that the demonstrators outside the jail could get out of hand. As always, some of the local small-time ruffians are now involved. By the way, Tom O'Rourke sent him a bunch of papers which arrived yesterday. He called and told us we could open the envelope but to please give them to Father Brown to read and decide whether or not they meet his needs. He has them in his cell.

"We let Father Brown wear our 'prisoner clothes' since he's been here because there was nothing else available. His other clothes were sent to the lab. He'll have to wear ours unless you have some other clothes for him."

I replied, "As a matter of fact, I do have his other clothes with me. I'll bring them in and let him pick what he wants."

I brought the bag of clothes in, and one of the deputies took it to Father Brown. I went to the desk to read the papers I was to sign, the papers authorizing his release. The papers stated Father Fred Brown was not allowed to have his driver's license, his credit card, his check book or more than $20 in cash at any time. He was also to be in the presence of a responsible adult anytime he was going to be outside the residence, to be arranged by Bishop Charles Butler. That address was to be sent to the Sheriff's office once it was determined. He was not to leave the state of Montana. The paper also stated I would be responsible to return him to the Springer jail when requested to do so. I signed and dated the paper and returned it to the desk officer. I asked him to make four copies, one for Fred, one for me, one for Tom O'Rourke, and one for the pastor of the parish where he would be staying.

Fred was waiting for me when I turned around. We shook hands as we greeted each other. He picked out a nondescript shirt and pants to wear. The bag of clothing was in his left hand together with a manila envelope which I assumed contained O'Rourke's documents. He said goodbye to the Sheriff and thanked him for his courtesy. He raised his hand in a wave to the other officers as we left.

We were both silent until we got in the car. Fred pulled the papers out of the envelope. "These are the documents I asked Mr. O'Rourke to prepare for me. I carefully read through them all, and they clearly state what I told him I wanted. I'm anxious to have you read them, and if you concur I would like to have them signed, notarized, and copies for you, myself, the bank and O'Rourke.

"But before we do anything about this, and I meant to say this first, I want to thank you from the bottom of my heart for what you have done to get me released from jail. I know it was basically your doing. One of the officers told me the plan came from outside the jail. I decided on my own you are the only person I know who might have such consideration and care for me. I deeply appreciate it, Bob, and feel undeserving of you and what you do for me."

"Fred, I'm not sure I really know what *you* have done, but being in jail seemed unnecessary based on what is known, and jail was certain to be draining for you both emotionally and spiritually."

He answered, "Interesting you should mention spirituality to me. It should be the other way around, me mentioning it to you. I'm not sure where that piece fits in or where it's going for me. At the moment I have no desire to bare my soul to any priest or even to you."

"You'll get to it in due time, Fred. Regarding the heavenly banquet, I think we can consider God the *waiter*."

We were on the road to Black Eagle and I still needed to find out where I should take Fred. I said, "Why don't we stop at the Cascade Bank and get your papers signed and notarized? I believe the bank is open until five. We can make copies there and notify the bank about your account."

"That's fine with me, Bob. I know you'll want to read them carefully before we get to the signing. They ask a lot of you but, as I said before, I have no family and no friends in whom I would have a spark of confidence. You've come out on the short end, I guess."

It took us a little over an hour to get to Black Eagle. On the way we chatted about everyday things. I mentioned Jane said to tell him he was in her prayers. He was surprised. "I had no idea your wife would be praying for me. Please, thank her. Prayers are always good. I doubt there are many people who pray for me anymore." Those last words were spoken in a dejected manner.

I parked at the bank, took the papers from Fred, and read through them carefully. O'Rourke had done a good job. I had no questions or arguments about any of them. We went into the bank and found the notary. When he was available, we sat down and told him what we needed; we signed each paper one at a time and had them notarized. There was a copy machine near the notary's desk, and Fred asked him to make five copies.

While Fred was waiting for the copies, I called Bishop Butler. When he answered, he told me they were expecting Father Brown at St. Kateri parish across the Missouri River in an area called the West Side, a poor section of Black Eagle. I was familiar with the area but had never been to the parish. Charles gave me the address. I told Charles what the stipulations were regarding Father Brown's freedom. He was grateful for the limitations they specified.

The population of the West Side is probably eighty percent Native American, or if you prefer, "Indigenous People." The parish was fittingly named for St. Kateri. When Fred heard the name, he asked, "Where did they get a name like that?"

I just happened to have the answer. "Kateri Tekawitha was of the Algonquin-Mohawk tribe and was converted to the Catholic faith at age nineteen. She became ill with smallpox, and during the last five years of her life she lived in a Jesuit mission village in New France, now Canada. She died in 1680 and was canonized in 2012. She is often called the 'Lilly of the Mohawks.' When I was in college, I met a priest who was touring the country giving talks about Kateri's life and raising money in support of her canonization. I have no idea why he was dedicated to her cause."

We arrived at the parish and found the rectory. The pastor was a man from Nigeria, Father Zenwaki. Bishop Butler talked to him earlier in the day so he was expecting us and had general knowledge of why Brown was going to be staying with him.

Father Zenwaki met us at the door and after introductions showed us around the rectory. He seemed to be a friendly man, a bit talkative and obviously pleased to have a companion in the house. It was a small house, but there was a separate bedroom with a bath for Fred. Father Z (as he said parishioners call him) said he did his own cooking and would be glad to share some of the kitchen duties with Fred. There is a housekeeper who comes in every Friday to clean the house, change the linens and take their personal laundry to wash.

It struck me forcibly how lonely this man's life must be. He is far from his native land and family, living by himself in a parish laced with poverty and surrounded by a congregation which still clings to a number of tribal customs and attitudes. His marked accent further complicates his life. I could understand most of what he said but more successfully when he was facing me. I wondered what he did with his spare time and assumed he must have lots of it.

Charles asked me to give Father Z a copy of the paper I signed for his release. I spoke to Fred and Father Z together. "Here is a sheet Bishop Butler asked me to give you. Father Brown has some restrictions placed on him at this time. Father Brown should not use your car or anyone else's car. These restrictions are important, and if Father Brown does not comply with them in any way, you are asked to call the Bishop's office and report the violation. Father Brown is free to accompany you when you go shopping or out driving or to activities you may want to attend. But you are not his nursemaid. You may leave him by himself when you go out. If that happens, Fred is expected to remain in the house until you return. Fred, you would be violating the

Bishop's trust and mine if you left the house by yourself. Keep in mind *what the alternative is.*"

    After my little lecture, I said goodbye to both of them. I reminded Fred to call me if there is a need. I made a quick call to Jane to tell her I was leaving. I brought Fred's things in from the car, and then was on my way home with a sense of relief but knowing it was only temporary. I began reflecting how deeply I was involved in the affair. I needed to get home to my "sounding board."

CHAPTER NINE

I got home a little after seven that evening. Jane was sitting outside waiting for me. As she stood and walked to the car, a sense of peace and contentment swept through me. I thanked God once more for the blessings of my life.

After her warm greeting, to my surprise she suggested, "Dinner is ready, so let's wait until after we've eaten to discuss the events of your day. But if the day is heavy for you, we can talk about it as we eat. We're having the spaghetti and meatballs you like and one of your favorite desserts, which is a secret for now. What's best for you?"

"I'll take the spaghetti and meatballs first and maybe we can sit and talk over a leisurely desert or two. There is nothing pressing at the moment. It is such a pleasure to get home and have a sense of peace, no matter how temporary."

Jane added, "Also to make things a little easier for you, the milking is done tonight. I asked one of Ted's boys to do it. I had no idea when you might be home, and they appreciate the money they get for the job." I told her I was grateful.

After dinner we sat on the porch with coffee and the secret dessert, cream puffs. I gave Jane an update on the day and showed her a copy of Fred's restrictions in his temporary home. I also showed her a copy of the papers O'Rourke prepared.

"Robbie, these papers certainly give you a great deal of responsibility regarding Fred. He has become a rather pathetic figure in my thoughts. He seemed so alone and isolated when he first came to Springer. It must be difficult for any priest to be new in a parish and know each parishioner has his or her own expectations to be met. He's only been here a few months now, and I see little evidence he formed any relationships with parishioners other than a rather casual greeting after Mass. It's rare to see him get beyond that or to believe anyone in the parish wants to get beyond that. I think you're the only one who has any contact beyond what I've described. Where does he go with his thoughts and feelings? Does he take them to God in prayer? And does that satisfy his need to be heard, to be responded to? He doesn't get as much attention as a clerk in a store, someone who delivers mail, or someone who pumps gas and checks the oil for us. How can he survive across the chasm from the rest of the world?"

"Well, Janey, it's the 'stick of wood syndrome' you and I have talked about many times. I believe people have emotional quotients just as they have intelligence quotients. And just as the amount of intelligence a person has varies from very little to a great deal, so the amount of emotional capability a person has varies. We have known a few people who demonstrate little ability to respond emotionally. It isn't just they can't express feelings, they don't have them. Some of these without-feeling people watch others and learn to *act like* they have feelings. But when the chips are down, they're not in the game. The width and depth of their feeling responses are limited by their lack of endowment."

Jane said, "Yes, I remember saying Fred seemed rather 'wooden' the day we met him. So why does he respond to you the way he does?"

I answered, "Possibly our interaction stretches him a bit but deep down it's a 'business arrangement,' sort of like he might have with a clerk in a store who was especially helpful to him. He did seem genuinely expressive when I brought him out of jail to go to Black Eagle. I'm an important person in his life, not emotionally, but usefully. I do things for him. He appreciates what I do. There is no mutual bond of affection between us. Fred has no real affection for me, and I have no great affection for him. Yes, I care about him as a person, one of God's children. For me, affection is an emotional interaction. It must be reciprocal. But I've lectured long enough. Now it's getting dark so let's tidy up here and watch some news before we go to bed."

Jane commented, "Thanks for going over this again with me. I know we talk about it and I understand it, but when there's a situation like your current

interaction with Fred it seems different. You've made it pretty clear for me."
Later when we sat down to watch some news, Jane asked, "What are your
plans for tomorrow and the rest of the week?"

"I think we need to get to some ranching before we're into wintry
weather. It's not too early to anticipate snow in Montana. I'd like to get the
bales out of the fields and into stacks. We'll finish where we started yesterday
morning so we can move the heifers down by mid-October if possible—certainly by the end of the month. After we finish there we'll stack the bales in
the north field. I plan to winter a few steers there, and we'll need some bales
at home for heifers having difficulty calving and for our four horses.

"It would be helpful if things regarding Fred quiet down for a few weeks,
although that's not likely to happen. The results of the autopsy should be
coming in soon, and I have no idea what that will bring. I feel it's not going
to be good news."

Jane responded in her usual supportive way. "Whatever happens, we'll
get done whatever needs to be done. We've dealt with problems of one kind
or another throughout our marriage. Nothing has ever tested our faith beyond its strength or our love beyond its depth. We'll manage, Sweetheart.
Fear not."

A week went by with wonderful fall weather. We finished stacking the
bales in the field where we planned to move the heifers. Then we stacked bales
in the north field for two days. We were about to go there for the third day
when the phone rang.

It was Tom O'Rourke. "Good morning, Bob. I have bad news. We have
the full report from the coroner's office. It is not good. First of all, stomach
contents revealed food as reported by Fred, and in addition there was semen.
The semen matches Fred's DNA, so undoubtedly Fred will be charged with
sexually assaulting a child. Secondly, there is still question as to the cause of
death. There are two possibilities: strangulation or traumatic head injury. Undoubtedly the county attorney will be filing charges, and Fred will need to be
returned to jail.

"The question of the moment is: do you want me to arrange transportation, or do you want to come for Father Brown and take him back to the
Springer jail? As we speak, your county attorney is drawing up the charges. I
just spoke with her on the phone. Unless one of us provides transportation,

she will have the sheriff pick Fred up within the next few hours and there would be a charge to you for that."

I responded, "In another half hour I would have been out in the field. You called at an opportune time. I'll go for him, Tom. The news is going to be hard for Fred to face. He's only been at Saint Kateri's about a week. I haven't heard from him, so I presume things have been going smoothly between him and Father Z. After he's back in jail, I'll give you a call if I may. I'd like to know your thoughts about the situation. I presume you will be his defense attorney."

Tom said he had not yet given Bishop Butler the news. "I'll let you know the bishop's reaction. Yes, I'm sure I will represent Fred. Call me after you drop Fred back in Springer."

Jane had overheard most of my conversation with Tom. "Rob, I agree with your decision to get Fred. He's got a long road ahead, and this will at least help him get started in a better way by your kindness. Even a stick of wood must be afraid when a fire is starting. And there is sure going to be a blaze in Springer."

I responded, "Thanks, Love. Some people will probably be critical of me when they hear I am helping a 'child abuser,' but be that as it may, I can't turn my back on another human being in such a harsh situation. I'll shave and clean up a bit and then off to Saint Kateri's Parish to get Fred. If I'm delayed in some way, I'll give you a call; otherwise I should be home for lunch. Maybe we can finish the bales this afternoon. It's a good day for field work."

I dreaded confronting Fred with the stark news of his return to jail and almost assuredly a trial. Somehow my heart was not crying out for justice and punishment. It was interesting for me to observe my own feelings and know how different they would be if I did not have the relationship I have assumed with Fred. I also mourned the loss of Tim and felt a desire to console Mrs. Quirk. I was seeing and was in sympathy with the opposing sides of a single incident. I sorted through and struggled with these thoughts as I drove to Black Eagle.

I didn't call ahead because I didn't want to tell Fred over the phone that he's going back to jail. For what it's worth, I thought it would be of some support to be there when the axe falls. It will not take him long to get his things together.

When I got out of the car in front of the Saint Kateri rectory, Fred walked out the door with a cheery, "Hello, it's good to see you. What brings you to these parts?" His good humor was not to last long. As we shook hands it was time for him to know. "There is bad news, Fred. The County Attorney in Springer is filing charges against you. I am here to take you back to jail. I want you to get your things together while I explain the situation as simply as I can to Father Z."

I'm not sure Fred was as surprised as I expected him to be. His question came calmly. "What are the charges?"

"I don't know exactly. Mr. O'Rourke called me and told me charges were being filed. His expectations were a charge of sexual abuse of a minor and possibly a charge of murder." Fred chose not to respond. He turned and walked toward the rectory mumbling, "I'll get my things and be right back."

I followed him into the rectory and found Father Z in the room he called his office. I told him I was there to transport Father Brown back to Springer. I had no idea what Bishop Butler had told Father Z, so I was as discreet as possible in my comments. Father Z said he was sorry to see Fred go and en-joyed having someone else in the house. He came out to the front door and said a cordial goodbye to Fred as we prepared to leave. Fred expressed his gratitude to Father Z for his hospitality and comradeship.

Fred put his clothes, shaving kit, and a box of stuff in the back seat and got in the front with me. I decided not to "devise" conversation but to let Fred talk when he was ready. We were almost halfway to Springer before Fred spoke. "I'm not surprised I'm going back to jail. Once they mentioned an autopsy, I knew they would find my semen in Tim's stomach. No matter what comes out in the courtroom, in the news or in common gossip, *Tim's death was an accident.* It is my fault we were there together. I'll never forget his death or forgive myself, but *it was an accident.*"

I did not reply and truly believe he did not expect a reply. What he said was only for my hearing, whether or not I believed. Did I believe him? Per-haps I did. In my presence the only expression of affection I ever heard from him was his love for Tim. Was he sincere? How can one tell? A person states, "I love so and so." The hearer attaches their own meaning of love to the statement. The speaker has their own meaning of the word when it is said. An observer attaches their own meaning of love to what is heard. The word is nebulous, the feeling is indefinable, the truth is quixotic. Strange that a word used so often really has no common meaning.

I pulled up and parked at the jail. We left Fred's things in the back seat and walked in. The officer at the desk greeted us. "Well, hello. You are going to be back with us, Father Brown. The angry people who milled about outside the jail quit showing up after you left. Now they'll probably begin again shouting curses and calling you names. They haven't been directly threatening and we have not found any guns among them. We'll keep you safe here, Father Brown."

Fred was very passive as they came to put him through the returning process. I said a quick goodbye and told him I was sure Mr. O'Rourke would be out to see him before long. "I will also stop by when I'm able. I'm pretty busy at the ranch these days."

As they led him away, Fred said, "Thanks for all you've done, Bob. It makes it easier to know you're out there."

I was back at the ranch a little before noon, once more with Fred's clothes and other items in the car. Jane had lunch ready. I told her about the morning trip and how Fred was dealing with his return to jail. We agreed he seemed to be accepting the situation reasonably well. I commented, "He acted almost like he didn't care what was happening or what was going to happen. I can't say he's at peace with it; more like he's lost his enthusiasm for life and has decided nothing in the future will be of any importance." Since Fred's return went smoothly I decided there was no need to call O'Rourke at this time. Ranch work came first.

After lunch we went back to the work of the morning and finished stacking bales. I reflected on the pleasant day and how good it felt to be in the field and accomplishing something that had a purpose, a goal, an endpoint and a definite value. As I often do, I became keenly aware of the blessings of this day and our life together.

Three days after Father Brown returned to the Springer jail, I had a call from Lucy Quirk. Tim's body was released to her. She asked if I could help with funeral arrangements. She had no date in mind but would like to have the funeral as soon as possible. I told her I would call the bishop and ask for a priest to say the funeral Mass and the burial Rite. I asked if she would like me to coordinate the service with the undertaker. She expressed gratitude for my willingness to make these arrangements.

I assured her we considered her a member of the parish community and Tim was thought of as a treasured altar server. I offered my condolences for the sadness of Tim's death and the unholy circumstances we all acknowledge. I assured her I would let all the townspeople know about the final arrangements.

As soon as I completed the call I contacted Dempsey Funeral Services, the firm usually employed by our parish members. I spoke directly to John Dempsey, the owner. He agreed to accommodate any date and time when I could arrange to have a celebrant for the services.

The next call was to Bishop Butler. When he came on the line, he said, "Hi, Bob. I've been waiting for your call in regard to the funeral for Tim Quirk. I hope we can agree on a time when I can come to officiate. O'Rourke told me the results of the autopsy and, needless to say, I am deeply sorry and would appreciate an opportunity to respond openly and publicly to the entire community on behalf of the diocese and the Catholic Church. I might add, as a comment just between the two of us, I feel some personal blame for this tragic event. I had concerns about Father Brown, but when I asked for references from every diocese where he had served before, the responses were 'a clean slate with no evidence of misconduct.' Unless charges are filed or there is open publicity, one is not going to hear about accusations or suspicions— at least not from diocesan sources—when the Bishop of the diocese is encouraging a priest to go elsewhere. I was told Brown wanted to transfer to Montana because he loved the beauty of the State and the less crowded environment. But I need to ask why you've called. Has Mrs. Quirk decided on a day and time for Tim's funeral?"

"That is the purpose of my call. The remains are released by the coroner. I've spoken to John Dempsey, whom I believe you know. Currently John is free as to day and time, so if you can check your schedule, Charles, we can set it up right now."

The Bishop paused and then spoke, "I'm looking at my calendar for the coming week. I'm free next Tuesday morning. Why don't you speak with Mrs. Quirk and arrange a time that best meets her needs? I could be there as early as eight o'clock, but I assume a bit later in the morning would suit her and also allow for better attendance from the community."

I replied, "That sounds great. I'll contact Mrs. Quirk to arrange the time, and then I'll let Dempsey know. As soon as it's settled here, I'll leave you a message. I'm grateful for your willingness to be the celebrant. Your presence will have a special meaning for her, and it will also reassure the parishioners that our needs are still in your mind."

"They are indeed, Bob. I'm hoping to get one of our retired priests to agree to fill the vacancy full time for at least the next year. I think an older man would fare well in Springer. It is fundamentally a stable parish, and your presence there will be invaluable to an older man. Thanks for helping out in the current crisis. I will see you next Tuesday. Bless you."

After we hung up I made the other calls and within the hour I left a message for the Bishop to let him know the service was scheduled at 10 A.M. the following Tuesday. Then I emailed all the parishioners and also called the local paper to give them the information for the weekend edition. I notified the local TV news station.

The morning was over by the time my calls were completed. Jane spent most of the morning gardening. As we sat down to lunch I told her about the plans for Tim's burial. Jane commented, "I think Bishop Butler's coming for the funeral will do a great deal to heal the wounds left by Tim's death. It should help ease some of the anger and vindictive feelings we have all shared these past days. Butler's a good man. And his idea of a retired priest taking over for a time would work out well and help restore the parish to a sense of worship and a spirit of fellowship."

I responded, "I agree completely. The bishop is making some wise and caring decisions about this tragic event. His presence will help mend the open wounds still festering.

"But you and I have to move on to some other matters, Love. It's time to bring the heifers back home to their winter pasture. If the good weather holds tomorrow, I think we should saddle up and go to the Wolfe Butte pasture and bring them home. I suggest we go right after breakfast. They'll be up and grazing in the morning hours so we can see them more easily, gather them quickly and have them trailed home by noon or at the latest one o'clock."

Jane replied, "Sounds good to me. Let's get up a half hour earlier. You do the milking while I fix breakfast. I'll put a couple of cookies and our coffee thermos bottles in my saddle bag for a morning pick-me-up."

The next morning I had our horses saddled by eight o'clock and we were on the road. When we got to the pasture, it felt like the cattle were expecting us.

We began moving them toward the gate which we left open as we came in. As they gathered, Jane rode closer to the gate and counted them as they went through. We had sixty-six, the number we brought there four months previously. I noted they all looked healthy, and if a good cattle man looked carefully, he might notice a slight rounding of their bellies. They were beginning to "show."

The herd moved along well once we reached the county road. They were in their winter pasture a few minutes past noon. We left them there to explore the land where most of them had been born approximately twenty-two months previously. It was also the pasture where they had their tell-tale encounter with the bulls.

When we got home there was a message from Tom O'Rourke asking me to get in touch. After we finished lunch I called Tom. When he answered, I just asked, "What you got?"

"Bob, I got the law to meet with tomorrow in Springer. Wondering if you can possibly join us. Patricia Benet, the county attorney, said she would like to sit down and talk with me and see what kind of an agreement we can work out regarding Fred Brown. I'd like to have you there for several reasons. You know Father Brown better than anyone else in the area knows him. Secondly, he clearly relies heavily on you in regard to his affairs. Thirdly, you are well known in Springer and you know the people well. And fourthly, if you need another reason, I would like to have you to sort through with me whatever alternatives the county attorney may offer. And there's one more: you can clarify things for Brown and help him clarify what he is willing to agree to."

I asked, "What time are you meeting Benet?"

"We agreed to meet at ten o'clock at the courthouse. It might be good if we had half an hour or so just to update before we meet with her." I decided I ought to stop by and say hello to Fred and give him an idea of what O'Rourke and I would be doing. It would make him aware he is moving toward a confrontation with the legal system. I told Tom, and we agreed to meet at 9:30 for coffee.

Jane and I spent the afternoon harvesting some green beans, peas, and carrots from the garden. Jane learned to can vegetables when she helped Helen with canning whenever we visited the ranch in the fall season. It seemed to be a tradition that came with the ranch. Working in the garden helped nullify the depressing shadows that darkened the past few weeks. We treasured the satisfaction of soiled hands and the newly opened earth that nursed the seeds we planted last spring. The ritual of holding God's new creations was comforting, encouraging, life revitalized.

The following morning Jane and I sat and talked for over an hour after we finished breakfast. We discussed the coming winter and some of the work we still needed to accomplish. High on the agenda was selling the yearling steers for a good price. We also needed to set up an arrangement to sell the wheat crop. Here we were talking about selling cattle and wheat, when I was about to leave for Springer and talk with a couple of attorneys about a man's life, a value far exceeding that of all the wheat in the county and all the cattle in the state.

I arrived at the Springer jail at nine o'clock. Sheriff Wilson had just arrived and stopped to say hello. I asked how Father Brown was doing. He replied, "Father Brown has presented no problems for us. He is respectful to all the guards and has not asked for any special treatment. He engages minimally with others. I could sum it up saying he seems isolated from everything around him. He strikes me as a disheartened man."

I commented, "His prospects are not good considering the results of the autopsy. The future holds little promise for him professionally or personally. His is a sad lot."

The deputy on duty took me to a visiting room and brought Father Brown. I offered my hand, which he shook somewhat reluctantly. My mind flashed back to the first time we shook hands and my negative response at the time. He said, "I'm grateful you have come, Bob. Even a person as unfriendly as I am prone to be, I cannot be comforted or consoled by isolation. My thoughts plague me day and night and are without distractions. I don't *feel* desperate, but I am filled with despair. Perhaps your presence will bring some momentary relief."

I felt hesitant to tell him why I was there but I also believe speaking directly and openly about the dreaded realities of life give clarity and encourage one's spirit to a more focused and eventually more appropriate attitude and response. There would be no benefit in delay. "Fred, I'm meeting this morning with Tom O'Rourke, whom you know, and Patricia Benet, the county attorney. We are going to discuss what legal indictments you will be charged with and what the outcomes of those charges may be. I feel certain you are looking at a prison sentence. There are two issues: first, the question of the charges, and second, how you will plead in response.

"After O'Rourke and I talk with the county attorney, we will meet with you here and discuss what options you have in regard to your plea. We will spend whatever time is necessary to help you make your decision. By the end of this day you should know what crimes you will be charged with and whether or not you will go to trial. This is a significant day for you. I hope there will be a pathway that leads to peace of mind and a future that holds some promise of restoring your self-respect and renewing your relationship with your Maker. I don't expect we will be back here until afternoon, but when we do come I urge you to ask whatever questions you have about what we bring to you.

"I should also tell you arrangements have been made for Tim's funeral on Tuesday of next week. Bishop Butler has agreed to come and be the celebrant. I have notified all our parishioners, and there will be an article in the weekend paper about the funeral. I have helped Tim's mother with the preparations. I should also tell you she appears to be more consoled these days." I opened the door, and the deputy came for Fred who shook my hand and said nothing as I left.

I met O'Rourke on schedule at the coffee shop. After a few pleasantries he laid out the possibilities. First of all there was the solid evidence of sexual abuse of a minor. It came under the heading of statutory rape. That alone carried the possibility of a prison sentence not to exceed twenty years. Second, there was Tim's death and ambiguity still present as to its cause. With the information from the crime scene, statements made by Father Brown, and findings of the autopsy, the coroner was still unable to say definitively what caused Tim's death.

Tom and I walked the few blocks to the courthouse to meet Patricia Benet, who is an intelligent, highly qualified woman. She was one of the major attorneys in Clover County until her election as county attorney five years ago. When we arrived, her secretary took us directly into Pat's office.

I had known Pat for some time because we met in several prior situations. I introduced her to Tom O'Rourke. She was all business. "Have a couple of chairs, gentlemen, and we'll get down to discussing the Father Brown case. By the way, I appreciate your quick response, Tom, to my suggestion we get together and put this to rest as soon as we can. The case seems to contaminate the life of this town. The sooner we clear it off the books the better for all.

"Let me discuss what I see as possibilities. Considering the DNA evidence regarding the semen, there will be a charge of statutory rape which covers the sexual abuse of a minor. I would advise your client plead guilty on that one.

"Second, we have a possible charge of second degree murder. To bring you up to speed on that, Bob, it would be a charge of murder without premeditation. The autopsy showed evidence of dark discoloration of the skin around the mouth area and the neck area, especially in the back. There were also tiny hemorrhages, called petechiae, found in the eyes of the victim. These findings suggest the possibility of smothering perhaps occurring immediately after the oral sex. These petechiae are not specific to asphyxia, so they don't rule out other causes of death.

"Frankly, my theory is that Fred was overwhelmed with the need to conceal his sexual assault on Tim. This suggests that Tim was an unwilling participant and was somehow coerced or forced to perform this oral sex act. Once the heat of Fred's passion was dissipated by ejaculation, he became overwhelmingly aware of his gross violation of boundaries physical, legal, and professional. His instinct of self-preservation overcame his reason. He withdrew his penis from Tim's mouth, put his hand over Tim's mouth, and held the back of Tim's head with his other hand, which is where his other hand may have already been forcing Tim's movements on Fred's penis. Thus the discolorations I mentioned before. If Tim died of asphyxiation, I could consider a charge of first degree murder since one could argue it was a deliberate act. However, if we consider Fred's probable emotional state, the defense would argue and possibly establish lack of deliberateness because of extreme emotional immersion. If a charge of first degree murder were accepted by a jury, life imprisonment is a likely penalty.

"Let's assume for the moment that smothering was not the cause of death and that Tim somehow struggled to free himself from Fred's grasp. The other obvious possibility is the fall and the blow to Tim's head on the rock. Fred says Tim was running. The severity of the head injury is in part due to the kinetic energy transferred to the blunt object in the impact. Running would increase that energy and cause greater damage to the head in striking the rock. The autopsy reports severe trauma to the left frontal area of the skull resulting in, and I quote, 'severe laceration on the scalp with deeper scalp hemorrhage, associated skull fracture, and intracranial hemorrhaging.'

"If indeed this is how Tim died, and Father Brown says this is what happened, we must still ask 'why was Tim running?' Was it really a game of tag? Tag after an episode of sexual abuse? Seems unlikely. Or was Tim escaping his abuser? Isn't it likely an abused child will run away if possible? To run into the woods to hide seems a natural response. What better place to hide given the situation we are all aware of?

"Assuming Tim was running to escape and in the process tripped and fell on the rock and the fall resulted in his death, then we have a charge of 'involuntary manslaughter,' also called 'negligent homicide' or second degree murder. If so charged and proven, the penalty is prison not to exceed twenty years or a fine of $50,000 or both.

"The only *proof* that Fred and Tim were playing tag is Fred's statement, which will not carry a great deal of weight if presented to a jury. The county may not be able to *prove* otherwise, but it would not be difficult to convince a jury beyond reasonable doubt that Tim *was running away* from his abuser.

"That pretty well states our case. Considering the circumstances of this boy's death and the wrath of the community over the loss of this now 'treasured waif,' I don't have much to offer you. I will say that a first degree murder charge is not a strong position, and I would prefer to settle this case as quickly as possible. A guilty plea to second degree murder and to sexual assault would settle the case more quickly and in my mind satisfactorily for all involved."

I was overwhelmed by what we were just told. O'Rourke was not visibly perturbed but neither was he ready with a quick response. Attorneys are probably good at concealing emotional responses in dealing with one another. They save their emotional exhibitions to sway juries.

O'Rourke gazed out the window in thought for two or three minutes before replying. "Ms. Benet, you have clearly laid out a difficult argument for me to respond to without some careful thought and review of all factual information. Of course, I also need to discuss options with my client. I'm well aware of the importance of moving this case forward as quickly as possible for the sake of the community and for the sake of my client. I can tell you I would prefer not to see this taken to jury trial. The publicity would dominate at least the local news media for the duration of a trial. The whole event would live in the memories of the townspeople for an extended period.

"And speaking frankly, the welfare of the diocese and of the Catholic Church must also be part of my consideration. I am, after all, the diocesan attorney. In that role I would like to ask your opinion on one subject. If Father Brown were to plead guilty, let's for the moment say on both counts, do you think that position would make someone more likely to sue the Bishop and the Catholic Church for compensation?"

After a few moments of reflection, Ms. Benet responded, "I've had no experience in this particular kind of situation, but my general experience in the practice of law is that some people are going to sue no matter what the situation or the possibility of obtaining compensation. Often the suit is primarily for vengeance. If a person is just angry and wanting revenge, compensation is not as significant if they can get revenge in some other manner such as damaging publicity or some sort of physical retaliation. In any case, money has its own attraction to most people.

"Also for your consideration, I have heard from fairly reliable sources that the Catholic Church will often offer a considerable amount of compensation in order to avoid litigation and the associated publicity. You might consider contacting the victim's mother after you've spoken to the bishop regarding the question. You can be sure an attorney has been or soon will be trying to encourage Mrs. Quirk to start a civil suit.

"Why don't you and Bob take the matter to Father Brown today and perhaps by late this afternoon we can meet again and reach an understanding and an agreement about how to proceed?"

"We'll do just that," Tom replied. "It's almost lunch time and I would invite you to join us, but Bob and I will undoubtedly use the time to discuss all this, and lunch together might not be wise in case this does go to trial. Questions might arise about professionalism."

Pat replied quickly, "Thanks for considering it—maybe another time. And I do have a crowded schedule in the next few hours. I will clear my calendar after four o'clock today with the hope we can reach an agreement when we get together."

As Tom and I left the county attorney's office the first thing mentioned by Tom was lunch. It was only 11:30, but perhaps we both saw food as an escape from or perhaps compensation for the rather dismal proposal Pat Benet laid out for us. I asked Tom if he liked Chinese food, and he replied, "Those are the best words I've heard all morning."

"Okay, let's drive to Spinekop for lunch. Ming's New Moon is a fine Chinese restaurant and not expensive. I presume you're putting this on your tab since I still serve as your assistant in some way."

We asked for an isolated table when we arrived at the restaurant. They accommodated nicely. We were both ready when the waiter came for our order, and it wasn't long before we had our food. We ate slowly and, as anyone might expect, talked about the morning meeting with Pat Benet.

Tom was feeling frustrated because there seemed to be no wiggle room in the situation with Father Brown. In the face of Benet's speculation about the "game of tag" being more likely a little boy's escape from an abuser, Tom could hardly expect to convince a jury to believe Fred's claim "it was a game." So whether Tim died from asphyxiation immediately subsequent to the sexual abuse or from his fall on the rock while running would make little difference for a jury.

As Tom was explaining this to both of us, a clarity came to me and I interrupted Tom's comments. "Wait a minute. If Fred smothered Tim after the sex act was completed, how did Tim get the head injury? It can't be a case of 'either or.' The head injury was there and severe enough to be fatal. The sexual act could not have occurred after the fall. So the actual cause of death had to have been trauma to the head. The time sequence clearly suggests the cause of death was falling on the rock."

Tom got the picture immediately. Or maybe he knew it all along and I was just getting it. "Yes, of course, the sexual act was part one. Part two was Tim running. Part three was Tim's fatal fall and death. So Fred is facing charges of statutory rape and murder in the second degree, negligent homicide. The injury to the head does eliminate asphyxiation as cause of death. If death came from Fred strangling Tim, the charge possibly could have been murder in the first degree as Pat said. I cannot encourage Fred to oppose the charges as Benet stated them. I don't believe I could get a jury to find him innocent of either charge. A trial would only prolong the pain of Tim's death for Mrs. Quirk, the wrath and unrest of the community, and last but not least the publicity and embarrassment linked to the Catholic Church. And I might add a trial would not do Fred a bit of good.

"I see only one reasonable course of action, and I am prepared to recommend it to Father Brown when we visit him after lunch. If he pleads guilty, justice will be decided by one of the district judges in Culver City which is our closest district court. My guess would be a judge is likely to give him a sentence of ten to twenty years in the state prison for each crime, and the judge *may* make them to be served concurrently. That's probably the best deal Brown can expect."

Tom's position seemed sound to me and I told him so. "I can't imagine Father Brown will oppose what you suggest. Going through the process of a trial would be markedly disturbing for him. It would be traumatizing. I suspect he would do anything he could to avoid it. My guess is he will continue to deny responsibility for Tim's death when we talk to him. But I have no doubt he will be willing to submit a guilty plea."

We left the restaurant and drove to the jail. Our meeting with Fred was as I suspected it would be. He said several times, "I didn't kill Tim. I loved him. He was my friend. He was like my child." The last statement struck me as so unusual I wondered what might be behind it. For a brief moment I was seeing Fred through a therapist's eyes. Then we moved on.

O'Rourke gave Fred a synopsis of our discussion with Ms. Benet. He did not explain the details of our meeting but was clear about explaining the two charges that would be filed by Benet. It only took a few moments of thought for Fred to decide on a guilty plea to each charge.

O'Rourke explained to Fred the two of us would meet later in the afternoon with Patricia Benet, the county attorney. Tom would inform the county attorney Fred will plead guilty to the count of statutory rape and the count of second degree murder. Later Ms. Benet would present these to the currently presiding district judge in Culver City. Within seven to ten days, Father Brown would be taken by the sheriff to appear before that district judge for sentencing. Ms. Benet and Mr. O'Rourke would also be before the court. If sentenced to the Montana State Prison in Red Lodge, Father Brown would be taken there by the sheriff's office within a stated period of time.

Fred was calm and his usual distant self as we said goodbye. I told him I would probably be at the hearing in Culver City and we would certainly have a long visit to discuss whatever concerns he had about his personal affairs.

I had called Jane a couple of times during the day to let her know what was going on. After we left Benet's office, I called her again to tell her I was on my way home. As I said goodbye to Tom, he told me he was thinking of going by Mrs. Quirk's house. He said he might talk to her about possible financial compensation from the diocese. I told him I thought he ought to check with Charles. As he walked away he said, "You're right. Guess I better wait until I've talked to the bishop to be sure he favors the idea."

CHAPTER TEN

O n the way to the ranch I suddenly realized tomorrow was the day for Tim's funeral. I had been totally absorbed with the legal issues. I forgot the significance the charges would have on members of our parish, most importantly Mrs. Quirk, and the people of the community. One of the most remarkable tributes to the memory of Tim Quirk was the plan to close the small local Mall and all the department stores and specialty shops on the day of his funeral. It was like a revival of old western traditions, the unity of the village.

I had contacted the four altar boys—Jim Mansfield, Pat and Joe Kirby, and Tom Brill—and asked them all to serve at the funeral Mass suggesting they not wear the white cassocks but just white shirts and black pants if they had them.

Jane had dinner ready when I arrived home. It felt so peaceful to be back on the ranch and to talk with Jane about the day. She grasped the substance of the legal issues and understood the direction O'Rourke took in his recommendations to Father Brown. When I talked about Fred's attitude, she commented, "I suppose Father Brown had little choice but to accept a guilty plea. In reality it didn't make much difference whether Tim was running for safety or running to play tag. He was there alone with a Catholic priest who was violating the rules of his current state in life. The priest was wrong in creating the situation and the situation brought about Tim's death. It does come out sounding like negligent homicide.

"It was such a foolish thing for Fred to do, but I remember the Latin quote I've heard you say, 'Penis erectus non conscientiam habit,' which I think you translated to mean 'an erect penis has no conscience.' Fred's uncontrolled sexual appetite wreaked havoc with his own life and caused the destruction of Tim's. Tim's loss of life will be a sad delicate memory for his mother and the people who loved him. Fred's loss of life has begun and will go on during his years in prison and whatever empty years may follow. I'm surprised I feel almost as sorry for Fred as I do for Tim."

After dinner we continued to talk about Tim and his mother and how Tim's death might affect her life. Jane suggested I call her and ask if we could pick her up and take her to the church with us. I called and she accepted my invitation. She surprised me a bit when she commented, "It will be easier for me to be there with you and your wife. I don't go to Mass very often, and I'm not sure I will feel very comfortable. I quit going to church a long time ago, but after Tim was born I went sometimes, mostly to encourage him to go. Then when he went regularly as an altar boy, I would make excuses, mostly lies, why I didn't go."

I responded, "Jane and I will be happy to be with you during the Mass and, if you wish, we will accompany, sort of escort you to the graveyard for the final rites. The undertaker has arranged for pallbearers from the parish. We'll stay with you and sort of guide you through the services if you like."

She quickly replied, "Yes, I would like that. Thank you so much for the call." I told Jane how grateful Mrs. Quirk was and how thoughtful Jane was to suggest it.

We picked Mrs. Quirk up at 8:40 the next morning and entered the church about five minutes later. The church was already half full and as we went up the center aisle, persons at or near the center came over to speak to Mrs. Quirk, offering their sympathies and many embraced her. Many were tearful. Mrs. Quirk was deeply touched and was softly sobbing as we reached the front row. She knelt in prayer with us after we entered the pew.

As we waited for the coffin to be brought in, Mrs. Sweeny and a small group of singers from the congregation sang the *Ave Maria* with Louise Sweeny at the piano. As the service began, Bishop Butler, following the four altar boys in white shirts and dark pants, entered from the sacristy to the sanctuary. The pallbearers brought the coffin to the front of the aisle and returned to their seats.

Bishop Butler blessed the coffin with Holy Water. When finished he turned and nodded to Mrs. Quirk and then spoke to the congregation. "We are gathered this morning to bid an angel farewell on the journey back to God. All of us mourn Tim's loss, but no one feels it as keenly or as deeply as his mother, who has not just lost a child but has lost a source of meaning in her life. Let me tell you, Mrs. Quirk, about a spiritual thought I've had for a long time. Our religion tells us that each of us has a guardian angel. I believe when children die in their infancy or in their years of innocence, God has a special need for them. Nine-year-old children are too young to commit serious sin. With population increasing all over the world, God gets a little short of guardian angels sometimes. So these innocent young children become guardian angels for family members still here. Mrs. Quirk, I believe it's quite possible there may have been a recent change. The next time you call on your guardian angel, try calling him Tim."

There weren't many dry eyes in the church as Bishop Butler continued with the Mass. He brought tears again during his homily. These are the messages I captured listening to Charles. "For my words to Mrs. Quirk and the congregation today, I go to chapter one, verse four of the second letter of St. Paul to the Corinthians. Paul writes of the 'Father of mercies, and the God of all consolation! He comforts us in all our afflictions and thus enables us to comfort those who are in trouble, with the same consolation we have received from him.'

"St. Paul has given us a strikingly pertinent message in these few words. It is my sincere prayer today that each of you will be consoled and comforted in the grief and pain of this present experience. St. Paul says 'we have shared much in the suffering of Christ,' but in response to that sharing Paul also says we must learn to share abundantly in our consolation of others.

"The message of Christ's everlasting love for us carries a simple addendum: 'Pass it on.' The New Testament is filled with evidence of Jesus' desire to console, to relieve the pain and suffering and loss endured by others. Matthew chapter five, verse forty-six: 'If you love those who love you, what merit is there in that?' If you are here this morning because you loved Tim who loved you, do you think there is merit in that? I ask you out of the love you have for Tim to extend your love from here to those who are not here, to *one* who could not be here. May the good Lord bless each of you and hold you in the palm of His hand where Tim rests this very day.

"It may seem inappropriate to bring the following message on the day of Tim's funeral. I remind you that God works in strange and mysterious ways. On November first, Father Timothy Matthews will be taking up residency in Springer as your full time pastor. Father Matthews is a retired priest of the diocese who has agreed to return to duty as a tribute to Tim Quirk, the deceased altar boy of St. Cyril's. Father Timothy will be a Sunday reminder for all members of the parish to pray for altar boy Tim, perhaps now serving as the guardian angel of Lucy Quirk."

When Bishop Butler left the lectern, I didn't know whether to clap or cry or run up and down the aisle or shake hands with Lucy, who sat between me and Jane. I saw Jane had her arm around Lucy, and both of them were drying their eyes. Suddenly there seemed to be something joyous in the air of St. Cyril's. Was I the only one who felt it or was the congregation caught up in the mood? There was a distinct note of joy as the choir sang "Here I Am Lord" at the offertory of the Mass.

At Communion time, Lucy clearly intended not to receive the sacrament. When I looked at her, she shook her head in response. I leaned over and whispered in her ear, "Lucy, God loves you and wants to know your love for Him. Just tell Him you're sorry for your sins and you will go to confession when there is a priest available. Join us in this sacrament as we all honor Tim." Lucy received Communion with the rest of the congregation.

As we left the church, signs were posted outside announcing the Springer Community Women's Society was hosting a luncheon at 12:30 for all who attended Tim Quirk's funeral. Lucy rode with us to the cemetery. We had not had occasion to go there since Don's funeral three years ago.

Bishop Butler said the rites of burial as the casket was lowered into the grave. Lucy was tearful and stood in Jane's embrace. As the mourners moved back toward their cars Bishop Butler approached us. He took Lucy's hand and said, "Mrs. Quirk, I have deeply grieved since Bob Lee first told me of Tim's death. Then when he told me later of the circumstances I was horrified and as the responsible bishop I experienced a sense of personal blame. I was the person who sent Father Brown to Springer. I am deeply pained with a sense of accountability for what occurred.

"I am going to ask our attorney, Mr. Thomas O'Rourke, to get in touch with you within the next two or three days. I know there is no amount of money that can in any way compensate you for the loss of your son. Nevertheless, the diocese wishes to give you a sizable sum as reparation for this tragic loss of life. Mr. O'Rourke will be prepared to settle this with you. Let me add I will keep you and your new guardian angel in my prayers. If there is some personal need you have or something the parish can do for you, get in touch with Bob Lee. He will act as my personal emissary in regard to your loss."

Lucy Quirk was quite taken by the Bishop's warmth and words. She thanked him for coming to Springer to say the Mass and perform the burial service for Tim. I have a strong feeling the parish will see Lucy more often than we did in the past.

Bishop Butler agreed to come to the luncheon with the three of us so we met him outside the Town Hall where the luncheon was held. Charles "worked the crowd" as a politician might do. But he was not being political. He just liked people and always did as I remembered from our seminary days. It seemed like the whole town was there. There was a warmth and friendliness in the room that bode well for a peaceful ending to this sad solemn period.

Many of those at the luncheon came to talk with Lucy, and perhaps for the first time she felt a favorable presence and genuine acceptance by the towns-people. Jane and I wandered through the crowded room exchanging comments with everyone we met. Our fellow parishioners were buoyed by the news of a new resident priest. I quietly commented to Jane that it was a brilliant move on the part of Butler. It helped to draw the curtain on the tragedy of Tim's death. Good has come from evil. And surely Lucy Quirk's life is newly blessed. How mysterious, how unpredictable the providence of God!

We were back at the ranch by midafternoon. We reviewed once more the events of the day as we sat with a cup of tea. We agreed that, all in all, it had been a blessed day and Bishop Butler's presence together with his message was a godsend to all.

Then our thoughts and conversation turned to the signs of autumn and the need to take care of ranch affairs. It felt like we lived in parallel worlds: one, the ranch with relatively simple routines encompassing cattle and wheat; and two, the parish with the unexpected complexities relating to pastor and altar boys and a tragic death. It was time to focus on the first of these worlds.

"Janey, we have to start making arrangements to sell the yearling steers and also to sell a large portion of the wheat. In the past I dealt with a couple of cattle buyers in Springer and was satisfied with their prices. I think I'll ask each of them to come out, separately of course, and look at the seventy-eight steers in the south pasture and give me a price for the lot. They'll probably truck them to the 'feeder market' in Highland. I'd like to get them sold and trucked out before the end of next week. The cold weather will be coming soon, and I want them sold before that happens.

"Once we're settled about the cattle I want to hire a couple of bulk grain carriers to come out and haul the wheat. We'll keep what we'll need for seed next spring to sow the three hundred acres that were fallow this year. We'll probably just take the grain to the elevator in Springer and sell it there. If we have it hauled somewhere else the charge for hauling will cancel out any better price we might get."

Jane responded, "You seem to know what you're doing in this ranching business. I'm sure your brother would be proud of you. And your father would be too. He'd be lost if he came back to earth and saw the equipment available and the way things are done. It hardly seems possible we're nearing the end of another year. I can't say I look forward to winter coming, but there is a certain beauty in the ethereal whiteness that only belongs to snow. I'm glad we took up cross country skiing when we lived in Minnesota. We had five months of skiing last winter. Maybe we should do some downhill this winter. The slopes up at Monarch have a great reputation."

I commented, "Now that you mention winter skiing, Babe, I have another idea. It's not connected with skiing other than it ties us down morning and evening. The two milk cows require our presence here twice a day. I know we can get Ted or one of his boys to do the milking when we're gone; but we still have the responsibility to see the cows are fed and sheltered in the cold and snow. Milk cows are a tradition of the Lee ranch and probably go back well over a hundred years to homestead days. But we're in Springer often enough to buy fresh milk and butter. What do you say we sell the cows to the cattle buyers when we sell the yearlings?"

Jane was completely agreeable. "I've had that thought lots of times, but I felt you connected milk cows sentimentally to your early years here. I would be happy if they were gone and you had no more milking to do. Do you think there is any chance Ted would like to buy them? We've been giving them fresh milk since we moved here, so they might consider buying the source. Why don't you ask Ted? I doubt he'll want them, but who knows?" When I saw Ted later, I asked him. He wasn't interested in keeping them.

I contacted the two cattle buyers and got a bid from each. The bids were practically identical. I sold them to the Lacy Livestock Company. I frequently dealt with their buyer. He also gave me a fair price for the two milk cows. He knew a couple who had a small farm and were looking for a couple of milk cows. He would send a small truck for the cows in two or three days. He scheduled Wednesday of the following week to bring two smaller livestock trailers to pick up the steers.

The following day the alternate parallel world was front and center. O'Rourke called me about 9 A.M. He had just heard from Pat Benet. Fred Brown was scheduled to appear before Presiding District Judge Martin Walsh at 11 A.M. this coming Friday. The meeting would be in the Culver City Courthouse. Tom suggested we meet at our usual coffee spot at 9 A.M. Friday. We could have some coffee and plenty of time to drive to Culver City.

I met Tom as scheduled for the coffee and doughnut. We talked about a variety of things as he drove to the meeting. As we neared Culver City I asked him what sort of sentence he thought Judge Walsh might give Fred. After a few moments, he responded, "It's hard to tell, but several factors must be considered. Is this a first offense? We don't have the answer to that since there was no trial and no need to research the question. Walsh might ask Fred the question, but I would advise Fred not to answer. Tim's age will likely push the judge to be harsher. The fact that Fred is a Catholic priest can weigh either way. Walsh is Catholic and I presume a practicing one. But is he a traditionalist or is he liberal? Which way he leans is more important than his being a Catholic.

"Fred is pleading guilty to two crimes, each of which can bring a sentence of up to twenty years. Fred is about fifty. One twenty-year sentence would bring him to seventy. I doubt the judge would give him twenty times two. It really is impossible to say. I don't know Judge Walsh personally, but he may be the kind of person who makes decisions based on what he had for breakfast."

We were getting into Culver City. I said jokingly, "Thanks, Tom. That was a big help."

We met Pat Benet outside Judge Walsh's chambers. We had a pleasant exchange as we waited to be called into the court room. Father Brown was farther down the hall with the sheriff's deputy. I was about to go speak to him when the clerk came out and opened the door for all of us to enter. There were signs: No Spectators.

Judge Walsh was seated and motioned for all of us to come forward. As we took our places at the front of the court, we were told to be seated. He asked, "What business is before the court?" Attorney Benet stood and said, "Your honor, we are here today to present the guilty plea of Father Kevin Brown to two charges."

Judge Walsh: "What are the charges in this case?"

Benet: "The first charge is statutory rape."

Walsh: "How does the defendant plead?"

Benet: "Guilty, your honor."

Walsh: "And the second charge?"

Benet: "Murder in the second degree."

Walsh: "Was this the same victim?"

Benet: "Yes, your honor."

Walsh: "And what is the plea?"

Benet: "Guilty, your honor."

Walsh: "To the charge of statutory rape, the defendant is sentenced to twenty years to be served in the Montana State Prison in Red Lodge. To the charge of murder in the second degree, the defendant is sentenced to twenty years to be served in the Montana State Prison in Red Lodge. Sentences will be served concurrently. If there is nothing further before the court at this time, the court is adjourned."

The deputy was taking Fred out of the court when I stopped them and said to Fred, "I'll come by to see you in Springer on my way home this evening. There are several things we must talk about." Fred looked calm and fairly relaxed considering how his life has just been washed away.

As Tom and Pat and I left the courthouse, I was not greatly surprised when Tom spoke up. "I once before asked you to go to lunch with us, Pat, but it was probably an inappropriate time. Let me make that offer again, and this time it seems extremely appropriate for us to get together."

Pat accepted the invitation and then the question was where we should go. Each of us came up with a recommendation based on meager experience with Culver City restaurants. The Silver Saddle became our mutual choice.

During lunch the conversation never returned to the courtroom or to any comments about Father Brown. I found that noteworthy. I suspect that may well be how attorneys manage to keep their distance from the aftermath of court proceedings. They apparently do not invest emotionally in the lives of their clients. Objectivity is their safeguard. They remain insulated behind their desks and law books. Quite contrary to my experience in psychiatry where emotion was the coin of the realm. It was more than that. It was not just a contact; it was a bond between patient and physician. There was not just a "you" and an "I." It was more like a "we." I sat there thinking I would never have made it as an attorney, while Pat and Tom went on talking about their personal lives, their families, and various other topics. My mind kept sneaking back to the court, the sentence and the wretched abusiveness of prison life.

Our lunch was good, and the time was well spent as we came to know each other better. We spent almost two hours over lunch. I finally suggested I would like to get on the road because I wanted to meet with Father Brown back in Springer. I wouldn't have been greatly surprised if one of them had said, "Who is Father Brown?" That's too harsh. Neither of them was quite that removed from the morning.

Tom and I chatted away on the drive to Springer exploring common interests and talking about our families. I learned he had two children, teenagers, and was divorced about two years. I couldn't help but wonder if he might have some interest in Pat Benet. I had noted she didn't wear a wedding ring.

Before he dropped me off at the jail, he told me the law requires guards from the prison to pick up any sentenced person within seventy-two hours of the court decision. As I moved to leave the car, we shook hands. He said, "If you're in Black Eagle someday and have the time, let's have lunch together. Give me a call. You have my number. I don't expect I'll be in Springer again for a long time unless I go through here on my way to Culver City." He smiled with the last comment.

As I got out of the car, I said, "That wouldn't be a trip to see Pat Benet, would it?" His smiled broadened as he drove away.

I wasn't looking forward to this last meeting with Fred, and I was determined to keep it as simple as I could but still cover all the bases. The deputy brought Fred to a room where we could talk. I didn't worry about concealed mics or two way mirrors. He was convicted and going to prison. The law needed nothing more.

I had a list in my head, so after some casual (how can one be casual in a situation like this) conversation, I started with Fred's belongings, all I had removed from the rectory. Fred had an answer for what to do with them. "Give them all to charity or just throw away anything not worth giving away."

I asked about the Tundra and told him the police had authorized its release from their yard. "What should I do with it?"

He replied, "Get the keys from the desk officer; you have my power of attorney. Just keep it. I'm sure you can use it on the ranch."

"No, Fred, I'd really have no use for the Tundra."

"Then give it to your wife," Fred said. "She might like it. I'm sorry I never really came to know your wife. She seems like a nice woman."

"Sorry, Fred, I'm sure Jane will appreciate the offer but we really cannot accept your truck." I considered asking him if he would like to give it to the new pastor but then it occurred to me it was a marked vehicle in the community. If people saw the Tundra around, it would remind them of the whole tragedy. So I continued, "Why don't you give it to Bishop Butler and let him decide where it can be used best in the diocese? Butler is a pretty sharp guy, knows his priests and knows his diocese. He'd find a good use for it, perhaps one of his St. Vincent de Paul groups. They shelter people and often arrange housing for them and help them move."

Fred replied, "That sounds good. It would be nice to know the truck may be of benefit to others, especially considering the sordid history I attached to it. And please, take it somewhere for a complete cleaning and if necessary new seats and floor coverings in the front."

I went on, "We also have your bank account to deal with. About how much is in the account?"

Without hesitation he gave me the figure, "As of the fifteenth of this month there should be one hundred and twenty thousand, give or take a couple of hundred dollars."

"What should I do with the money, Fred?" I asked.

His quick reply, "First, transfer it to your account, Bob. Then keep it. You'll find a good use for it. Invest in more cattle. I don't know. I don't want it. I'll never benefit from it. I'll never need it." For the first time, I could see

Fred pushing himself to stay calm and to control the things hammering at him inside his head.

"Do you have any family to give it to," I asked.

"I have no family. I never had a family. I had two adults I lived with, and thankfully they're dead," he said in a grim, harsh tone. I didn't want to unsettle him if I could help it but the question of his bank account needed to be resolved.

I tried again, "How about a friend, someone from the past, someone who did you a favor, someone who deserves the return of a kindness?"

For the first time he sounded caustic and sneered as he answered, "You were a psychiatrist and worked with peoples' emotions and feelings most of your life I suppose. After these months you've known me and all the times we've talked, how is it you have not discovered *the me* in this life? *I don't feel, I don't emote.* I'm an empty opaque jar with an air tight lid. I'm an invisible tree in a crowded forest of living trees."

He made me feel I offended him. The feelings he denied had unwittingly surfaced in his response. I certainly didn't want to push him further. "I didn't mean to offend you, Fred. Let me make another suggestion about the money. I understand Bishop Butler is giving Mrs. Quirk a fairly large sum as compensation for the loss of her child. Would you consider giving the Bishop fifty or sixty thousand and then give the rest to some charitable organization such as Catholic Relief Services? CRS provides all kinds of help to people all over the world."

Fred looked at me in that unconsciously pleading look I've seen before. "That would be all right with me. In a way it might contribute to the wrong I've done to Mrs. Quirk and to the Bishop. Go ahead and do what you have suggested but only give fifty thousand to the Bishop and fifty thousand to Catholic Relief Services. The remaining twenty thousand or whatever is left I want you to keep in your account. Before you comment let me add one more statement. After giving the hundred thousand as I just agreed to do, maintaining the remainder of funds in your account and for your use is an essential part of the money arrangement. It's a deal breaker.

"Now I will tell you why I want these funds to be yours. I have thought about this every day since I knew they were doing an autopsy. It was then I realized I'd be going to prison and I began thinking about the request I'm going to make. It is not easy for me to make a request that pertains to *my well-being*.

It suggests *dependency* and I've never known the wealth of another's care. I am asking you, Bob, to visit me at the State Prison not just once but once in a while. You can call the money transferred to your account 'payment' and not a gift if that makes you more comfortable accepting it.

"I dislike trying to force you into something. But I'll beg if need be. Your visits will help me maintain my sanity and provide an avenue for me to bring God into my life again. I don't have much life to live, nothing to live for and every day in prison will drain what little I have. I'm down to the crusty edge of life, Bob."

I could feel the blighted world Fred was in and clearly destined to become more and more barren until it thinned to despair. It was not his words; it was my conscience, my heart, my bones that answered him. "Quiet yourself, Fred. It's a deal. I'll use the money for gas, for meals, for motels if I get stuck in Red Lodge in winter storms. I *will come* see you. I'll try to come every month or two if possible.

"After you get to Red Lodge, write me a note and let me know the days and times for visits. I assume they will give you messages but I will also write and let you know in advance when I expect to be there. So this is it for now, until I see you again."

I extended my hand. Fred took it in both of his, saying, "Bob, you have responded to me in a way no one else ever has. Is it some generosity of your soul or is it because I have always desperately avoided the barrenness, the aloofness I experienced from others? You must see something beyond what I see in myself, something not attached to me as a child abuser and now a murderer. Yes, I did kill Tim but it was not by the rock. Nor was it my intention. I loved Tim deeply and soulfully. He brought back my memory of the only love I had as a small child. That's what brought me to kill him. I'm confused. I don't know things as I should. I don't do things as I should. I don't even say things as I should. Something is missing or was never there. Someday you will help me put it all together."

I put my left hand on his right shoulder as I withdrew my right hand from his. "It's time to say goodbye, Fred. We will have the opportunity and the time to talk again. Maybe we can track some strings of your life and loose some knots along the way." He let go of my hand slowly, went to the door, opened it and walked out. The deputy was waiting.

It was past six o'clock. I called Jane and told her I was on the way. She said, "There is a surprise for you when you get home, but I can't wait until then so I will tell you now. The buyer of the milk cows picked them up this afternoon. You don't have to milk tonight, Rob. Dinner will be waiting. Hurry home but drive safely. I'm anxious to see you whether or not you tell me about your day."

It felt so good to be in touch with the love of my world, especially since the day had seemed to wander through the dark alleys of life and the lonely paths of sadness and loss that confront us all.

CHAPTER ELEVEN

I don't think I've ever been more appreciative to be with Jane than I was that evening. I clearly am not cut out to be an attorney or work in any area of law. You can call it sentimentality or compassion or whatever you want, but it's definitely not for me. In fact, one question has already presented itself; how will I be able to deal with my own feelings when I visit Fred at the State Prison?

We had a pleasant dinner and chatted about the kids and how each of them was doing. My brother's son, John, had written, and Jane read the letter to me as we finished dinner. He was asking how ranching was going for us and was the harvest completed. I felt certain Jane in her gentle wisdom had deliberately avoided asking me about the day. She knew I would get to it when ready.

As we sat leisurely eating freshly baked cherry pie, I brought up my rather extensive report on the day's events. "The court proceeding was not much like you see on television. There were no spectators allowed. It was simple: 'What is the charge? How do you plead? Guilty. Twenty years in the Montana prison. What is the second charge? How do you plead? Guilty. Twenty years in the Montana prison. Terms to be served concurrently.' It goes on almost mechanically. Everyone present knows their lines.

"Father Brown was unemotional about it all and was whisked away by the sheriff's deputy as soon as court was over. I told him I'd see him later at the jail. Pat Benet and Tom and I had lunch at the Silver Saddle. They made no reference to the morning. It was as if nothing unusual had occurred. I suppose in their world the morning was nothing unusual. They just played their role in a priest being sent to prison for what could be the rest of his life. The food was good; the conversation was disappointing.

"Tom drove in the morning so he brought me back to Springer. I found out Tom is divorced. I think he has an interest in seeing Pat Benet again. You met Pat a couple of times at meetings in Springer. As I recall, you two hit it off quite well.

"Seeing Fred at the jail was a strain for me and left me feeling rather morbid. Getting home and chatting with you during dinner helped relieve me of the melancholy. The talk with Fred had several surprises. He told me to give his belongings to charity and throw away old stuff. He wanted me to take his Tundra, and when I said I had no need of it, he offered to give it to you. So there is evidence he does know you really exist. In fact, he commented he was sorry he never got to know you. And I don't think he was buttering me up. He meant it. I suggested he give the Tundra to Bishop Butler and let him give it to whatever person or situation he thinks can get the best use of it. He accepted that idea. That reminds me, I have to go to the jail to get the Tundra keys and then arrange delivery. We talked about his bank account which is about one hundred and twenty thousand dollars." I continued the money story and how it was finally settled, including the prison visits to which I had agreed. I looked at Jane for her response.

And it came. "Fred has become attached to you, and I suspect that's an unusual experience for him. It surprises me he would actually take the risk of asking and being turned down. That would have been devastating for him. He's in a desperate situation, making the risk even greater. You know you did the right thing, Robbie. And I can't imagine you responding any differently than you did. Since you will have that twenty thousand in your account, maybe I'll go with you on occasion. Even Red Lodge must have a couple of art shops or clothing stores or antique shops where I could spend some time and some money." Jane was smiling as she referred to our teasing topic, money.

Once the kitchen was tidy, we spent the evening going through some pictures of Don and Helen, their kids and ours. Jane and I both dislike being asked to look at pictures on cell phone screens or iPads and such devices. We like the wonderful old fashioned sitting around with friends and passing actual pictures to hold in your hand and study the details. Later as we were going to sleep, I nudged Jane and said, "It sure was a good day to get rid of the milk cows."

The following day had marked signs of winter. The sun comes later over the eastern horizon. There was a chill in the air the sun was not going to conquer until well after noon. The Big Mountain, as we called the one nearest the ranch, had a snow cap from the night before.

During breakfast we talked about getting the wheat hauled and harvesting the vegetables from the garden that we could keep for a while or "can" for later days. I always thought it was strange to say you "canned" something when you really put it in jars. Jane, the Philadelphia girl, had learned to can from watching Helen who had learned from watching my mother who had learned from…and how many generations back does the story go?

When we finished breakfast, I said to Jane, "I'm going to put the back hoe on the caterpillar and dig a small root cellar in the side of the hill past Ted's home. I'll dig it beyond freezing depth so we can store the potatoes there. Once the potatoes are in it, I'll use straw and old gunny sacks to cover them. With the pack of snow, they'll never freeze. We'll have potatoes in the spring and seed for the garden.

"If you'll start getting the corn that's still on the stalks and picking the peas and beans and rhubarb and whatever else you can can, I'll come and work with you as soon as I finish the home for the potatoes."

Jane laughed and said, "When you said 'can can,' I thought you were asking me to dance. But instead you want me to work."

I finished the root cellar in about two hours. Then I pitched in and worked with Jane. We had about half of the vegetables picked and cleaned and ready for Jane's canning before lunch time. After lunch I called the Cargo Grain Carriers and scheduled two bulk grain carriers for late morning on the following Tuesday.

I decided I should bring Bishop Butler up to date on Father Brown. I called the office even though it was Saturday. He answered the phone himself. I said, "You're answering your own phone. Are you too poor to hire any help?" He laughed and replied, "I've been thinking about you, Bob, and wondering how everything is going with Father Brown and the town of Springer."

"All is going reasonably well, Charles. Brown will probably be picked up within the next couple of days for the trip to Red Lodge. The hearing was just *pro forma*. Fred was sentenced to twenty years on each count, to serve concurrently. I'm sure Tom filled you in.

"There's another area I need to inform you about if you have a little time."

"All afternoon" was his reply.

"Well, Fred is not a poor man. He has one hundred and twenty thousand dollars in his bank account. He's probably the richest priest in the diocese, except for yourself of course." Chuckle for that one. "He told me how he comes to have the money. It was in confidence, and I am unable to speak further about it. I believe you know I have his power of attorney and whatever powers I need to enter his bank account and act in his behalf. He asked me to give all his possessions from the rectory to charity. He wanted to give me the Tundra. I declined and suggested he donate it to the diocese and let you decide which priest or parish or organization could best use it. He agreed.

"He wanted me to transfer his money to my account and keep it for myself. I had no problem saying 'no' to that. I told him Tom O'Rourke informed me you were giving an undisclosed sum to Mrs. Quirk as compensation. I suggested he give fifty thousand dollars directly to you and the rest to Catholic Relief Services. He agreed to do so but only if one condition was met. I am to give fifty thousand to you and the same amount to CRS. The remaining twenty thousand I am to keep in my account. And that's a *sine qua non* attached to the money deal." I went on to tell Charles about the plan to visit Fred in prison and the twenty thousand to "cover my expenses."

Before ending our conversation, I said, "Your kindness and your shepherding presence at Tim Quirk's funeral has not only brought calm and peace to the community but has inspired the respect and allegiance of the parishioners of St. Cyril's. And Lucy Quirk is an outspoken fan of yours."

Charles spoke quietly, "I'm grateful things have worked out as well as they have. I regret ever sending Brown to Springer, as you well know. Undoubtedly it is good his behavior came to light. It is most unfortunate it cost a boy his life. When will this sorry behavior within the priesthood come to an end? Oh, I know it will never end, but there is a culture of dissent among our priests which spreads an attitude of permissiveness and preeminence in their lives that I believe is both unhealthy and unholy. Sometimes I think they are but a tribe of men who have gone astray and have lost their bearings because they have lost contact with the blessed presence of women in life.

"More and more I find our clerics put increasing effort and time and often manipulation into 'building church' instead of 'building the reign of God.' At times I envy the simplicity of some other faith groups who clearly focus on 'building the reign of God.' They are not bent on strengthening and protecting an aristocracy of isolated men, like we seem to be doing more vehemently each day.

"Thanks again, Bob, for your help throughout this sad business and in so many other ways. I'm entrusting Father Timothy Matthews to your care when he comes the first Sunday of November. I know you'll give him your support.

"I admire the sensitivity and compassion you have shown and continue to show Father Brown. The Lord will surely bless you for visiting him in Red Lodge. Perhaps you will help him return to peace with his heavenly Father. I presume he fared poorly with his earthly father or he would not be where he is."

I commented, "Your last remark is interesting and so accurate. The church is caught up in eliminating potential child abusers from the seminary. They seem to rely on psychological testing and a variety of 'insights by the experts' to determine whether someone is a suitable candidate for the priesthood. They focus excessively on the individual candidate and pay little attention to the family background from which the individual comes. They should have one of their experts interview and visit the family, perhaps a couple of unannounced visits. I don't believe child abusers are products of normal, healthy family life."

Charles replied, "Your comment is something I will discuss with the seminary professors I know. I think some of the seminaries are struggling with the problem and others are trying to deny it's as serious as it is. We're all praying for wisdom and guidance. Bob, please give my regards to Fred and tell him he is remembered frequently when I say Mass."

I had one more question, "About the Tundra, Charles, one day soon we'll bring it to Black Eagle. Where do you want us to leave it?"

He replied, "Leave it at the office please. And when you're here drop in and say hello. It would be nice to see you both."

After finishing the call, I found Jane working in the kitchen getting everything set up for the work ahead. I reminded her it was Saturday and she wouldn't be able to start the canning until Monday. She looked at me and replied, "Robbie dear, when I don't know what day it is, you'll be long gone, and if I don't remember the day then I'll still remember you. Now don't be nagging me. I'm just getting everything in perfect order so I can look at it all day tomorrow and admire the start I've made."

Of course I had to reply. "You're a wise and capable woman and a great canner of garden produce. You know that's why I married you. As if you ever saw a garden before you came to the ranch."

We sat talking again after dinner. I told Jane about my conversation with the bishop and the comment he made about the priests being like a tribe of men who have wandered off by themselves and left behind the beneficial presence of women. Jane said, "I imagine there aren't many bishops in today's church who even think that way, much less make such a comment. Was he tying that in with Fred's abusive behavior, or was it just a general comment?"

"It was a general comment, but it came up in our conversation about Fred. I believe Charles might connect child abuse with the lack of women's participation in the full life of the church. I tend to believe there is some connection, but I'm not quite sure how it fits together. Several years ago there were some studies which attempted to uncover reasons for the high rate of child abuse among Catholic clergy. As I recall, the only possible cause they came up with was the isolation of seminarians from the outside world. On the basis of that, I would argue that the most significant part of the outside world from which they are isolated is the feminine segment. I wonder if seminaries have any female employees on their staff these days. There was not one woman in our building or on the grounds when I was in the seminary. Possibly some of the stilted attitudes and pretentious policies have improved since then.

"To a considerable extent, isolation from feminine influence continues to be an important piece of the priest's life. I suspect even now when the average priest looks at a child, he is not immediately and naturally aware there is a mother in that child's life. If Lucy Quirk had accompanied Tim to Mass each time he was there, would Fred have picked Tim out as quickly and as easily as his mark? I'm only speculating. I don't think anyone has clear answers to these questions but there is certainly cause to wonder and to search for reasons."

Jane commented, "We've always talked about things like this, Rob. We have the same interest in lots of areas and certainly this is one of them. Father Brown was not atypical in the obvious attitude he had toward women. Weeks ago I knew it wasn't just me he overlooked."

I realized we should make plans for Sunday. "Sweetheart, we better give some thought to our Sunday rather than sit here solving all these problems of the church. Suppose we drive to Black Eagle in the morning, and for a change of pace, we'll go to Mass at St. Kateri's parish where Father Brown was during his brief release from jail. I'll introduce you to Father Z, someone a bit different than the priests we've always known. You will be struck not only by the poverty of the parishioners but also by their warmth and sense of community."

Jane put her hand on my arm in a light caress. "I'd love to do that since you don't have to milk the cows before we leave. And what will we do after Mass so we don't have to rush home?"

I knew her implication and responded, "Okay, okay. I know I've spent years rushing home from Mass so we could get to work on one or another of the house projects we always seemed to be doing. My sainted father probably frowned every time he saw you making me work on the Lord's Day."

Jane's reply, "Ha." I thought the Sunday Mass at St. Kateri's was 10:30, but I called to make sure. The parish phone message told me I was correct.

We got up later than usual the next morning and had a leisurely breakfast before we left for Black Eagle. Father Z's homily was a little difficult for Jane to understand and I have problems with it when he speaks rapidly. We waited to say hello to Father Z after Mass. He was cordial and grateful we had visited his parish. I told him Father Brown pled guilty to charges of statutory rape and second degree murder and was sentenced to twenty years in the State Prison. The press made the story common knowledge, so it was hardly news.

As we were driving away I asked Jane if there was any particular place she would like to go. She replied, "Let's go out to Giant Springs for a visit. It must be twenty or more years since we went there with Don and Helen. And we never toured the old copper foundry that provided about thirty percent of the jobs in this area before it closed twenty-five years ago. That should be worth seeing and learning more about its history."

"Sounds good to me, Love," I replied. "Suppose we head out to Giant Springs and then we can stop for lunch at the Copper Crest which is just a few blocks from the old foundry."

Jane added another idea. "When we leave the foundry, let's drive down to central park and walk around the Missouri river area. We'll be able to see the giant falls of the Missouri that stymied the Lewis and Clark expedition back in 1805, requiring portage and delaying the expedition several days. And if that ice cream vendor is still in the area, let's get cones like a couple of kids and walk around until they're gone."

It turned out to be a wonderful day. We got home before dusk, had some leftovers, and watched a movie. Then night prayers and slumber land.

Monday morning I was raring to go and decided I wanted to get some things wrapped up and settled. I told Jane my thoughts for the day. "Can you come to Springer with me this morning? We'll pick up the Tundra at the police yard and you can drive it to Black Eagle. I'll drive our car and we'll drop the Tundra at Butler's office. Then we'll go to the Cascade Bank. With my legal documents in hand, I'll get Fred's money transferred to our account. After the required time lapse, I'll write the check for Butler and the check for CRS and the whole matter will be settled."

Jane hesitated before answering and during her moment of hesitancy I realized canning vegetables was on her schedule. But she couldn't resist the Tundra. "Well, I planned on canning vegetables this morning, but I think these I picked will be fine until this afternoon. They're in a cool place and they'll stay fresh."

We left thirty minutes later and accomplished all I planned for the morning. We had a brief but pleasant visit with Charles when we dropped off the truck. When we got home, I wrote and postdated the two checks, balanced the checkbook, and breathed a long sigh of relief.

Later, as I was basking in the satisfaction of my day, Jane came into my little office and said, "Did Fred ever tell you what to do with the secret letter from his secret friend about that secret subject?"

I answered, "Thanks for bursting the balloon that was just carrying me through the white billows of today's beautiful sky. Until you spoke I hadn't noticed the tag on the balloon. It reads, 'To be continued.' That subject never came up again between Fred and me. I wonder what 'Bishop Bill' will think when his check comes back marked 'account closed.' He'll uncover the reason within a short time. In his position he has connections. He will ask enough 'innocent questions' of other bishops or perhaps even of Charles. Before two days go by he will know Father Brown is in the Montana State Prison and why he is there.

"The thing he won't know is what happened to the letter that cost him a bucket of money over the past years. Who has it? Where is it? He'll eventually know I handled all Fred's affairs after he went to prison. He'll spend some restless days and sleepless nights over it. He has no idea whether he is still in jeopardy. He wouldn't dare ask anyone about it directly. He may hazard asking Fred through a visit or by letter. No, the visit might be picked up by the press. A letter would be safer, but he would have to word it carefully. I believe all mail to prisoners may be opened by prison staff and may be read. What do you think I should do with it?"

Jane was ready. "I think you should ask Fred when you visit him. I wonder if the letter is still on his mind. He has no need of it any more unless he is feeling vindictive and wants that guy to keep hanging by his thumbs.

"Now I'm going back to my canning and don't forget you volunteered to fix dinner and promptly at 6 P.M. or I'll go out to eat—in the back yard with my carrots and peas and corn." Just after lunch I had promised I would fix dinner since Jane would be canning.

The following day Cargo Grain Carriers came and hauled the wheat to town. Considering the amount they hauled and what was left for spring seed, the yield was close to twenty-eight bushel per acre, an excellent yield for dry land farming in Montana. Don's children should be pleased with their share.

Jane and I had lunch about 12:30. I did what I could to help her during the afternoon. I suddenly realized the coming Sunday was the first Sunday in November and Father Timothy Matthews would be coming to say the ten o'clock Mass. The diocesan chancellor was coming from Black Eagle to do the installation ceremony in place of Bishop Butler.

It looks like a quiet week ahead. The weather has become mildly threatening. The frost is heavier on the grass in the early morning and there is a chill in the air that remains until the afternoon. Harvesting the garden was timely.

Jane finished her canning before lunch on Wednesday. I suggested we ride out and look at the heifers we brought from the Wolf Butte land. Cattle can be restless when they're moved to a new pasture. They explore the fence line as if they're looking for a way to get back to where they used to be. They remind me of people who have a penchant for the same behavior. They keep trying to get back to a prior time in their life, although back then they were looking for something new and different. Like the cattle, some people seem to have an instinctual longing to return to the transient seeming-security of the past. I recall patients who fit that description and found difficulty moving forward in life.

We rode out after lunch with light jackets. The autumn chill was persisting today. We went to the pasture and rode the fence line. I found a couple of spots that needed fence repair. We saw several deer scattered on the prairies and Jane spotted an elk grazing in one of the coulees. We saw a colorful flock of Chinese pheasants.

In the past Jane and I hunted deer with my brother Don during some of our visits. Now that we live here, it feels more like the deer and elk are our neighbors so we don't kill them. I still shoot coyotes if I see them. They kill calves. Wolves are scarce in this area of the state. For years there has been a battle between the government and the ranchers. The government declares wolves "an endangered species," but ranchers shoot them because they too kill young calves in the spring.

When we got home, I sent an email to our congregation and the local weekend news reminding them our new pastor was coming on Sunday.

On our way to Mass Sunday morning, we talked about doing the same thing when Fred Brown first came to the parish. It was heartwarming to see all the parishioners again. The pews were nearly full, and all parishioners appeared to be present in spite of the gravely disrupted summer. Lucy Quirk came into the church with us and was happy to accompany us to the front where we usually sat.

Father Jack Tracey was there to introduce and to officially install our new pastor, Father Timothy Matthews. The installation took but a few minutes and then Father Matthews said his first Mass with us. All four altar boys were part of the ceremony. Father Matthews officiated with a reverence and respect that was impressive. His sermon was well received. At the end of Mass he paused briefly before he left the altar and told us what parishes he had served in before he retired two years ago. He mentioned briefly why he felt called to the priesthood when he was young. His parents were kind, charitable people who were both professional caregivers. He wanted to work with people and felt a desire to give his life to God's service. He felt called to return to active duty at this time because there was a shortage of priests and the faith of the laity was being threatened by an increasingly materialistic culture.

Father Matthews stood outside greeting everyone after Mass. There was no line. He just walked around shaking hands, chatting, chuckling from time to time, telling people to call him Tim or Father Tim if they were more comfortable with that bit of formality. I suspect he will continue to be called Timothy as long as altar boy Tim is in our thoughts.

It has always been a pleasure for me to see someone in life who enjoys what they do. I found myself enjoying Father Timothy. Jane and I spent over an hour visiting with other parishioners and our new pastor. A spirituality, a peace, a bonding from some distant time seemed to fill the gathering. We were one. And hidden not too deeply, not too secretly was the spirit of angel Tim.

Late the following week I had a brief note from Fred. It read: "Dear Bob, This is the first chance I've had to write. It took several days to go through processing. There are many restrictions here. Visiting hours are on Thursday and Saturday 2:30 to 4:30 both days. You need to fill out a Visitor Questionnaire before you can visit. One is included in this envelope. Please come whenever you can. No need to tell me in advance. Fred."

The questionnaire was two pages and rather tedious to complete. I had to look up dates for when we lived where, provide information on immediate family members with addresses, and include my professional background and numerous other questions. It would be five days after the prison's reception of the questionnaire before I could visit. The questionnaire had the five-day notice at the top, so I was sure Fred knew it would be at least that long before I could visit.

I went over the questionnaire with Jane. She remained supportive of my plan to visit saying, "I assume you won't have any difficulty making it to Red Lodge and back in one day. I dislike being here without you, but if it turns out you can't get home some day because of bad weather or anything else, I assure you I'll be fine. I note there's a one hour limit on visiting. I have no doubt you will get Fred to fill the time even though he never seemed to be much of a talker. He probably has no one to talk to there. I presume he's in a cell by himself."

I responded, "I wouldn't be surprised if he's in solitary confinement. I doubt if he's with the general prison population. Child abusers become victims of the other prisoners and even of the guards, from what I've heard. Other prisoners will sodomize him right and left if they get the opportunity. I wonder what percent of the general population would take the opportunity to do some physical harm to a child abuser if they had the chance. It's likely the initial impulse when someone hears about child abuse. 'They ought to castrate that guy' is not an unusual verdict people easily recommend. I think it's our nature to be extremely protective of children. Yet we know parents more commonly abuse their children physically or mentally or emotionally. Just for discussion, what type of abuse by an adult would you see as most damaging to a child, Love?"

Jane's answer, "Sexual abuse of course."

"Why?" I asked.

"Because it's just abhorrent, repulsive, vile," Jane replied.

I asked another question, "Which type of abuse do you think would be the most difficult to recover from?"

Jane's reply, "Sexual abuse of course. A child will never recover from sexual abuse."

I continued, "I've asked the questions and, of course, I don't really know the answers and perhaps they are no general answers. Each case is different. Much depends on who does the abusing and how severe the abuse is.

"But I would argue that perhaps the most vicious abuse is emotional abuse. Emotional abuse is usually hidden and unrecognized. It typically occurs surreptitiously. No one sees; no one knows. Even the person being abused quite possibly isn't aware it's happening. But the result may be indelibly destructive. Since no one is aware it's happening, often including the victim, the damage may never be repaired and continue as an emotional handicap, an undisclosed and unrecognized wound throughout the victim's life. This is not an unusual finding in psychiatric care. One finds persons in their forties, fifties, and older whose lives have always been limited or difficult or even dissolute because they carry the unrecognized emotional scars of their earlier years.

"Mental abuse would probably come next in my book. Again there are often not distinct and definite markings when mental abuse takes place. Lack of educational opportunities, failure of parental encouragement, and an attitude of disdain for intellectual matters come under this heading. Sometimes it is subtle, attached to what is not said more than to what is said, more to what is not done than to what is done. The damage is often not recognized. Result: the child may go through life thinking they are stupid, a true handicap.

144

However, events may occur which help the individual finally realize the intelligence they do have. They blossom.

"Finally, physical abuse and sexual abuse are more likely to present rather clear evidence that abuse is occurring, someone is clearly suffering mistreatment. The physically abused child is keenly aware of the abuse. Sadly enough, the sexually abused child is sometimes not aware it is abusive behavior and can be led to believe otherwise at the time, even to believe it is love. Those sexually abused eventually tend to clarify for themselves the existence and extent of the abuse and being aware of something is the first and necessary step to overcoming the effects of the mistreatment. I should add that some children who are sexually abused defend themselves by developing a sheltering amnesia which may come to the fore during therapeutic encounters.

"Considering all these factors, sexual abuse of children may not be the worst type of child abuse except when emotional abuse is also involved, which is frequently the case. I think sexual abuse of a child is abhorrent to adults because it is a violation of an area of life that most of us have learned to guard protectively, sometimes excessively, which can bring later complications. Small children learn their sex organs are *private* even while they are on display to mothers and fathers and doctors and at times older siblings. Then for many, religion steps in to strengthen a sense of sequestered, mysterious and perhaps 'nasty' body parts. Social and cultural taboos join the chorus, and sexual parts and privacy become of overwhelming concern for the individual. The resultant subliminal sexual attitudes can become a handicap in the natural and healthy performance of sexual acts for otherwise healthy adults.

"I do not mean to minimize the seriousness of child abuse. But I wonder sometimes if most of us, in our own severe and relentless attitudes, don't somehow make it more difficult for the sexually abused to undo what has been done to them. If they act out in sexually inappropriate behavior, are they unwittingly getting revenge on those responsible for their proclivity? I have never worked with a child abuser who was not emotionally and/or sexually abused as a child.

"I admit I'm speculating and not sure this all makes sense. But you keep listening, and I keep talking as if I know it all. Perhaps the bottom line is: persons who have been sexually abused can find resolution of the damage once they recall the abuse and deal with it openly in therapy. Similarly emotional abuse must also be faced before it can be resolved."

Jane is always patient with these lectures of mine and often contributes wisdom of her own. She sat thinking for a while and then, "You've had considerable experience with all of this in your prior practice and the variety of people you worked with. I think it's difficult for most people not to see sexual abuse as despicable behavior and a crime. You have a broader view of the whole realm of sexuality."

As I pointed I said, "See that book on my top shelf titled 'Just Love.' It is a very scholarly work written by a Sister theologian. It explores sexual attitudes and sexual behaviors back through the centuries and in other cultures. It provides a much broader background in which to consider the whole subject. I suggested the book to Fred, but he showed no interest. You might have a look at it sometime."

Jane replied, "For the moment I think I'll stick to the views I have but keep an open mind to all the things you and I talk about. I'll listen and learn."

The rural delivery of the day had not yet arrived, so I walked to the mailbox and left the prison visitor application. I'm almost anxious to get started on these prison visits. I wonder how Fred is dealing with the situation. In addition, I have to admit an increasing professional interest. There are questions already in my mind. What was his childhood like? Was he molested as a child? Why did he choose the priesthood? Have there been prior violations with children? How does he view this errant behavior? And on and on.

Jane and I went to Springer to do some general shopping a couple of days later. I stopped by the rectory to see Timothy Matthews, our resident pastor. The phrase, 'our resident pastor,' sounds good. His presence reminds me of the time when Joe McDonough was here before he retired back to Ireland. The parish is becoming active again. The parishioners will undoubtedly be calling him Father Tim or just Tim when the name no longer reminds them of Tim Quirk. Someday there will only be one Tim, Tim Matthews; except for Lucy Quirk, whose own Tim will always be the only Tim.

As I approached I saw Timothy raking leaves in his yard. As I got out of the car, he called a cheery, "Hello, Bob. Have you come to give me a hand?"

"No, not today, Father. But if you really need some help any time give me a call. I'm usually available. Now that the harvest is over I can spare the time. But it looks like you're quite able to handle that job."

Timothy replied, "I'm doing okay for an old man. I say that but in fact I don't feel like I'm seventy-three even though I probably look like I am. It does me good to be out here doing yard work. I was getting kind of stale in retirement. I was living in that home for elderly retired religious in Black Eagle and all they do is talk about their past lives. You can imagine how exciting it is to sit around and listen to the old fogies exaggerate or invent the notable events of their past. But I'm being uncharitable. Anything on your mind now that you're here?"

I responded, "Yes, as a matter of fact. I was wondering when we should restart Sunday school. I was teaching the second and fourth Wednesdays of each month through the school year with the exception of the fourth Sunday of December."

He replied, "Sounds good to me. We've past the second Sunday so let's start on the fourth this month. By that time the young people will be tired of hearing from me."

I assured him that was not true. I went on to tell him how many attend Sunday school and while I was on the subject I thought I should tell him my position regarding the Sunday school guide that comes from the chancery office.

About the guide he had no problem. His comment, "I think the guide is primarily developed and circulated by the National Conference of Catholic Bishops. That bunch needs some new blood and some up-to-date theology to become more relevant in the real world. Since you're here I want to ask you what you think about having a parish council. Do you know if the parish ever had one?"

"Well, Timothy, I don't really know. I'm a relative newcomer, although we visited here for years before we finally moved here a short time before Father Brown came. We always came to St. Cyril's when we visited in prior years. I heard they had some sort of parish committee when Father Joe was here. I'm sure you knew Father Joe Donovan."

He replied, "Joe was a contemporary of mine in the seminary. He did his last two seminary years in Seattle with the Sulpicians. Before I forget, how is Father Brown? I know you were good to him and I thought you may have heard something."

I answered, "Actually I had a letter from him just two days ago. Prison life must be hard for him. It must be hard for anyone, but a priest who was a child abuser must be a prime victim for other inmates and possibly for some of the guards. I plan to visit him and will probably go there in the next two or three weeks."

Timothy replied, "When you see him, give him my best wishes and tell him I will pray for him. In another two or three weeks when I'm more comfortable with the parishioners and a little better known to them, I plan to ask them to remember him in their prayers. Will you give some thought to my comment about some sort of parish committee to work with me? I dislike calling it a Parish Council. Makes it sound too formal, too business-like. This is not a business. It's a group of Christians trying to live a good Christian life."

I answered, "You describe it well. Off hand, I can tell you now I think your idea of a committee would be well received by the people. They haven't felt like it was *their* parish in a long time. I will tell Father Brown about your prayers for him. And after I visit him I'll let you know how he is." I told Timothy I had to get going because I was due to pick up my wife.

He thanked me for stopping by and commented, "Please, come again. You're always welcome. A few other parishioners have stopped by. It strikes me as a friendly group of people here."

I drove to the Mall, parked, and walked through the inside area knowing I would find Jane somewhere there. When I found her (with only a couple of small packages), I suggested we have lunch at the Cheesecake Café. We visited as we ate. She showed me the new scarf and the house slippers she bought. I always admired her taste in clothing. I spoke of my meeting with Father Timothy and how different he was from Fred and what an asset to the parish. We agreed his presence would help us all move forward from the tragic events of the past two or three months.

The next couple of weeks went by quickly. Each of us found a variety of jobs to do, some we had previously postponed. Jane did some mending that was put aside and some thorough cleaning in preparation for the winter months. I did a variety of catch-up items and minor repairs around the buildings. I spent three days checking and mending fences.

Most of the fences have some wooden posts we cut and hauled from the nearby mountains. In recent years Don replaced most of the recently rotted posts with steel posts driven into the ground with a sledge hammer. One of my fond childhood memories was going with my dad and two or three of my brothers to get posts in the mountains. It was an all-day trip. On occasion we arrived home after dark. But we had a number of fence posts and lots of fire-wood for the kitchen stove and for heating the house in the winter in two "pot-bellied" stoves.

CHAPTER TWELVE

The day came when there was a return letter from the state prison. It enclosed my authorization to visit the prison with the provision I meet with the warden prior to visiting a prisoner. The form letter included a telephone number. I called and made an appointment to meet with the warden two days later, Thursday at 2 P.M.

Jane and I have never been to Red Lodge. As I was thinking about the trip I decided it would be nice to have Jane with me on this first view of the area and the town. I would be meeting with the warden at 2 P.M. and then I would meet with Fred, a visit limited to one hour. All visits ended by 4:30, so no matter how things worked out with the warden or with Fred, I would be out of there by 4:30 at the latest.

I found Jane in her workroom where she does her sewing and some of her art work. She was going through her paints and I suspected she would soon be doing some landscapes. I got her attention. "Janey, what would you think about accompanying me on Thursday when I go to Red Lodge? We've never been in that part of the state and this is our first opportunity to see the area. The prison is about six miles out of Red Lodge. My appointment with the warden is at two. We could leave here fairly early and drive around the town to get some idea of what's there. We'll find a place for lunch, and then I'll drop you in a shopping area where you can cruise around for two or three hours. After I see the warden, I'll have an hour with Fred. So I should be finished by four but no later than 4:30 because that's the end of visiting hours. We'll be home after dark, but there won't be any cows to milk."

Jane walked over to me with that lovely smile on her face, put her arms around me and said, "You'll have to say please."

"Please" came easily.

Jane continued, "I'm so glad you asked me. I was thinking you'd have that long drive home after seeing Fred and your head would be full of thoughts. I always worry when you're driving alone and I fear you might become preoccupied after a tense or trying situation. I know how invested you become in emotional exchanges with others and the kind of impact they sometimes have on you. It will be far more comfortable for me to be with you on the way home than to be worrying about you driving home alone. So count me in."

I hadn't thought about it the way Jane did. "You are absolutely right. I would have rehashed my meeting with Fred all the way home and something in it may have distracted me. And you know I'm not too fond of driving after dark. If I could see Fred promptly at 2:30 until 3:30 I could make it home by dusk. But this will work out much better."

Wednesday passed quickly and Thursday morning we were on the road by 9:15. It was a cloudy day with a forecast of twenty percent chance of rain. We took the road to Black Eagle and then went almost directly north toward Red Lodge. For about fifty miles we paralleled the Missouri River and then we turned east of its continued route. We crossed the Blackfoot River and were soon in the Bitterroot Mountain region of the state. It was a beautiful drive. I suggested to Jane, "Love, you can bring your paint equipment sometime when I'm coming to see Fred and I'll drop you at one of these rest stops and pick you up on the way home."

Her smiling reply, "I'll drop you at one of these rest stops for good."

We arrived in Red Lodge just before noon. The internet said the town had thirty-two thousand residents and was the sixth largest town in Montana. Its principle business was the Montana State Prison. We drove around town for a half hour to get some reference points. There was no Mall, but there was a main street with a number of shops on both sides stretching about seven blocks. We decided to try the Central Avenue Café for lunch.

After lunch we agreed to meet in front of the same café when I return from the prison. I would call Jane when I leave the prison and I would pick her up wherever she was. I kept elaborating on unnecessary planning. Jane said, "Rob, you're starting to worry about it. Please, don't. The stores on Main Street will keep me occupied for hours. I want to get an idea about each one in case I come back-I-hope-I-do." I left Jane outside the café. She was right. My tension was building.

It was a quick drive to the prison. Visitor parking was a medium walk from the main building. There must be ten or more buildings on the grounds. I know there are nearly two thousand inmates, all male. There are several "general cell" buildings, three "special management" buildings, and two buildings for "serious mental illness" and "serious behavior management." The prison has nearly one thousand employees.

I was searched as I entered the Headquarters Building where the Warden's office was located. The guard directed me to Superintendent William Craven's office. The door was open to the attendant's desk. I showed him the appointment card I was given when I came in the building. He asked me to be seated; it would be a few minutes. It was five minutes before two. At 2:15 the attendant's phone rang. He picked it up and without a word motioned for me to go in.

Craven was a big man and husky, also fatter than was good for him. He sat behind a wide desk, made no motion to get up and waved me toward a chair in front of the desk. I said, "I'm Bob Lee and here to see Fred Brown."

His response was curt. "I'm the warden, and we have no Fred Brown. Do you mean Charles Brown?"

I could see we were off to a bad start. Later I wondered if there is ever a good start with this man. He never smiled, never changed his expression. It was flat and cold. I have the bad habit of forming first impressions based on the first few seconds when I meet someone new. I don't really form the impressions. They just develop. It was already in my head: this man is narrow-minded, cruel, sadistic, dangerous, power hungry. After my first impression fades, and it almost always does, I have the good sense to form an opinion based on realistic interactions with the person in question. I doubted further interactions would change this initial one, and I hoped there would be no need for further ones. I responded, "Yes, I guess I do mean Charles Brown. We knew him as Fred Brown."

Warden: "We insist prisoners use their birth name. His is Charles Frederick Brown. He is allowed to use Charles Frederick Brown if he wishes. When you say 'we knew him,' who is the 'we'?"

I answered, "Fred, I mean Charles Brown was the pastor of our church in Springer for a few months before he was charged with a crime."

The warden continued, "Charles Brown was not just charged with a crime. He was charged and convicted of two crimes. That's why he is here and why he will remain here for the next twenty years at least if I continue here as warden."

I found the nerve to ask, "How is Father Brown accommodating now that he's been here nearly one month?"

The warden's reply was caustic. "It's not Father Brown. It's Charles Brown. If he's not defrocked, he should be, and as far as we're concerned he is. He didn't fare well initially. My rule is to house every new prisoner in one of the general population buildings. After we observe them for at least three days, and more if necessary, the officers of the unit report to me regarding their behavior.

"Apparently Charles Brown had considerable difficulty adjusting to the other prisoners in the building, resulting in episodes of physical interaction and minor physical injury to Prisoner Brown. Based on reports coming from officers on the unit, Charles was found unfit to remain a member of the general population. As a result he is now housed in a special management building where he has meals in his cell. He spends all his time in his cell except for sixty minutes each day when he can be in the yard by himself. In short he is isolated from other inmates because of his hostile and unmanageable behavior. If at some later date he exhibits a reasonable change in attitude and behavior, it is possible he could be returned to a general population building."

I had the audacity to ask, "How would you know if there was a change in his attitude and behavior?"

Caustic response, "That's what we are trained to know. Have you read the rules of the prison for all visitors and do you agree to comply with those rules?"

Like a school boy, I replied, "I have read them and agree to comply."

And the teacher dismissed me. "You may now visit Charles Brown. He is not Father Brown and will not be addressed as Father Brown by you or anyone else who visits or any member of my staff. Inquire from the clerk on the way out of the building where you can find Charles Brown."

As I left the Warden's office, I felt a cold chill throughout my body. I had spent too much time with an icicle. The person at the front door of the building gave me directions to the building that housed Charles Brown. I had been looking forward to seeing him, but those positive feelings were darkened by the warden's words and my mental images of what had probably happened to Charles.

I showed my pass and went through another body search as I entered his building. I was taken to a small room poorly lighted by one ceiling bulb and no window. There was a table and two chairs, all firmly attached to the floor. After waiting two or three minutes the door opened and the guard came in with Charles in handcuffs and shackles. The guard said it was 2:36 and he would be back at 3:36 to get prisoner Charles. If I wanted to leave prior to that time or if I was in any distress or discomfort, press the bell on my side of the table and a guard would respond immediately. He seated Charles in the chair facing me and left the room.

The physical changes in Charles were beyond what I had been imagining. He had lost perhaps twenty-five pounds; there were bruises and welts and healing wounds on all the body parts I could see, face and neck, hands and arms. His walking was awkward, with an obvious limp favoring his right leg. He sat with his cuffed hands in his lap. He looked at me as if dazed and searching for a name to attach to my face. I wasn't certain he recognized me. I said, "I'm glad to be here to visit you, Fred."

Fear creased his face and he vigorously shook his head. "Charles, I'm Charles."

I responded, "I'm sorry, I was told to use the name Charles. That other name is not to be spoken." The exchange appeared to enhance his awareness of who I really was.

I waited giving him time to orient himself to my presence and his own in this stark room. He looked down at his hands and feet as if to be sure the irons were still there. I decided to support his struggle to reality and said, "I'm Bob Lee, Charles, and I've come from Springer to visit you here at the Montana State Prison." He was suffocating in his lost self, and each word seemed to be supporting his need to find more air, another breath of life. I waited a few moments and then added, "Charles, you've been here about three weeks now. I'm sure the time has been something of a nightmare for you. I spoke with Warden Craven today. You are now in a special unit where you will be more isolated but also more protected from other inmates. You were in a general unit for the first several days and I am aware those days were a terrifying and painful experience. We don't need to talk about those days. We don't need to ever talk about them if you prefer not to. Let's just talk about how you are today and how you spend your time." I was trying to find some ground where he could feel safer and more present.

For the first time he looked into my eyes and seemed to widen his own in recognition of who I was and acknowledgment of an existing relationship with me. The words came slowly, "Bob…Lee….yes…how good of you to come."

I said, "Charles, you and I talked about my visiting you when you were still in Springer. After you got here you wrote me a note and told me the visiting hours. This is the first chance I've had to visit. The rules of the prison allow me to visit with you for one hour. If you find that too long to talk today, just let me know. I can press this button and the guard will come for you."

At the mention of the button, Charles waved his hands in a clear indication not to even think of pressing it. At least he was beginning to express himself. He began, "I have so much to say, but I feel I've almost lost the ability to put thoughts into words. I sometimes go days without speaking a word. There is no one to hear them. Most of the guards never respond even if I speak to them. I'm outside in the yard each morning and each afternoon, but I'm alone except for the guards with guns in the towers. It's difficult to keep my thoughts focused because I have no boundaries in my head. Walls and fences are everywhere but none inside me. Sometimes my thoughts get focused on things from the past. I have no walls to keep them out or separate them from the present. The painful past comes up and I want to run away from it but there's no place to run inside my head. The prison is inside my mind. I can't stop thinking. I can't escape. There are walls and fences but no STOP signs in my head. There are DO NOT ENTER signs on the outside of my head. I can't get out. I can't live in my mind and I can't get out of it. I know I'm rambling and I know I'm mixed up, but it's all a jumble and my brain is crumbling. I don't know how I can stand this exile another day or even another minute. Then I get calm and for a brief time I'm just tired of it all and it almost feels peaceful."

I said to myself, "At least we got the cork out of the bottle." And to Charles, "Maybe it's good for you to just say whatever comes into your mind. It might release some of the tension that's been building up."

Charles continued, "When I first came in and was in the general population I thought they would kill me. Sometimes I wished they would. There was no recourse. The guards ignored it when the other prisoners stripped me and then threw refuse and feces and filth at me until I was covered with it. Then they'd drag me to the shower and hold my mouth open while they urinated in it. I was too empty to throw up and too weak to get up. I think every prisoner in the building and some of the guards raped me.

"The chaplain came through the area once a week and a prison inspector came through every other day. I didn't dare complain. They told me they'd cut out my tongue if I complained or they'd castrate me, one or the other or both. I felt ravaged, and sometimes in the worst of it all I felt like I deserved it.

"Even since I moved to this unit, I still think of those few days before I came here. The vivid memories live in my head and destroy my attempts to relax or to rest for fear they'll put me back there. The worst part of every day is when I go to bed. These recent memories kindle the fear and helplessness of childhood days."

As he spoke Charles seemed encouraged by his own words and his ability to express his thoughts freely. He no longer looked as fearful or as apprehensive. I decided to wait before responding. His mind was wading through the mire. It was likely he had more to say.

"Then came the worst part, the old memories from which I've tried to hide for years. Memories from when I was a child. The anger, the verbal threats, the beatings from my father. The strangely affectionate, bizarre fondling from my mother. I had no place to hide. Hiding only made my father more dangerous and my mother more weird. Well, now I've gone from the recent horror of this place to the horror of my childhood. You didn't come here to listen to all this, Bob."

I responded carefully, "Charles, feel free to talk about anything you want to talk about. I'm a pretty good listener and you don't have many listeners around here. Make use of the opportunity with any words you want to say, any subjects you want to just think out loud about."

Charles seemed eager to use the opportunity. "I was an only child. I think my father hated me and my mother doted on me. It was a weird childhood. I felt like a pawn in some vicious game that went on between the two of them. I don't remember my father's presence much until I began school. He worked for the railroad and was sometimes gone for days. And when he was home he spent a lot of time with his drinking buddies. When I was six or so he tried to get me to play catch with him. He was drinking and telling me how great he'd been at baseball. I was afraid of him. I didn't do well at catch, and he'd curse me for it and send me into the house. I've never cared for sports of any kind.

"After my failure at playing catch and more importantly my unwillingness to put much effort into it, my father seemed to forget I existed except when he came home drunk. Like most alcoholics I've known, he seemed to need to be angry at someone as if that someone was responsible for his drinking. In fact, he was so good at recriminating comments he sometimes had me feeling guilty for his alcohol abuse. He would quiz me on every aspect of my life and find fault in every area. My homework, my grades, the cleanliness of my room, my manners, my prayers, my eating, my clothes, the way I sat, the way I talked and on and on. Once his anger began it increased almost always to a beating. He never hit me where marks would show. With the beatings he would call me names. His favorite was, 'you little bastard.'"

I knew Charles was trying to escape from these thoughts that fill his mind at night and flow over into each day. All the brutality and isolation of prison are merciless on their own but retreating to the past only confronts him with what he's talking about now. My silence encouraged him to continue.

"When I was two or three, my maternal grandmother gave me a large teddy bear. I used to drag him around the house and then at night his head would be on the pillow by mine. Teddy was my faithful and trusted companion. He knew all my secret thoughts. I loved him like he was real. I was probably nine the last time Teddy slept on my pillow. It was the night my drunken father came home late and came into my room. When he saw the teddy bear, he hit me in the face and jerked the teddy bear away. His tirade of loud cursing woke my mother and she came in the room. My face was covered with blood from my nose and upper lip. She started screaming and my father was cursing. He threatened to kill her and slapped her as she approached my bed. She grabbed at the teddy bear and caught one arm. The two of them pulled the teddy bear apart and the stuffing fell all over the floor.

"That scene remains vivid in my mind. I see it happen all over again. I never got over the loss of the teddy bear. Later on my mother put some of the stuffing back in the teddy bear and sewed it shut but it was never the same. I continued to sleep with it, but I kept it under the covers where it slept between my legs. I used to pretend it was not me but the teddy bear that played with my penis. I've never loved any person like I loved my teddy bear.

"My father died in a railroad accident when I was fourteen. My mother said they found he was drunk at the time. I never told her I was glad he was dead. I never said that to anyone before today. But I was glad he was dead.

"My mother had her own oddities. In fact, she was quite strange. She was a perfectionist in many ways, a poor match for a slob of a husband. I felt like she was always breathing on the back of my neck. She felt she had to know everything I did, everything I felt, everything I thought. I learned the importance of secrecy early in life, long before I began school.

"My mother's perfectionism dominated my body, but not my mind or my will. I lied to her about everything. She supervised my cleanliness and my clothing. It was like a passion for her. She bathed me every evening before I went to bed. It was a ritual, absolute, no argument. To be honest, I accepted and in some strange way enjoyed the bath ritual. I even looked forward to it. She filled the bath tub about half full and then kneeling beside the tub she let me get in by myself as she held my hand. After I sat down to get wet she had me stand again and used a wash cloth to rub soap all over my body. The strange and awkward thing for me even to talk about is the way she washed my genitals. She played with my penis like it was *her* favorite toy. She used to talk to it and say 'what a teeny little weeny you are.' When some hair started to grow in the area, she would feel for gonads. She would handle my scrotum carefully and talk about 'two tiny marbles in your marble bag.' Each time she bathed me she would lift me out of the tub and place me on a scale she kept in the bathroom. I remember how my body stiffened in resistance to the feel of her bare hands.

"Just before my twelfth birthday she was bathing me and soaped my genitals in her usual way. Then she was sponging me off with water. When she got to my genitals, she took my penis in her fingers and kissed it, licking it a couple of times. She said, 'Goodbye little fella, Charlie will have to take care of you now because he's going to be twelve soon. Be careful of girls; they can hurt you and make you ill.' I can't remember my mother ever touching my body in any way after that day. Oh, she might pull at my coat sleeve or hand me my jacket. Things like that, but never my skin.

"I must be wearing you out, Bob, with all this blather. And I can see by your watch it's 3:30. We can finish with my mother the next time you're here. I finished with her when I went to the seminary at age sixteen. She died two years later. I was expected to go to the funeral so I did. I couldn't even pretend to be crying. Good riddance to bad garbage."

I hated to leave Charles in the midst of the negative, isolated, and somber mood he seemed to be in. On the other hand it was better than his state of mind when I came. And I told him so, "It's been difficult for you to talk as you have, Charles. At the same time I believe it is good for you to expose some of these deep wounds that have grown and festered in you all your life. If you think the words were harsh and bitter, let me tell you that harsh and bitter events don't heal by themselves. Events like you have related need to be opened up, looked at, examined and learned from, because they carry over into life.

"We only have a few minutes left. I will plan to come over four weeks from today, same time, same place. Before I go, with your permission, I would like to say something from the Canticle of Zechariah." Charles nodded his consent.

I recited: "In the tender compassion of our God the dawn from on high shall break upon us, to shine on those who dwell in darkness and the shadow of death, and to guide our feet into the way of peace." The guard opened the door. Charles and I shook hands as he nodded his gratitude. I said a quiet prayer for him as he walked away.

I felt a self-protective numbness as I walked out of the building and searched for my car. I needed to find Jane not so much for her sake as for my own. I called her on the cell, and she told me which store she was in. I said, "I'll park nearby and find you. I should be there in about ten minutes."

Jane made clothes for herself and our granddaughters. The Needle Store had material and all the makings for her talents. Because of our sensitivity about privacy, Charles was not mentioned when we got together. Jane talked about her shopping and a couple of items she bought. We agreed to go back to the Central Avenue Café for a cup of coffee and a pastry. Then we hit the road for home, planning to stop for dinner at the Park Plaza Restaurant in Black Eagle.

Once we were on the highway Jane asked, "Would you like to talk about it?" I accepted the prompt and told her about my talk with Charles. I began with my visit to the warden and included my impression of him as a cold, mean, unsavory man. I explained about the various levels at the prison and how Charles had been with the general population three days for "evaluation" according to their rules. Without details and specifics, I gave Jane some idea of how abused Charles was during that time.

I commented, "I'm going to use the name Charles now when I speak of Fred. It's the name the warden insists on and anyone who doesn't use it will be punished. Of course, if I use it the warden couldn't punish me so he would punish Charles. I think the warden has a personal score to settle with Charles. I wonder if he's Catholic. It's my guess he's either a Protestant who hates Catholics or he's a traditional Catholic who hates priests who don't meet his standards."

I explained how isolated Charles is in his present environment and how his physical isolation drags him back into the emotional isolation of his childhood. I decided to tell Jane about Charles' description of his father's brutal behavior and his mother's highly intrusive and markedly peculiar behavior. I would rather have waited for another time when we could be sitting together and I could watch her face and hold her hands. Of course, we were physically close in the car, but when you can't look in someone's eyes or reach out your hand at a special moment, there can be an unbridgeable distance. My concern was based on the fact that Jane's childhood had been replete with hostile, intrusive, and demeaning interactions with significant adults.

I decided to approach the subject carefully. I said, "Charles had some difficult interactions with his parents. My telling you about these now might be upsetting to you, and I don't want to interrupt the pleasantness of this time together. It's a pretty drive, and with the sun behind us we'll see some nice mountain views. I have no problem postponing the 'parent stories' until later this evening or even until tomorrow. They are not weighing me down."

Jane thought a bit and then answered, "We're together and are having a nice day. I enjoyed my time in Red Lodge. Our life is fulfilling in every way. I couldn't ask for anyone or anything more at this time in my life. That childhood you didn't refer to directly out of thoughtfulness no longer haunts me and hasn't for a long time. The big blue sky of Montana and the openness of the life we have are comforting and reassuring. Let's hear Fred's, I mean 'Charles,' story."

We reached Black Eagle about the time I was finished giving Jane the details Charles had shared with me about his early life. I finished by saying,

"Once more I've spoken with a child abuser who was himself abused. The abuse from his mother was quite unusual in my book. I've heard stories from patients about physical and/or sexual abuse by fathers. I've talked to women who, as children, were raped by their fathers and eventually bore their first child by him. I have seen men who were molested by their father, rarely by their mother. I suspect a more frequent sexual interaction between father and son involves sadistic punishment of the son, as may well have been the case for Charles.

"Charles's mother's sexual interaction with Charles borders on bizarre and hard to diagnosis. If she took some sort of sexual pleasure from seeing Charles naked, she could be called a voyeur. If she took sexual pleasure from touching his genitals, she could be called a pedophile. But there is no suggestion that her behavior was stimulated by sexual desire or produced any sexual satisfaction for her. It would be fascinating to know the story of *her* sexual development.

"We ran out of time when we were talking about the mother. Perhaps Charles will choose to tell me more. It seems she was a doting, jealous mother and found his naked body such a treasure she couldn't refrain from helping herself to those parts all others knew to be *private*. It would be safe to say she would never have approved of any girl who came within an arm's length of Charles. Remember how angry Charles got when I made the 'Teddy Bear' comment. Now I understand why. I've been doing all the talking again, Love. Here we are at the Park Plaza. I'll drop you off and find a place to park."

"No, Robbie, I'll come with you and we'll walk back together. It's a good time to stay close."

In a public place we automatically find other non-private things to talk about. And so we did throughout the course of our dinner. We enjoyed the meal and the time, taking well over a leisurely hour before we got on the road for home.

It was twilight when we drove into the yard. I started thinking "everything looks the same" and then I realized we left only ten hours ago; why shouldn't it all look the same? It was one of those days that has a fullness stretching beyond its own time. Jane and I put sweaters on and sat on the porch for a couple of hours in the cool air of evening, reviewing the day's events. As the evening wore on stars began to share our space and we watched them multiple like floating candles in a dark blue ocean of sky.

Jane read our scripture for the evening and then we talked about our lives and what we each gathered from the readings. We always say our night prayers together. It was a good night to sleep. As I was thinking that, Charles came to mind. I added a prayer asking that he might sleep well this night.

The next morning introduced a stormy-looking day, and this time of year snow is a likely product. By noon the verdict was in as flakes began to fall. I'm prejudiced, but in all the places we've lived I don't think I ever saw snowflakes as large as those that often fall early in Montana snowstorms. The other end of the spectrum is a Montana blizzard when the flakes look and feel like white frozen drops somehow still flaked. The weather report did not indicate a major storm, and once there was a thin white blanket on the ground the clouds moved on.

CHAPTER THIRTEEN

The coming Sunday was the second of the month and time for the first Sunday school class since Tim's death. I was a bit anxious about facing the group again, wondering what they were feeling, questioning what I should say. Should I just take up the next recommended lesson in the Sunday school guide, a lesson which focused on the Holy Trinity? We had missed the lessons for earlier classes, so we were clearly out of sequence and not ready for this.

I questioned whether I should discuss the events of the past couple of months which surely must occupy their family discussions as well as peer talk. So what perspective could I and should I take as their teacher? I asked Jane's opinion. "Hey, Sweetheart, I have a question. I'll have the Sunday school class the day after tomorrow. Do you think I should talk about Tim and Charles (Fred to them), and if I do, should I go into details about Charles's sentence and about my visit to the prison? It seems to me I can't face them in that room without making some reference to Tim. They are certain to be thinking about some of the conversations in the past that involved Tim. He was the focus of the class a couple of times."

Jane took her time about answering, which didn't surprise me. She rarely answers such questions without some careful thought. Finally, "It seems to me the kids are going to expect you to say something about it all. They know you've been involved in some way in most of what happened. Your name came up in family conversations and in their talk at school. Like it or not, your name has probably been mentioned in some way each time the subject is discussed.

"I don't think it's a question of should or should not, but a question of how much? The specific charges and his confession of 'guilty' are probably well known to them. They will be curious about what's happening to Charles now. And adult conversations have probably stirred some curiosity about what happens to him as a priest. What does the future hold for him? I see no reason why you shouldn't tell them about your visit with Charles, about his name, about the general abuse he experienced—I wouldn't go into the details—and the isolation he is in now. Questions about his future will be there, but the bishop has the answers and there's not much reason for you to speculate. One other item to consider: What if they ask how he was convicted, what was the evidence? What if one of them asks about the stomach contents in the autopsy? Nothing gets by some of these kids. Be prepared."

I replied, "You've covered all the bases, Love. And I think you're right on. These youngsters are so informed these days, not just from adults they talk to, but from one another and from the social media. They've probably read many of the newspaper articles about the case of Tim Quirk and Father Fred Brown. The one area they won't know about is Charles's prison life and what it's like. I agree, I think it's something they should know. It might touch some compassionate cords in a few of them.

"You raised a good question about the autopsy report. If that comes up, I'll have to deal with it square on I guess and say something like 'that report shows that semen from Fred's penis was in Tim's stomach. When the mouth of one person is in contact with the genitals of the other person, it is referred to as oral sex. The police decided that was what happened between Tim and Father Brown.' How does that sound?"

Jane thought it sounded straightforward and clear. I said it was helpful we talked about it, especially the question she brought up about the autopsy. I'll be prepared if it is asked by one of the class. On the other hand the kids may have already discussed those details among themselves.

Sunday came and we went to Mass. It seemed strange to be at the church and see the rectory and garage and remember conversations with Charles in each place. I thought about my "undercover work" to get Charles' things.

Lucy Quirk now sits with us in one of the front seats. It appears she will become a faithful Catholic since Tim's funeral and a regular communicant. She visits with us and the other parishioners after Mass. Most of the parishioners stay for a while and visit with one another, and Father Timothy circulates and talks to everyone. There is a growing sense of community. In fact Father Timothy asked Archie Brill to select and work with three or four other parishioners to review how the parish runs and what changes might be of value. Everyone is pleased with "our pastor."

The youngsters were rather quiet as we gathered in the basement for this our first class since the class that might have been our very last. I asked them about their families and a few things about school. Then I said, "Would you like to talk a little while about the death of Tim and the arrest and departure of Father Brown?" All heads nodded in assent but no one spoke. Was the subject too frightening or too sad or possibly too embarrassing to verbalize? I broke the ice.

"I will first tell you I visited Father Brown in the State Prison two days ago. I'll tell you some things about my visit and also some things about the State Prison and what life is like for him there. Because Tim was part of this little group, it might be helpful for us as a group to talk about what happened to Tim and the reason Father Brown is where he is."

I told them some things about visiting Father Brown and then asked if there were any questions or comments. Mary Mansfield opened the discussion that followed by asking, "Why would Father Brown ever have taken Tim up to that area all by himself? I thought priests weren't supposed to be alone with children. They weren't just alone; they were out in the wilderness." After that all kinds of comments and questions poured out of everyone as if the dam finally broke.

And yes, the question of semen came up. Louise, Mary's sister, asked that one. "What is semen and if it was Father Brown's how did it get in Tim's stomach?" I answered as I had practiced with Jane. I didn't feel anyone was embarrassed.

It was obvious from comments and questions that parents had approached the entire situation in a variety of ways in talking with their children. I also noted the children apparently avoided talking to one another about questions they had. They seemed eager for information not out of curiosity but to understand what actually occurred. Some reported wild rumors. The wildest rumor mentioned was: Tim was really Brown's son and Lucy Quirk came up with the idea of doing away with Tim. Beyond belief! How and where could something like that get started!

Once they felt comfortable talking, they came up with questions about details they had heard. I answered questions that did not invade anyone's privacy.

Before class ended, and I did keep them almost ten minutes extra, I told them I had something I wanted them to think about during the next two weeks. "Here's a question for you. Who can tell me what one request in the Our Father has a conditional clause? Anyone? What request is conditional?"

And then Joe Kirby said: "As we forgive those who trespass against us."

"You got it, Joe. Until next class I want each of you to ask yourself: does that apply to Father Brown? Ask the question when you say, 'Forgive us our trespasses.' See you in two weeks."

Later I wondered if I had gone too far in my comments about Charles. Would some parents object if their son or daughter brought up our conversation at home? I went to my usual resource for confirmation and approval of offhand statements I make or questionable positions I take. Jane showed no hesitation in giving her full approval. Of course, she may be slightly prejudiced.

We celebrated Thanksgiving in our usual manner. Our three children, with their spouses and children, visited from Wednesday until Sunday. Laura and Bill came from Minneapolis with their two girls, Casey just finishing high school and Tara who is a sophomore. Edward and Marie came from Boise with their son, George, who is a freshman at Loras College in Dubuque, Iowa. Joe came from Columbia, Maryland, with his friend Mike.

This holiday has become our traditional family day. We all spend Christmas in our own homes. Laura and Marie get along well with Jane and pitch in easily in all the "makings" of the days. Thanksgiving is the "story day" and the "passing around picture day." The late teenagers maintain contact through Facebook but always have more stories to tell. They talk "school and careers and dating" a good bit of the time. George is happy with Loras, but the girls look more toward the University of Minnesota or possibly St. John's in Collegeville.

Jane doesn't care for sports, so this is my chance to watch football and hockey with Edward and Bill and Joe and Mike. And George joins us occasionally. I can honestly say this is a happy family, although like all families minor incidents occur like who gets the extra piece of pie.

Father Timothy decided to say Mass at 10 A.M. on Thanksgiving Day. We all went without objection even from the teenagers. I had time after Mass to visit with Father Timothy. I told him about my experience with the Sunday school class. He found it interesting and was supportive of what I did. In fact, he said he wanted to go over it in his mind and possibly say something similar in one of his homilies.

As he was talking he came up with another idea and threw it out for my response. He said, "Here's a thought. What would you think if I scheduled a parish meeting some night next week in the parish hall, a meeting about these events of the summer? I would make some comments and ask you to tell us about your visit with Father Brown. Perhaps you should talk first and then I'll follow up and remark mostly on what you've said. I was not part of any of it so in a sense I am an outside observer and would be commenting as such."

I was surprised at his proposal and replied, "I think it would be of benefit to our parishioners. Those months remain in our memories and continue to chafe in our thoughts and probably also in our hearts. As I'm sure you know, my professional attitude is basically, 'Bring it out, look at it, examine it, make peace with it.' What I found in the Sunday school class is present throughout the parish. In addition to parishioners, how would you feel about inviting everyone in the community to come?"

"Excellent, excellent," was Timothy's response. "But the parish hall probably wouldn't be big enough to hold the whole crowd that might come. I think we should move it to the Town Hall. Yes, definitely, the Town Hall. I'm sure many townspeople would be there. Let me talk to the Mayor, Marge Sullivan, to arrange the whole thing. Marge is a member of the parish and, I'm sure, would be supportive."

Interesting how an almost insignificant incident can suddenly turn into a major event. The development of this one was providential in my book. The two of us fed our own enthusiasm as we talked. We agreed on the Friday or Saturday evening of the following week, depending on availability of the hall, et cetera. Timothy would ask the local paper and TV station to announce the meeting once all was decided.

During our conversation Jane came over and said she would ride home with one of the others and leave our car for me. As I drove home I wondered if I had accepted this whole idea too quickly. But going back to the experience in Sunday school quelled my doubts. The town of Springer needed to open the boil and drain the seepage and recover their sense of unity and communion. Wild rumors also needed to be put to rest.

Thanksgiving dinner was beyond gourmet standards. Jane and Marie and Laura had surpassed their best. The fellowship and warmth of the family enhanced the blessings of the morning. After dinner I mentioned the plan Father Timothy and I developed for the following week. Everyone commented in strongly supportive words.

Our family visit came to an end early Sunday morning. Edward and Marie and George were driving to Boise and got an 8 A.M. start. Laura and her family and Peter and Mike were catching morning flights back home and left the ranch at the same time as Edward and family. I can't really say it's ever a sad goodbye to see them go, perhaps because they don't totally leave. They're still with us, not just in the other room or in the yard nor within arm's length. They remain within heart's length.

On Sunday Jane and I went to the usual 10 A.M. Mass. At the end of Mass Father Timothy announced the upcoming talk and discussion night to revisit the events of the months prior to his arrival in Springer. He mentioned his discussion with me and told them I had visited Father Brown the preceding week. He said he is in contact with Mayor Marge Sullivan (nodding in Marge's direction) and they are making arrangements for the use of the Town Hall. He said, "As of the moment the most likely evening will be next Friday at 7:30. There will be an announcement in the local news and local TV station. There will also be posters in some of the shops. I hope all of you can attend. We are inviting the people of Springer. It is my hope the evening will bring a sense of peace and closure for all."

After Mass people almost lined up to ask me about Father Brown. I didn't go into any details but simply said he had some frightening and harsh experiences at the prison but at the time of my visit was basically in isolation and managing satisfactorily. Jane and I didn't leave for home until almost an hour later.

By Tuesday afternoon Father Timothy called and confirmed the talk for Friday evening at 7:30. During our conversation I mentioned what I said in class about the conditional phrase in the Our Father. Timothy's response, "That's an interesting way to approach the topic of forgiveness. I never used the phrase that directly. I rattle through it several times a day but this slows it down to a thoughtful process."

With a bit of a chuckle, I said, "Tell you what, Timothy. I'll leave that approach for you to use Friday evening. I'll set them up for it and you use it to strike home."

I could hear Timothy's smile in his words, "We'll make a great team, Bob."

Jane and I were mostly house bound during the week. It snowed pretty steadily on Tuesday and Wednesday. The inch on Tuesday didn't prevent the cattle from grazing. But on Wednesday I saddled Ben and rode to the pasture to feed them. It was almost ten below zero on the thermometer outside the garage. This was sheepskin weather.

I made my way to the pasture through some heavy snow drifts. The cattle were sheltering in the shed or standing around the corralled bales. Feeding the cattle in the snow and cold of winter has always been a blessed experience for me. It always remind me of "feed my lambs, feed my sheep."

The snowstorm passed on after a couple of days and by Friday we were full-time sun. We went to town for the 7:30 meeting in Town Hall. Town Hall capacity was eighteen hundred. There must have been two thousand people there that evening. Mayor Sullivan was up front with Father Tim and Lucy Quirk. We joined them in the front row, nodding and saying hello to numerous people from church and from the town. I waved to Sheriff Wilson and Deputy Carr as we went by their row. I also greeted Pat Benet who was sitting a couple of rows from the front. It was a remarkable turnout.

The evening went beautifully. I know no better word to describe it. The mayor introduced Father Matthews who, after some brief comments mentioning his recent arrival to Springer, introduced me.

I talked about twenty minutes, beginning with my first impression of Father Brown as a quiet, rather reserved man and not too easy to know. I noted that his arrest, his incarceration, his legal charges, his guilty pleas, and his sentencing were all handled with professional dignity and fairness by those involved. I said, "After his conviction, Father Brown asked me to be his executor in all legal matters and arranged to give me full power of attorney. These arrangements were made in the presence of Tom O'Rourke, Father Brown's attorney. Father Brown stated he had no family members with whom he had contact and no friends to whom he could transfer these responsibilities.

"My being teacher of the Sunday school resulted in several contacts with Father Brown prior to his arrest. He asked the sheriff to call me when he came to the Columbus Hospital with the deceased son of Mrs. Quirk. I tried to be of help to him in a variety of ways until he was taken to the State Prison in Red Lodge. Before going, he asked me to visit him and I was able to do so approximately a week ago."

I continued and told them essentially the same things I told the class about my visit. I talked about my interview with the warden, his dispassionate attitude and pitiless comments about Father Brown. The audience appeared to have a keen interest in the harsh and unnecessary duration of Father Brown's stay on the open prison ward. My description didn't leave much to their imagination. I was more forthright than I had been with the Sunday school class. I ended saying, "Jane and I pray for Father Brown every night and ask the Lord to ease the ever-present loneliness of his life, to smooth the sharp barbs of memory, to soothe the untreated wounds of childhood. I do not tell you details about his childhood because I treat them as a confidential matter. But in all my years as a psychiatrist hearing horrors of parental abuse, I've never heard anything as shocking as what Father Brown told me during my visit. The childhood from which he came brought him to the barren life he lived and to the abysmal behavior that ended in the death of Lucy Quirk's little boy.

"I want to thank Father Timothy for proposing this meeting, arranging the evening and offering an opportunity for the community to hear, reflect and perhaps pray about the disturbing and sad events that recently confronted us all. Father Timothy now has some additional remarks."

Every word Father Timothy said had a gentle, warm tone to it. He expressed his gratitude to the bishop for giving him the opportunity to serve the people of Springer. He said, "As a parish we have not prayed openly for Father Brown although he must certainly, at least for the present, remain prominent in our minds. I am going to suggest to our congregation that we add his name to the list of those we pray for each Sunday. As I speak of that, I recall a question Bob Lee asked me a few days ago. The question: which words in the Our Father have a qualifying or conditional phrase? Anyone?"

Joe Kirby (who had answered in class) raised his hand and when Father Timothy pointed to him he responded, "Forgive us our trespasses as we forgive those who trespass against us."

Father Timothy went on. "Thank you, Joe. Yes, we ask the Almighty to 'forgive us as we forgive those who trespass against us.' So I raise the question for all gathered here to think about, to pray about. We all agree Father Brown is guilty of a dreadful and shocking crime, a crime no one here could ever consider condoning. And Father Brown is being duly punished. Do we want more? Is his present punishment not enough? What benefit can anyone obtain from continued anger, hatred, or desire for revenge? As you reflect on what we have spoken of tonight, consider the blessings in your own lives in spite of the frailties of your humanity, and let the blessing of forgiveness fill your hearts and reach out to others including Father Brown.

"There is one more person here who has asked me if she could speak to you tonight. To those who do not know her, let me introduce you to Lucy Quirk." There was no applause for Father Timothy because the fact that Lucy Quirk was going to speak was spell-binding. It was a surprise, almost a shock, the dead boy's mother speaking to this group! The room was completely silent as she stood up and walked to the microphone.

"Thank you, Father Matthews. Yes, I am Tim's mother. And I know how Tim died and I know who caused his death. I was not the best of mothers to Tim. I didn't spend much time with him. I spend more time with him now. I didn't talk much with him before. I talk more with him now. We weren't very close. We're closer now. Perhaps he is now my guardian angel. I lost a son. I found God again. I ask God to forgive my failings. Every night I ask God to forgive and to bless Father Fred Brown."

For a moment, a silent numbness filled the room as Lucy started for her seat. Then everyone stood and the rafters shook with applause and cheers and the silence of angel wings. It was a heart-moving moment that will live for long in the hearts of everyone who was there.

Mayor Sullivan stepped to the microphone and thanked everyone for coming and praised all who had participated in what she called "a heartfelt evening of fellowship and good will in this peace-filled loving town of ours."

It was one of those times when no one wants to leave. They want to live in the warmth and peace and communion of the moment. Jane and I stayed another hour or more. Lucy Quirk was overwhelmed by everyone crowding in to speak to her, shake her hand, give her a hug. Jane and I spent a few minutes with Pat Benet. She was interested in my visit to the State Prison and my impressions of the warden. She confided that the State Bar Association has had several discussions about the warden and the prison program.

When we left the hall there were still two or three hundred people savoring and prolonging the experience. On the way home we both acknowledged how tired we were but how exhilarating the evening was. I agreed with Jane's summation: *It was a grand evening.*

Chapter Fourteen

The following morning while we were having breakfast, I told Jane I was thinking of visiting Charles on Thursday. I suggested she consider coming with me. "The weather is getting increasingly unpredictable. You know how quickly a major snowstorm can show up in Montana. I don't want to get caught in Red Lodge without you. I would visit Charles from 2:30 to 3:30, but it gets dark about five o'clock, and starting home I wouldn't be very far from Red Lodge by sundown. I don't relish the idea of driving home so late in winter months. Snow comes quickly and unexpectedly, especially in the mountains, and roads become icy.

"We could get an early reservation at one of the motels and take what we need to stay over. There's even the possibility we could get stuck there for a couple of days or more. We were in those mountains years ago, and I remember traffic being slowed for long periods waiting for snow plows to clear some of the mountain passes. I'll get Ted to feed the cattle if our return is delayed. Thursday morning before we go I'll put out enough bales for a couple of days. I can call Ted if we'll be late getting home on Friday."

Jane didn't hesitate, "Do you think for a moment I would possibly give up the opportunity of going with you wherever and whenever you're going and no matter how long you're going to stay? I'll pack this afternoon." The last comment with a beginning smile.

It was settled. I contacted the Red Haven Motel and got a reservation for Thursday evening. I've heard good things about the Red Haven. I made arrangements with Ted about feeding the cattle.

We were up early Thursday morning. After breakfast I rode out and left sufficient hay for the cattle for two days. By the time I came home, Jane was packed and ready. She does my packing and keeps a list of what I need when we travel. Great service!

The trip went well. We stopped at Snowtop Lodge in the Bitterroot Range for an early lunch. It's a popular ski resort so the stop gave us an opportunity to get information about possibly spending a few days there sometime after the first of the year.

We arrived in Red Lodge about 1:30. I had asked for an early check-in. The motel was not far from the downtown area. The main stores were within walking distance for Jane. There was about four inches of snow on the ground but sidewalks and roads were clear. I said, "Janey, I'll be leaving for the prison in a few minutes. I want to get a full hour's visit with Charles as early as possible. Should we meet back here when I return or should I call you on your cell and meet you wherever you are?"

Jane smiled, which told me she was going to be funny. "Why don't you come back here so you can see all the things I bought if there's still enough room for you to get in the door?"

I replied, "I'll knock so you can hide all your purchases in that little purse you have in your hand. I'll see you shortly after 3:30, Love."

"Tell Charles we pray for him. There's no need to tell you to be kind to him. I'll see you soon, Rob. Drive carefully. Avoid the warden."

I went through the admission routine at the prison and was sitting in one of the cell-like rooms with Charles at 2:32. The guard left the same instructions as before. My first impression: Charles was more relaxed, bruises continuing to heal, referring only to physical bruises. Some emotional bruises never completely heal. Charles reached his hand out first and said, "Thank you for coming back, Bob. After all I told you during our last visit, I thought you might not return. I can hardly put up with myself and could never put up with my parents. In fact I don't really put up with people very well. I hope it's not a strain for you to be with me."

I thought I'd test his cognitive acuity a bit so I said, "Based on what you just said how do you put up with me?"

He was mentally tracking well because he replied, "You're not like anyone I knew before. Or perhaps more accurately, you don't treat me like anyone else I ever knew."

I thought I would add another layer, "Charles, that may be because you never let people know you like I know you."

He smiled and said, "You may be right." That comment was a surprise.

I started in a new direction saying, "What's been going through your mind since we met a few weeks ago? You've had lots of thinking time."

He looked at me as he replied, "I told you a lot about my father last time and some things about my mother. I pretty much dismissed my father from my life when he had a fatal accident as a result of alcohol abuse. I was fourteen. All he ever was in my life was a danger and a demon, all in one."

Charles began talking as if he'd been preparing what he was going to say and could hardly wait to get it all out. I couldn't help thinking what a good patient he would have been and it was unfortunate he had not somehow found his way into therapy years ago. "Talking to you about my mother's bizarre sexual aggressions toward me brought other things about her into my mind. I have always tried to avoid anything that might remind me of her. I don't try to blame either of my parents for the mess I've made of my life. I have to take responsibility for the degenerate human being I am."

I interrupted him briefly to say, "Yes, we are each responsible for our own behavior, Charles, but our adult behavior is greatly shaped by those who influence our early image of who we are and how we fit into the world."

Charles went on, "I never thought I fit into my parents' world. I didn't want to fit into it. My mother's world was creepy with her obsessive religious delusions. I think I can call them delusions. She was always talking about 'the devil's work' and how careful we had to be to avoid *occasions* of sin. She used the word as if it had some meaning for me. It didn't. She usually attended early morning Mass, and when she came home she would go around the house holding her rosary beads and waving them in the air as if she were chasing a ghost away. I guess it was her 'evil spirits' she was shooing away. I think she went to confession three or four times a week.

"I never saw my parents touch one another. They must have touched me when I was little, but I don't remember either of them touching me except in the negative ways I mentioned the last time you were here. They rarely spoke to each other. They slept in different rooms. Her bedroom was covered with holy cards and pictures, and she had votive lights all over the house. My father used to tell her she would burn the house down someday. Looking back, I think she probably drove him to drink.

"They sent me to a Catholic school starting in first grade. She insisted it had to be the only school for me. That's about the time she began saying, 'the greatest blessing a family can have: a son who is a priest.' I did well in school and became an altar boy when I was eight. We lived two blocks from the church. My mother was always making over the priests as if they were saints. She asked the pastor if I could be the altar boy at weekday Masses. He agreed I could serve morning Mass the first week of every month. I liked wearing the cassock and surplice. It felt like I had a dress on with a blouse over it. I can't understand that attraction. I'd rather have died than be a girl.

"My mother used to bake all kinds of cakes and cookies for the nuns who were my teachers. Sometimes I'd hear my mother talking to one of her 'cookie and cake' nuns, telling them how she thought I should be a priest and asking them to pray I would be. On occasion one of the nuns would say something to me like 'don't you think you'd like to be one of God's priests, Charles?' or 'I will pray you get a vocation to the priesthood, Charles.' I felt like saying 'I'd rather get polio.'

"I was never interested in girls. They were all like my mother, strange and possessive, interested but invasive. I wasn't attracted to men or boys either. They always acted superior, and eventually most were cruel like my father. Even in grade school I felt like a misfit. I never played sports. I knew the boys who played sports took showers together after games. I didn't want to see anyone's genitals or to let them see mine because I knew mine couldn't compare in size, from what my mother told me."

Charles stopped his recitation and seemed to be lost in thought. I decided I'd ask about his decision to become a priest. "As you were talking about all of this, Charles, I began wondering how you found your way into the priesthood."

His thinking went on for a short time and then, "Don't you think it should be obvious from what I've already said, Bob?"

I countered with the comment, "But you saw your mother's religion as delusional, weird, more like superstition. How could you decide you had a vocation? Did the nuns convince you?"

Charles looked puzzled for a couple of minutes and then replied, "After all I've been thinking about and from what I've just said, I think I'm just now getting the answer to your question. I decided to become a priest when I was in tenth grade. At that time my diocese sent priest candidates to live in seminary-like high schools in junior year to begin their training. My father was dead about two years. Now I needed to *get away from my mother.* Going away to high school was my answer. I've always thought I went because the nuns and my mother convinced me I had a vocation. Not so. It was to get away from my crazy mother.

"All these years I've lied to myself and asked why God doesn't help me live this vocation I was called to. I wasn't called to serve God. God didn't want me any more than my parents did. I used God to get away from my mother and maybe I've been trying to get away from God.

"My mother died two years before I was ordained. It was too late for me to change my mind. But of course I never considered doing so. She had several strokes and was in a nursing home for three years before she died. I remember feeling relieved when they told me she was dead. I dreaded the possibility of having her around for my ordination."

When Charles hesitated I had a comment to make. "You are not the first person to end up in the priesthood and much later discover it is not a life for which they are suited. Like you, they thought they had a vocation, a sort of mysterious communication from God designating them for lofty service to this sacred ministry. They are *special* and will always *be special.* They are not like other young men who question what they want to do in life and look into a variety of possibilities, seeking the advice of others, doing some research and deciding to try a certain field with the plan that if it doesn't work out for them they'll be open to the pursuit of something else. But when one believes *God has called,* it's difficult to believe one has an alternative."

Charles listened and seemed to understand what I was suggesting. "It never occurred to me I could do anything or be anything other than what I was. I just needed to plod along alone, always alone."

This remark gave me the opening I hoped would come. "Charles, was Tim the first boy you were attracted to?"

He sat thinking and perhaps wondering how much he wanted to tell me. He slowly got to it. "Tim was the second boy I ever had active sexual contact

179

with. The first boy was in Louisiana. I had been ordained eight years by then. He was ten years old. His parents found out. They threatened to expose me. I offered to pay them thirty thousand dollars and to leave the diocese. They accepted, and I transferred to a Missouri diocese."

I interrupted, "Were you originally from the Louisiana diocese?"

"No, I was ordained for the Tulsa diocese in Oklahoma. But I left there because I, as they said, 'behaved in an inappropriate manner with students' at the Catholic grade school in the parish. It was in the gym, and I was participating in their wrestling matches. The instructor was present at the time, but when the pastor heard about it, he spoke to the bishop and I was removed from the parish. A year or two later there was a similar incident reported to the bishop. That was when I went to Louisiana with the aid of the bishop. I started in Oklahoma, then to Louisiana, then to Missouri, and from Missouri to Montana. I requested the move to Montana because I was becoming unduly attracted to a twelve-year-old boy who often served Mass for me in Missouri."

Charles spoke freely and without feeling as if he were reporting someone else's history. It was all matter-of-fact, almost like a salesman telling you about his various customers. I wondered if he ever felt real passion for anyone or anything.

I remembered how much he talked about his love for Tim after Tim's death. In view of all he just told me, I wondered if Tim was just another kid he briefly fixated on. I asked, "What kind of feelings did you have for Tim?"

He looked surprised. "I was just thinking about Tim and how much I loved him. I believe I can honestly say, 'I loved Tim more than I ever loved anyone.' More accurately, he's the only person I ever loved. Tim reminded me of myself, and at first I felt sorry for him. He was awkward physically and verbally. He seemed to be without any real friends. His father was gone, and his mother showed him nothing except her own questionable sex life. He seemed so all alone in the world. He was truly a kindred spirit. I loved Tim like I loved my teddy bear."

Like Tim used to blurt out things, Charles blurted out, "I killed Tim, Bob. I didn't mean to. I truly loved him. I didn't know he was dying. I had my penis in his mouth and had just ejaculated. I hadn't ejaculated in years. I was in an ecstasy of some kind. I grabbed his head before he could move away and I pulled him tight to my pubic area to keep my penis in his mouth. He was waving his arms, and I interpreted it as pleasure he was feeling. Then he stopped flailing.

As my mind cleared and I came back to lucidity and reality, he was dead. He suffocated. I panicked. I thought of the rock, had seen it there before. I picked Tim up, carried him out and hit his head on the rock. I thought that would explain his death and there would be no questions and no one would ever know what really happened. Then I brought him to town. It sounds cold-blooded and deliberate as I tell you. I was in another world during the sexual act. I had never experienced such frenzy of physical and emotional satisfaction.

"I wasn't planning to tell you that. There is really no need for you to know or for anyone else to know. No one can understand what strong feelings of love and need I had for Tim. It felt like he was part of me. He was my 'alter ego,' I guess. Don't think ill of me, Bob. Don't walk away. Everyone else in my life has."

Charles began crying softly. I said, "I won't walk away, Charles. Perhaps you were the one who walked away sometimes in the past. But the past is gone; let's let it rest." And somewhere inside I thought, "A stick of wood can't cry."

Our time was about up, and I thought, *We can't leave everything just as it is.* We have to have more thoughts with more words, words not to hide things but to expose, clarify, patch together the hanging shards of Charles life. From what Charles told me before and from the rules of the prison I'd read, Charles has one hour in the yard each day. He can take it as one full hour in the morning or half an hour morning and afternoon. Attorneys are authorized to be with their clients during yard time. Since Tom O'Rourke gave me his card, I've carried it in my wallet. It is his professional card and on the back is typed: "Robert Lee (the name is written in) is a qualified and authorized employee of this firm and at his own discretion may act in my behalf."

I said to Charles, "We need some additional time to talk. You can have an hour in the yard at 10 A.M. tomorrow. This card from Mr. O'Rourke will authorize my seeing you at that time, representing Mr. O'Rourke. Is that all right with you?"

"It's a godsend, Bob. I'll be expecting you. Could you say that Zechariah thing again before the guard comes?"

I did. The guard opened the door as I spoke the last words. And Charles walked out of the room.

Jane was waiting for me at the Red Haven Motel. When I saw her, I knew how grateful I was she came with me. Not just because I needed to stay over until tomorrow, but my confidante, my best friend was here to talk to. And that's what we did for the next hour. I told her about my meeting with Charles and the reasons I had for staying over to see him again in the morning.

As always Jane had no problem with the change of plan. She said, "I'm glad you're going to see Charles again. It would have been difficult for him and probably for you to leave as things are right now. It sounds like there is more he will benefit in talking about. I'm sure you are aware that in actual fact you are practicing psychiatry without a Montana license. Or don't you agree?"

I could hardly argue Jane's point but pushed her comment a bit further. "You don't think he's likely to sue me, do you?" That brought her smile and moved us both to other subjects.

Jane said she enjoyed visiting the variety of shops in the downtown area. I told her she could drop me at the prison in the morning and take the car so she could spread her shopping to stores farther away. She was happy with the stores she could walk to and would spend Friday morning in the same area and added, "There are a couple of items in the antique shop I'd like to look at again."

Although we liked the Central Avenue Café on our previous visit, Jane said, "Let's try something new tonight, something where there's music and maybe a place to dance."

I was all for the idea, commenting, "We haven't danced to live music in months. Let me check at the desk and see what they recommend."

On the Motel's recommendation we went to the Glacier Diner. We were pleased. The food was good. The Shannon Brothers played piano, guitar and sang. At our request they played a number of our favorites. We had Jack Daniels with our coffee and danced for almost an hour. It was a relaxed and pleasant evening and certainly took my mind off the events of the afternoon.

Friday morning I arrived at the prison at 10 A.M. As I checked in, I showed Tom O'Rourke's card. The desk officer studied it for short time and then said, "I need to talk to the warden about this before I let you go through."

He called the warden and from what I heard him saying, it seemed like the warden was not going to approve my visit. I said to the officer, "You might let the warden know that Mr. O'Rourke is the vice-president of the State Bar Association." After he told the warden what I said, my request had new life. I got my pass into the yard with Charles.

The yard was a different setting for our talk. There was snow on the ground, most of it packed down by the other prisoners who visited the yard several times daily. It was a sunny morning with temperature in the forties. Charles and I found a bench protected from the slight breeze and warmed by the sun.

After greeting each other Charles opened the conversation and was obviously prepared to continue on from yesterday. "You know, Bob, before I came to Montana, I changed my name from Charles Frederick Brown to Fred Brown. It really was not to hide my identity. The main reason I did it was because I was tired of being who I was. I felt disgusted with myself. I was not only a 'nobody,' but I was ashamed and worried about my attraction to boys. I was determined to make some changes. The 'new name' was a beginning.

"The time that first boy told his parents and I had to pay my way out of it remained prominent in my mind. What if it happened again and the family wouldn't accept pay to keep quiet? What if it was reported to the authorities? I wasn't too afraid of being reported to the bishop. I always believed I could talk my way out of it if I was confronted by the bishop. I know the church has stricter rules about it all now, but they still want to avoid scandal if it can be tucked away somewhere, somehow. And the shortage of priests weighs into the whole issue, favorably for the offender of course.

"For some reason I always thought of Montana as a great place to live. It seemed so open and free and clean. But once I arrived, my fantasy quickly faded. When I was in the Cut Bank area before I came to Springer, I was making physical contact with young boys playing touch football. It wasn't the game. It was the contact, the touching. I always knew the touch might someday, would someday, wander to the genitals.

"When Bishop Butler moved me here as pastor, it gave me new hope. In spite of my feelings of innate worthlessness, here I was a priest with my own parish to manage. It was encouraging. It was, in fantasy at least, a new start. Then I met Tim, and within a week I was visualizing sexual contact with him. My disease was not going away or improving. It was only worsening.

"I was molested once when I was an altar boy a couple of years older than Tim Quirk. He was a priest in Tulsa. I became his favorite playmate; you know the kind of play I'm referring to. It went on for a couple of years until he was arrested and put in jail. Several lawsuits were filed against him. Several years later when I was in the seminary I heard he disappeared from the diocese and no one knew where he was."

I tried to be offhand as I casually asked, "Do you remember his name?"

"Oh, yes. Peter _____." (Name withheld—the Peter I'd met.) "I heard the authorities caught up with him and took him back to jail in Oklahoma.

"Peter even explained some of his 'tricks' (as he called them) to me and how he found boys who were willing compared to those who weren't. In fact, the first trick I learned was the one that caught me. He did sleight of hand tricks with coins. He'd have 'the target' find which hand the coin was in. Then the target closed their eyes while he hid the coin. As the hiding places changed, the coin was of increased amount. Sometimes he'd hide the coin in his shoes. Then he'd hide it in one of his pants pockets—two in front, two in back. When you put your hand in a front pocket, he expected you to feel his erect penis. If that didn't work, he told me he had a pair of pants with the bottom of one front pocket cut off. In this case there was no coin, so eventually you reached in the pocket without a bottom.

"He also told me he tested for 'ready boys' by finding some excuse to try to lift them. If he could get behind a boy and put his arms around the boy's waist and lift him up, he could tell whether or not the boy was a 'possibility.' Do you know why that works, Bob?" I said I had no idea how that would indicate anything to anyone. Then before Charles could answer, I remembered *the scale in the office.*

Charles continued, "If the boy stiffens as if he is uncomfortable or resistant to the arms around his waist, he's an 'unlikely.' If the boy seems to have no discomfort, it indicates he may well accept more physical contact."

Without thinking I said, "Is that why you had the scale in the sacristy, Charles?"

To my surprise he looked embarrassed. He said, "You probably think someone like me can't be ashamed or embarrassed by their behavior. I despised my behavior. I was crass and insensitive enough not to be ashamed of it. But today I am ashamed of it because *you* know about it. Your opinion is important to me. No one else's opinion ever was. They were just others' opinions and went directly into the mother-father box, the 'to hell with them box.' Yes, that's why the scales were there. I 'weighed' each altar boy a couple of times. Tim was comfortable when I lifted him onto the scale. I had fondled him once in the sacristy before anyone else came in. But the day he died was the first time we ever did that."

Charles looked off into the distance which suggested he might be about finished talking. I assumed he was now thinking he'd have to continue to live with all he had told me and the fact that someone else knew. I waited for a time. He turned his face toward me, "Bob, I'm glad I told you all these things. Somehow it relieves my mind but not my guilt feelings. I fear I'll never be unburdened from the guilt." We had a brief exchange.

Me: "Do you sincerely want to remove the burden of guilt?"

Charles: "Yes I do."

Me: "Have you talked to the chaplain? What's his name by the way?"

Charles: "We say hello. He's Pat Sullivan."

Me: "Do you want to make peace with God?"

Charles: "I confessed to you. That's enough."

Me: "I think you better talk directly to God when you feel ready. I don't have that kind of connection. God will be waiting."

Charles: "I'm sorry for the crappy life I was given and doubly sorry for the life I lived."

Me: "The life you were given led to the life you lived. God's aware of that. I hope you can remember the connection."

Charles: "That's no excuse."

Me: "Not an excuse but it is a reason. You don't need an excuse. God's aware of the connection."

Charles: "Oh, I guess maybe I'm sorry for it all."

Me: "Just let God know that, Charles."

I continued, "I've been anxious to tell you some news from Springer and here I've let it go so long we don't have much time left. The new priest caught up with the mayor and the two of them arranged a public meeting in the Town Hall. The meeting was to review the events of the last few months and to attempt to lift the town's spirits. There must have been two thousand people cramming the hall. I spoke about forgiveness, and then Father Matthews gave an excellent talk on the same subject and suggested the parish add your name to the Mass intentions each Sunday. At the last minute Mrs. Quirk stood and told everyone how she prays for you every night and how she talks with Tim and spends more time with him than she used to. She says he's her guardian angel now."

Charles's eyes filled with tears as I told him the details of the evening. He just sat there with his tears and the picture I had presented of the Town Hall meeting. This hour would soon be over. It was time to get some closure. I put my hand on Charles' arm, saying, "Thank you, Charles, for talking to me as freely as you did. I hope you will find some relief and a greater sense of peace from your 'confession,' as you put it. You know we are into December so I won't plan on coming back until after Christmas. Jane and I stay home for these holidays. Maybe I can come over between Christmas and New Year's. How does that sound?"

Charles reached out his hand. "You are welcome any time. Your visits have been more of a blessing than you can ever know. I have gained an understanding I wish I'd had years ago. After your story about the people of Springer and especially of St. Cyril's, maybe I *can begin* to pray."

I took his hand in both of mine. "Don't dwell on Tim, Charles. He's at peace. Tim's mother, the parish of St. Cyril's and the Lee family and many others from the town, those who pray for Tim, also pray for you now. That you will find peace of heart and mind and spirit. Merry Christmas, Charles."

Before I left Charles asked, "Would you say that Ezekiel thing again? The thought is so consoling to me." As I ended the prayer, the guard came out and took Charles. Good timing, God.

Jane was packed and checked out and ready to go when I got back to the Red Haven Motel. We went to the Central Avenue Café for a quick lunch and then set our GPS for Springer. There were some delays in the high mountains but we got home before dark. And Jane put a quick dinner on the table while I brought in the bags and checked the mail and phone messages.

As you might expect we talked about Charles on the way home. I reviewed the significant family history in which I found nothing supportive, compassionate, or even encouraging. The history of his *vocation* contributed nothing truly positive. Regarding his vocation I commented, "How could a seminary have accepted this boy (he was really a boy at the time) without knowing his history and the factors that were *compelling* his vocation? They could not have done any psychological testing or careful interviewing. He would never have passed. They could hardly have done any assessment of his family background. He was then much as he is now, certainly no better. We saw how he functioned as our pastor. His performance, even forgetting about

Tim, was at best mediocre. And his enthusiasm and charisma were minimal to absent." I told Jane in generalities about his behavioral misadventures.

When I told her about Peter, the priest in Minneapolis, she said, "Unbelievable coincidence, unbelievable coincidence."

I commented, "I believe child predators have a sense about who might be vulnerable to their advances. Perhaps it's not only a sense; it's also information they gather about the child, information about family presence or absence, parental interest or neglect. Children who have inadequate parental concern and supervision are unconsciously looking for an adult to fill some of those gaps in their life. Children who lack expressed parental affection must be readily susceptible to the 'friendly' hand on their arm or shoulder of their admired and respected parish priest."

CHAPTER FIFTEEN

Saturday was spent catching up with whatever was left undone since Wednesday. I rode out to check the cattle. The snow had melted enough they could pasture.

Sunday Mass was a warm, friendly, and deeply spiritual experience. It felt peaceful to be with our friends saying the prayers we always say. When the list of petitions was read, it included Father Fred Brown. Father Matthews decided to use the name Fred, the name by which we all knew him.

Another couple of weeks went by, and we were, as always, surprised that Christmas was two days away. We used to decorate elaborately for Christmas. It was Jane's artistic talent at its best. But when we came back to live at the ranch, Jane suggested we let God do most of the decorating for Christmas and God usually obliged bountifully. Before our move, Jane had given the bulk of our decorations to Laura, where they are still used and enjoyed in her house.

Jane was busy preparing our usual Christmas dinner with all her cooking skills. We had an additional two inches of snow during the night. It was continuing this morning, and the weather prediction was for another eight or ten inches today. I put on warm and protective clothing, head to foot, and told Jane I was going to feed the cattle. Jane came over and checked my winter clothes to her satisfaction. As she did so, she said, "You know I always worry about you when you go out in a blizzard like this. The weather station didn't call the storm a blizzard, but looking out the window tells me it is. The wind is blowing very hard. You'll have trouble seeing and so will your horse. Be careful, Robbie. When can I expect you home?"

"Sweetheart, you know I'll be careful. I always am. I should be home in about two hours. But don't worry if I'm late. Some of those heifers may be calving soon, so I'll want to check them out carefully."

I kept Ben in the barn when the weather was this bad. I gave him a few oats as I saddled up and got ready to go. I took a lariat just in case one of the cattle was caught in deep snow somewhere. If it were, I'd get the rope around it, fasten my end to the saddle horn, and Ben and I would pull it out.

As I rode toward the field I reminisced about ranch life when I was a boy. I have memories of a Christmas Eve when we all went to Midnight Mass in a sleigh my father built. He drove the team of horses. We all had warm clothing plus horsehide robes to cover us. The earth was covered with snow, and the sky had a first-quarter moon and the stars in the clear Montana sky were as numerous as "the sands of the seashore." We visited with relatives for an hour after Mass and arrived home about 3 A.M.

The cattle checked out fine, and I put out bales for two days. I was home in two hours and greeted with a kiss as always. We reminisced during lunch and then sat for a couple of hours talking about our life and the general turmoil the area had experienced during the last six months. We were planning to go to Midnight Mass. It would not require a lot of preparation since warm clothes and winter boots become far more important than style in this kind of weather. And we were all country people by birth or by adoption into this world of harsh winter weather.

Midnight Mass is always a unique experience. The story of the Infant born in a manger is gripping of its own accord, but to live in an area where imagination can almost recreate the scene is awe-inspiring. At the end of Mass, Father Tim invited everyone down to the basement room for coffee, tea, cookies, and milk. The people congregated for a second time and stayed an hour or more visiting with one another. It was exhilarating to watch and participate in the warmth and goodwill of the night. Many asked me about Father Fred. I spoke of my last visit and the brighter mood in which I left him.

We were treated to a spectacular display of aurora borealis on the way home. The northern sky was alive with a variety of changing colors reaching almost to the summit. When we got home we sat in the cold on our open porch to view the colorful rays from millions of miles away rising from behind the Highwood Mountains up to the heavens. Jane commented, "Can't you almost hear the heavenly chorus?"

We woke late Christmas morning because of our late night. We fixed breakfast together and sat in our robes by the fire I'd made. Jane and I agreed many years ago, probably soon after we were married, that we would not do Christmas presents for each other or birthday presents or even anniversary presents. In that early discussion, we agreed we would buy the things we needed and things we sometimes liked but didn't need. It never required a special time.

Since we did not exchange presents, it was difficult for us to buy presents for other adults. We did okay with gifts when our children were young, but after they reached maturity we left behind the joy and burden of shopping for things. We sent checks on gift days. We each had several gifts to open, gifts in the mail from our children and grandchildren.

The morning was spent by the fire opening the presents and more importantly recalling memories and news of each of the children and grandchildren. We never grow tired of those conversations. We had a light lunch around noon and then got out the pictures we accumulated through the years. We spent the afternoon as we had the morning with the added pictures show.

There was an interlude of about two hours during which we talked on the phone to each of our children and grandchildren. They all seemed to have adopted our practice of doing Christmas at home. We keep in close contact with them on a regular basis but Christmas needs a special time of well-wishing.

I kept the fire going all day, and it kept us company adding a crackle or a spit here and there. Jane served a wonderful dinner, the usual turkey but with elegant sides of little baked mysteries of vegetable and fruit. Key lime pie had become our traditional Christmas dessert years ago and was continued this day.

Together we cleared the table, put things away and washed-dried the dishes. We got on our robes again and sat by the fire with a glass of wine. We reminisced about how we met, how we fell in love, and as always ended up talking about our gratefulness to God for the gift of our life, our love, and our faith. We read the scriptures for the day, said our night prayers, and went to bed with the peace of Christmas in our hearts.

December twenty-sixth was a cloudy morning and became a dark, dreadful day. We finished breakfast. It was nearly ten o'clock. The phone rang and

I answered. A woman's flat voice asked to speak to Mr. Robert Lee. Of course, my first thought is "something has happened to one of our children or grand-children."

Me: "This is Bob Lee."

Voice Again: "Robert Lee?"

Me: "Yes, Robert Lee."

Voice: "Are you the Robert Lee who has legal responsibility and power of attorney for Mr. Charles Brown."

Me: I felt a chill in my bones. "Yes, I am that Robert Lee."

Voice: "This is Geneva Johns. I am the assistant to William Craven, Warden of the Montana State Prison. Warden Craven has asked me to call you and inform you that Charles Brown is dead."

Me: "What happened? How did he die?"

Voice: "I am to inform you he died of a self-inflicted injury."

Me: "What was the injury? When did it happen? How did it happen?"

Voice: "I am to inform you it happened last evening."

Me: "What happened to him? How did he die?"

Voice: "I have given you the information the Warden authorized. The warden also asked me to inform you that beginning at noon today you have forty-eight hours to pick up his body. If his body is not picked up within that timeframe, it will be cremated and placed in an area on the State Prison Grounds. Goodbye." She hung up.

I was angry. This woman was a female mockup of the warden. She was hard, cruel, wicked, and I came up with a number of other adjectives. But my emotions moved quickly on to consider the loss of Charles, a man I had come to genuinely care about. What a sad ending to a sad life. Somehow his crime had faded into the past. From the conversation with Geneva, he killed himself. And I began to see him as having a more positive attitude in our meeting just a few days ago. He spoke more positively. His voice was stronger and brighter. He seemed to be relieved of his tendency to negative thought patterns and his opinion of himself showed some hint of confidence.

Jane heard my conversation on the phone and was standing beside me waiting to hear the details which I then told her. It was a shock to me because of my last visit with Charles, and it was a shock to Jane because she had heard me talk about his improved attitude. Jane was a bit more down to earth at the moment. She came over and as she put her arms around me asked if I was going to call the bishop and perhaps Tom O'Rourke. Before I responded she added, "Who should we inform in Springer and how should we go about it?"

I should call Bishop Butler first. When I got him on the phone, he said, "Somehow I feel this is not a Christmas call. It's a day late for that. What's on your mind, Bob?" I had a hard time keeping my voice from showing emotion as I replied, "I had a call from the prison warden's assistant a few minutes ago. She said Charles Brown committed suicide yesterday. She didn't say 'suicide,' she said 'of a self-inflicted injury.' She would give me no further information. She said I had forty-eight hours from noon today to pick up his body or they would cremate him and bury the ashes on the grounds."

Bishop Butler gave a deep sigh and responded, "That's sad news. May the Lord grant him everlasting peace. He was still a priest of this diocese— even in prison, so I feel the diocese has responsibility for his funeral. I'll have Clark's Funeral Home get the body and I or one of my assistants at the Cathedral can just say the internment prayers as he's buried in Mount Olive Cemetery."

I was surprised by his statement and said, "Charles, don't you think there should be a funeral Mass, perhaps privately but still a Mass?"

He answered, "You're right of course. I was just thinking of him as a prisoner and as a murderer. He was a priest for twenty-plus years and perhaps did a great deal of good during that time. My picture of him as a child molester stays in my mind and becomes almost synonymous with his name. That's unchristian and unfair on my part. Yes, of course. First, I'll arrange to have his body brought to the mortuary here. Then after I've given the matter some thought I'll let you know what further arrangements are made."

I wanted some further advice. I asked, "Do you think I should go ahead and give this information to Father Matthews and perhaps email the members of the parish and let them know? I would also like to call Tom O'Rourke and see if he can find out something more about the statement: 'Died by his own hand.' That doesn't tell us much and I'd very much like to know exactly how he died. It's not easy to kill yourself in the Montana State Prison. There were some suicides a few years back and preventative measures were taken or were supposed to be taken. Tom can maybe put some attorney pressure on and get a little more detail."

Butler answered both my questions. "By all means, let Matthews know and the parishioners. They will tell the town. And I think it's a good idea to get Tom to find out a little more if he can. A lawyer should be able to get them to expand on the meager information they gave you. I'll be in touch when I have more to say about burial. Thanks for your help, and blessings, Bob."

I stopped him from hanging up by quickly saying, "One thing more. I will fax you a copy of two pages I have which give me power of attorney, heir to his possessions, and almost any other legal power available. Could you get these to the person from Clark's who is picking up the body and ask them to please get all his personal possessions and bring them back here with the body?"

He replied, "When I receive your papers I'll have someone take them to Clark's."

My next call was to Tom O'Rourke. I told him about Charles death and my inability to get any adequate information. He commented again about the State Attorneys Association's recurring issues with the prison. He asked what the bishop's plan was and I told him. He said, "There is one thing I can do. When they bring the body to Clark's Funeral Home, I'll ask the coroner to have a look at it, sort of off the record. It's far too late to do an autopsy, but we could get a professional opinion about the death."

"I appreciate that, Tom. I became increasingly interested in and I might say attached to Father Brown. He had a difficult childhood, and it never ceased to pursue him and eventually destroy him."

Tom replied, "Have you forgotten about 'free will'?" Then he said, "Goodbye" and hung up before I could reply. I would have liked to give him a few enlightening comments about his 'free will' statement.

I decided to drive to Springer to tell Timothy Matthews about Fred's death. He was as shocked as any of us. He's one of those people that start off looking for a solution the minute they become aware of a problem. "Bob, why not have the funeral here? I think the parishioners are ready for it and I think the town is ready for it. If you asked Lucy Quirk, my guess is she would give a strong 'yes.'"

My initial unspoken reaction was "I can't believe he's saying this. People wouldn't tolerate Fred's body back in this town." And as I stood looking at the source of the surprising funeral suggestion, I remembered the Town Hall meeting and the 'gala' in the church basement after midnight Mass. Maybe Timothy was right on.

I was still not convinced so I searched for a problem to slow Timothy down on the path he was taking. "Father Timothy Matthews, do you honestly believe the people of this town will allow a pedophile priest, a murderer no less, to be buried in the one cemetery that holds all our deceased loved ones?"

He answered very simply, "Yes." Then we talked about his idea for several minutes. I questioned whether the bishop might come to say the Funeral Mass. He nixed the idea. "I don't think we should even invite the bishop. Don't forget he's the hierarchy, that part of the church which is ultimately held responsible for this continuing worldwide scandal. I think he would be wise to keep his distance from the whole thing, and Butler is smart enough to do just that."

In the end I agreed with Father Timothy and encouraged him to approach the parishioners and the Mayor and Mrs. Quirk. I suggested he contact Lucy first and then the Mayor and lastly the parishioners. We agreed he should contact the Mayor not actually for permission but at least for tacit approval.

When I returned home, I talked to Jane about Father Timothy's response to the news. She was not surprised and completely agreed with the idea. Finally my series of calls and contacts about Charles' death seemed complete. It's a little awkward for me to keep using two different names for one man, using the name as known by the listener. In Springer he's still known as Fred, in spite of my telling them what the prison did about his name. To all others I use Charles as his name. Jane and I float easily from one name to the other.

It was two days later when I had the call from O'Rourke. The local coroner had examined Charles' body. O'Rourke said the results were shocking. "Charles was castrated, and his testicles were found in his mouth. Someone at the prison said they were there so as not to lose them. The external pudental artery, a branch of the femoral, supplying blood to the skin of the scrotum and adjacent areas was the major source of exsanguination. The coroner said it looked like it was deliberately severed. The man who picked up the body from the prison said the person at the prison told him Charles castrated himself with a plastic knife from his food tray. No man is capable of doing that with a plastic knife. 'Death by his own hand' is an obvious lie. This happened Christmas Eve. Undoubtedly some of the regular guards were on leave, and those who were there may well have been celebrating with booze and/or drugs. In any case, Charles was assaulted and must have died an excruciating death.

"And at this point in time I don't believe there is anything we can do about it. They undoubtedly have records made out to support what they have said. And they have guards who would perjure themselves to keep their jobs and protect their buddies. The body was no longer in their possession when *our* facts were *discovered*. They would argue that we manipulated the findings in an attempt to slander the warden. The fact that the State Bar Association is in the process of investigating the prison administration would only add support for their position. That sums it up, Bob."

I replied, "Thanks for getting involved, Tom. Maybe you can use the results at a later time in your investigation. Charles is dead either way. And all the rest of us can do is pray for him. There's probably no point in sharing any of this with anyone else." Tom agreed and we ended our conversation.

I decided to see how Father Timothy's funeral plans were going. He answered my call with his cheery, "Good afternoon. This is Father Tim."

He knows my voice so I started, "How are plans for the funeral coming, Timothy?"

He responded, "Just fine, Bob. Lucy Quirk was supportive of the idea. The Mayor thought it was a good idea and doesn't expect objections from anyone in the community. When I talked with Bishop Butler, at first he reacted with the same strong doubt you had, Bob. But when I told him you were in agreement, he decided a public funeral in Springer would be a salutary occasion. He agreed it was perhaps better not to try to hide the event but to let it be openly conducted and supported by the Church."

I had raised another question when Timothy and I talked before, so I brought it up again. "Where is Fred to be buried?"

I think Tim was waiting to tell me. "Bob, you know the part in the scripture about 'the lion and the lamb will lay down together,' well Lucy Quirk suggested Father Brown be buried next to her son, Tim. Now what do you think of that level of forgiveness and peace and grace and blessings for the town!"

All I could say in reply was, "You must be a miracle worker, Timothy."

And he had more to tell me. "I called the Clark Funeral Home, and they will be available for Father Brown's funeral in Springer either Wednesday or

Thursday of next week. I was about to call you and ask you which day you would prefer. I'm available any day." I told him either day was fine with us.

Timothy said, "Well, let's decide on Wednesday if that's good for you. I've cleared both days with Lucy. One thing more and this is Lucy's special request. She asked me to ask you if you will do the eulogy. Of course I've been in touch with our parishioners about the funeral. I've asked for volunteer pall-bearers. In no time about ten responded. I took the first six responders.

I said, "Looks like you have it all tied together, Timothy. I compliment you on your attention to the details and your ready interaction with every-one involved. I suppose there may be other people from the community who will come. Do you want me to call the paper and have them put in the notice with day and time? We didn't talk about time but I presume you're planning 10 A.M."

Timothy replied, "Yes, 10 A.M. Wednesday morning. I have to call Clark's and notify parishioners and while I'm at it I'll give the paper and the local TV news a call. So we're set for next Wednesday. I'll see you in church, and I'm speaking of this Sunday."

Jane heard most of the conversation from her sewing room which is open to my office. Her first remark, "So you're going to be giving the eulogy, Rob-bie. I'm glad. And Fred will be pleased."

I replied, "I just hope he's where he can hear me."

Later that afternoon I began working on the eulogy. My pattern for talks is to write them when I first know about them. Then I read them over and over changing a word or a phrase or redoing something until it reads the way I want it to sound. I'm compulsive about it and turn it into a life's work for a short time.

Sunday Mass felt like a prelude to a big day coming on Wednesday. The same spirit permeated the atmosphere at St. Cyril's. Lucy approached me after Mass and thanked me for accepting her request. I rather boldly asked her why she had consented to the Mass in Springer and why she asked me to give the eulogy.

She slowly pieced together her answer. "Something inside me tells me Father Brown truly cared about Tim and tried to act paternally toward him. Perhaps Father Brown hadn't had a good experience with paternity. His sexual behavior was unforgivable, but so was mine. And Tim witnessed mine. I can hardly throw stones. About the eulogy: you too had a paternal attitude toward

Tim and he cared about you. Now we're burying Father Brown. You seem to have an open mind about life and about people, and somehow you're able to fit everyone within your boundaries and without judgment. You're a good man."

Lucy Quirk's words were deeply touching. I marveled at the depth and sensitivity of this woman. My first thought was how much she has changed; but she hasn't really changed, she has discovered her true value and is using it well.

We shared the morning's events on the way home from Mass. We were rather surprised about the flexibility of the parishioners. They seemed to be welcoming the opportunity to have Wednesday's funeral for Charles. Jane commented, "Don't you get the impression they're almost making a hero out of Charles? It's all sort of topsy-turvy. He wasn't a celebrity. He was a criminal. I perhaps have a greater appreciation of what happened than any of them do, thanks to your involvement in the whole thing. But I'm not about to consider him 'priest of the year' or give him any honors. What do you think is happening, Rob?"

I answered as I tried to think it through. "People probably become more vulnerable after a tragedy has occurred. And Tim's death was truly a tragedy. They know that. There was a disturbing period of time when people were restless, angry, uncertain, probably even fearful. When violence occurs, I think we innately look for safety to counterbalance life around us. Fear and doubt partner in such times and people respond with an inner desire to get back to the peace they previously had. In a primitive way we gather 'round the camp fire.'

"Tim was buried, but the fear and anger and uncertainty wasn't buried with him. It will be buried with Father Brown; at least that's my thinking. They would not say that's why they're lining up for the funeral. It is not a conscious decision. They will talk of the need to forgive and this is the Christian thing to do. All that is true. But at another level they're looking for inner certainty that the dangers in life are over. In an exaggerated way, 'They buried the angel, now they'll bury the devil.'"

Jane was rather surprised by the last statement. "I hope you don't include that last remark in the eulogy. They would not take kindly to it, as I am sure you are aware. You're wearing your psychiatric hat now."

Monday morning I had a call from Tom O'Rourke. He had Father Brown's belongings in a small box. He was on his way to Culver City and said he would drop the box off at St. Cyril's rectory. I thanked him for his help. A couple of hours later Father Timothy called to let me know he had

Brown's belongings. I said I'd be in within the hour to pick them up. I asked Jane if she would like to ride in with me. She said she would because she wanted to find a certain kind of material to go on a dress she was making for our granddaughter.

On the way to Springer we speculated about what would be in Brown's belongings. Jane said, "I doubt there will be anything personal. What would he have that he could keep when they locked him up? From what you told me about the rectory, personal belongings weren't important to him."

I agreed. "He was certainly not into worldly possessions. I doubt the prison would keep things for him. They'd throw them in the trash. He probably kept his breviary and his rosary beads unless they considered the rosary a dangerous weapon. Maybe a couple of holy cards and a book or two. We'll soon know."

We were at the Mall. "I'll be back in about ten minutes unless Timothy has something to discuss. He's a man of ideas and loves to talk about them and his talking sometimes is a little lengthy. Do your shopping, and when you finish come to the Mall Café. I'll be there with a cup of coffee."

Timothy opened the door as I reached for the doorbell. "Welcome to the humble home of your poverty stricken pastor," was his opening remark.

I replied, "And Happy New Year to you too, my friend. Are you demanding ransom for this prized box?"

"I'll get it with no further delay," he smilingly responded.

The box contained Charles' breviary with the name 'Fred' blotted out with ink. The warden probably did that. There was a small paperback of Thomas Merton's spiritual writings. There was a lead pencil two inches long with a bit of lead still visible. When I saw it, I remembered what O'Rourke told me in one of our conversations about the prison. In their "new standards of practice" to avoid suicide, prisoners could be given paper and pencils for letter writing but pencils could be no longer than two inches. In order to obtain a new pencil, they had to turn in the old one. There'll never be any more suicides from pencils at that prison!

Charles' pencil would not be of interest to us except he had written something with it. On one of the flyleaves of the booklet there was writing. It had a cramped, hardly legible style, probably the result of trying to hold a two-inch pencil. It follows.

Autumn Leaves
Strip my soul,
Shred my sins, Lord
Let them fall in the debris
Of hidden failures

Strip my heart,
Take the dreams, Lord
Let them rest between
My awakenings

Strip my mind,
Hide the promises, Lord
Let them be enjoined
With other emptiness

Strip my body
The weary parts, Lord
Let them refuse me
In their negligence

The trees are bare
With no sign of life, Lord
I pretend to live
In my absence.

I have no idea when or why Charles wrote this. Was it his or had he remembered it from another day? My heart told me it was his. It said so much about him and where his mind must have been when we talked. Father Tim and I read it silently, and neither of us commented. The Montana weather fluctuated as it usually does this time of year. We had eight inches of snow a few days after Christmas and two days ago the temperature went up to forty-eight degrees. Winds came from the south and the chinook turned most of the snow into slush.

The morning of the funeral was cold (five below zero) but with a beautiful blue sky and sunshine that made you almost believe it was warm. The church was crowded by 9:50 when we got there. We weren't concerned because our seats were reserved with Mrs. Quirk in the front pew. There was only standing room by the time Mass began. We were well beyond congregation numbers.

The four altar boys in black pants and white shirts entered from the sacristy, followed by Father Timothy in white vestments. Priests used to wear black for funerals, but the Mass is now considered a Mass of resurrection so white is worn. The pallbearers brought the casket to the front of the aisle. Father Timothy said the prayers and the casket was covered with white as a sign of resurrection.

Myrtle Sweeney led the choir singing "Make Me an Instrument of Your peace." Father Timothy proceeded with the Mass. After he read the Gospel he continued with a brief homily, speaking of the Risen Christ and the belief in resurrection by all Christian faiths. Then he extended the idea of resurrection to all who live with belief in God and love for others as is "written in the hearts of all." Considering the variety of attendees his words not only captured their attention but reached out to the goodness "dwelling within us all" as he described it.

It was time for the eulogy. I gave Jane's hand a squeeze as I stood up and walked to the lectern. I began: "This morning is unique to the town of Springer. Gathered here in St. Cyril's Catholic Church are seven or eight hundred people of various faiths and some perhaps of no faith. And the gathering is to commemorate a parish priest, a man who died in the state prison, a murderer, and perhaps worst of all in the eyes of most, a sexual predator.

"As I thought about this unique occurrence I asked myself: what really brings this unlikely group of people together here this morning? Is it curiosity, fellowship, charity, the aftermath of anger, the harboring of bitterness, the resolution of doubt? Or is it because you smell the flowers? Let me tell you why I use those three words: *smell the flowers.*

"Father Fred Brown never smelled the flowers. I visited Fred on two occasions in the Montana State Prison in Red Lodge. He talked about his childhood and why he became a priest. He told me stories about his parents and his relationship with them, stories that sent a chill through me in the listening. Those stories gave me a view and some understanding of his early life. As a result I gained some appreciation for the emptiness of his adult life.

"In early years a child is completely dependent on parental care. Even though that care might be neglectful or abusive, the child's body continues to grow and their mind continues to develop. But if parents fail to demon-strate the presence of their attachment to and affection for the child, that child's emotional development does not mature as it should and possibly does not develop at all.

"It is our emotions that provide us with the ability to 'smell the flowers.' Of course I'm not speaking of the sense of smell. I'm speaking of our feelings which provide another dimension to, another relationship with, another view of the world around us. Our emotions introduce us into a world where we appreciate and respond to the love of family, the warmth of friendship, the beauty of a lovely day, the delight of a child, the joy of someone's laughter, the embrace of a breeze, the splendor of the stars, the gift of someone's presence, and yes, the sadness of someone's absence. These are the 'flowers' of life: fresh, full of color, vibrant and calling to us; and when they fade and die, they still live in our memories.

"Fred couldn't smell the flowers of life because his parental care was mea-ger, barely sufficient to sustain his body and mind and without the nutrients that nurture and grow emotional life. There was no rich loam of parental love to cause Fred's feelings to sprout and to bloom. Fred never knew there were flowers to smell.

"Fred was truly handicapped as he went forth at a young age to face the world. Others misguided him into seminary life and those years led him into the priesthood, providing a continuation of a barren life without attachments. Then in some mysterious manner Fred one day reached out to a young win-some boy, a small flower in God's world, a flower that stirred new and unfa-miliar feelings in Fred. We are all familiar with the sad result of that first blooming and the final tragedy of Fred's life.

"Recently the townspeople of Springer came together to review those heartbreaking events and to come to terms with them. Now we know we are a people of compassion and forgiveness. We know and respond to the flowers of life, the lily white flower of Tim Quirk and the momentary weak blossom that was Fred Brown.

"I hope you will take home this thought from Psalm 34:18, 'The Lord is close to the brokenhearted and those who are crushed in spirit he saves.' My first visit with Father Brown in the state prison revealed a spirit crushed to the earth. My second visit showed a man who was struggling to face the de-mands of his situation with thoughts turning heavenward.

"At the end of our visits, I recited this passage for Fred from the Canticle of Zechariah: 'In the tender compassion of our God the dawn from on high shall break upon us, to shine on those who dwell in darkness and the shadow of death, and to guide our feet into the way of peace.' The shadow of darkness in Fred's life became the shadow of death on Christmas Eve.

"I end by repeating the request already made by Father Timothy that we keep Father Brown in our prayers. Pray he may be with his Heavenly Father, who loved him since he was knit in his mother's womb.

"There is one fact I want to note in this eulogy. There is a rumor Father Brown committed suicide. No matter what you may hear or read in the news, there is incontrovertible evidence that Father Brown did not commit suicide."

The remainder of Mass continued prayerfully. On the way to the cemetery, I remembered what Father Timothy told me. When Mayor Sullivan asked Mrs. Quirk how she felt about Father Brown being buried in the Springer cemetery, Lucy responded saying there was a plot next to Tim and she'd be pleased if Father Brown were buried there. Father Brown was buried beside Tim after final prayers by Father Timothy Matthews.

On our way home Jane and I talked about the peace and divine presence that filled the morning. Jane brought up something I hadn't thought about in some time. She asked, "Rob, what have you decided about that secret letter? You still have it. Are you going to keep it?"

I replied, "With all the other things on my mind, the letter sort of slipped away. What do you think Fred would want me to do with it?"

Jane answered, "If Fred's in heaven, I'm pretty sure he'd want you to return it rather than to keep it, burn it, or throw it away."

I said, "I think you're right, Love."

The following day I got a plain envelope addressed it to the auxiliary Bishop in the parish he serves. I went to the bank, took *the special letter* out of the safe deposit box, enclosed it and mailed it Special Delivery. The book is now closed.

ACKNOWLEDGMENTS

My gratitude to all those who have listened to the shaping of my story and especially to those who have made recommendations, especially Rev. Joe Heim, Dennis Mauro-Huse and Sara Rubloff, LCSW-C.

11-19